MISS MAITLAND
PRIVATE SECRETARY

Rising into the white wash of moonlight came Suzanne

[Page 45]

MISS MAITLAND
PRIVATE SECRETARY

BY

GERALDINE BONNER

AUTHOR OF "THE EMIGRANT TRAIL," "THE GIRL AT CENTRAL,"
"TREASURE AND TROUBLE THEREWITH," ETC.

ILLUSTRATED BY
A. I. KELLER

D. APPLETON AND COMPANY
NEW YORK   LONDON
1919

CONTENTS

v

Contents

MISS MAITLAND PRIVATE SECRETARY

CHAPTER I

THE PAHTING OF THE WAYS

CHAPMAN PRICE was leaving Grasslands. Events had been rapidly advancing to that point for the last three months, slowly advancing for the last three years. Everybody who knew the Prices and the Janneys said it was inevitable, and people who didn't know them but read about them in the " society papers " could give quite glibly the reasons why Mrs. Chapman Price was going to separate from her husband.

His friends said it was her fault; Suzanne Price was enough to drive any man away from her — selfish, exacting, bad tempered, a spoiled child of wealth. Chappie had been a first-rate fellow when he married her and she'd nagged and tormented him past bearing. Her friends had a different story ; Chapman Price was no good, had neglected her, was an idler and a spendthrift. Hadn't the Janneys set him up in business over

Miss Mcdtland Private Secretary

and over and found it hopeless? What he had wanted was her money, and people had told her so; her mother had begged her to give him up, but she would have him and learned her lesson, poor girl! Those in the Janney circle said there would have been a divorce long before if it hadn't been for the child. She had held them together, kept them in a sort of hostile, embattled partnership for years. And then, finally, that link broke* and Chapman Price had to go.

There had been a last conclave in the library that morning, Mrs. Janney presiding. Then they separated, silent and gloomy — a household of eight years, even an uncongenial one, isn't broken up without the sense of finality weighing on its members. Chapman had gone to his rooms and flung orders at his valet to pack up, and Suzanne had gone to hers, thrown herself on the sofa, and sniffed salts with her eyes shut. Mr. and Mrs. Janney repaired to the wide shaded balcony and there talked it over in low tones. They were immensely relieved that it was at last settled, though of course there would be the unpleasantness of a divorce and the attending gossip. Mr. Janney hated gossip, but his wife, who had risen from a Pittsburg suburb to her present proud eminence, was too battle-scarred a veteran to mind a little thing like that.

As they talked, their eyes wandered over a delightful prospect. First a strip of velvet lawn, then a terrace

The Parting of the Ways

and balustraded walk, and beyond that the enameled brilliance of long gardens where flowers grew in masses, thick borders, and delicate spatterings, bright against the green. Back of the gardens were more lawns, shaven close and dappled with tree shadows, then woods — Mrs. Janney's far acres — on this fine morning all shimmering and astir with a light, salt-tinged breeze. Grasslands was on the northern side of Long Island, only half a mile from the Sound through the seclusion of its own woods.

It was quite a show place, the house a great, rambling, brown building with slanting, shingled roofs and a flanking rim of balconies. Behind it the sun struck fire from the glass of long greenhouses, and the tops of garages, stables and out-buildings rose above concealing shrubberies and trellises draped with the pink mantle of the rambler. Mrs. Janney had bought it after her position was assured, paying a price that made all Long Island real estate men glad at heart.

Sitting in a wicker chair, a bag of knitting hanging from its arm, she looked the proper head for such an establishment. She was fifty-four, large — increasing stoutness was one of her minor trials — and was still a handsome woman who " took care of herself." Her morning dress of white embroidered muslin had been made by an artist. Her gray hair, creased by a " permanent wave," was artfully disposed to show the fine

Miss Maitland Private Secretary

shape of her head and conceal the necessary switch. She was too naturally endowed with good taste to indicate her wealth by vulgar display, and her hands showed few rings; the modest brooch of amethysts fastening the neck of her bodice was her sole ornament. And this was all the more commendable, as Mrs. Janney had wonderful jewels of which she was very proud.

Five years before, she had married Samuel Van Zile Janney, who now sat opposite her clothed in white flannels and looking distressed. He was a small, thin, elderly man, with a pointed gray beard and a general air of cool, dry finish. No one had ever thought old Sam Janney would marry again. He had lost his wife ages ago and had been a sort of historic landmark for the last twenty years, living desolately at his club and knowing everybody who was worth while. Of course he had family, endless family, and thought a lot of it and all that sort of thing. So his marriage to the Pitts-burg widow came as a shock, and then his world said: " Oh, well, the old chap wants a home and he's going to get it — a choice of homes — the house on upper Fifth Avenue, the place at Palm Beach and Grasslands."

It had been a very happy marriage, for Sam Janney with his traditions and his conventions was a person of infinite tact, and he loved and admired his wife. The one matter upon which they ever disagreed was Suzanne.

The Parting of the Ways

She had been foolishly indulged, her caprices and extravagances were maddening, her manners on occasions extremely bad. Mr. Janney, who had beautiful manners of his own, deplored it, also the amount of money her mother allowed her; for the fortune was all Mrs.

Janney's, Suzanne having been left dependent on her bounty.

His wife, who had managed everything eise so well, resented these criticisms on what should have been the completest example of her competence. She also resented them because she knew they were true. With all her cleverness and all her capability she had not succeeded with her daughter. The girl had got beyond her; the unfortunate marriage with Chapman Price had been the climax of a youth of willfulness and insubordination. Suzanne's affairs, Suzanne's future, Suzanne herself were subjects that husband and wife avoided, except, as in the present instance, when they were the only subjects in both their minds.

Presently their low-toned murmurings were interrupted by the appearance of Dixon, the butler, announcing lunch.

" Mrs. Price," he said, " will not be down — she has a headache."

Mrs. Janney rose, looking at the man. He had been in her service for years, was one of the first outward and visible signs of her growth in affluence. She was

sure that he knew what had happened, but her face was unrevealing as a mask, as she said:

" See that she gets something. Will Mr. Price take his lunch upstairs? "

"No, Madam," returned the man quietly, -" Mr. Price is coming down."

It was a ghastly meal — three of them eating sumptuous food, waited on by two men hardly less silent than they were. It wouldn't have been so unbearable if Bebita, Suzanne's daughter, had been there to lift the curse off it with her artless chatter, or Esther Mait-land, the social secretary, who had acquired a habit of talking with Mr. Janney when the rest of the family were held in the dumbness of wrath. But Bebita was spending the morning with a little chum and Miss Maitland was lunching with a friend in the village.

Chapman Price, as if anxious to show how little he cared, ate everything that was passed, and prolonged the misery by second helpings. Mrs. Janney could have beaten him, she was so angry. Once she glanced at him and met his eyes, insolently defiant, and as full of hostility as her own. They were vital eyes, dark and bold, and were set in a handsome face. At the time of his marriage he had been known as " Beauty Price " and it was his good looks which had caught the capricious fancy of Suzanne. In the eight years since then they had suffered, the firmly modeled contours had grown

" You've done one thing to me that you're going to regret —"

The Parting of the Ways

thin and hard, the mouth had set in an ugly line, the brows had creased by a frown of sulky resentment. But he was still a noticeable figure, six feet, lean and agile, with a skin as brown as a nut and a crown of black hair brushed to a glossy smoothness. Many women continued to describe Chapman Price as " a perfect Adonis."

When they rose from the table he stood aside to let his parents-in-law pass out before him. They brushed by, feeling exceedingly uncomfortable and wanting to get away as quickly as their dignity would permit. They dreaded a last flare-up of his temper, notoriously violent and uncontrolled, one of the attributes that had made him so unacceptable. In the hall at the stair foot they half turned to him, swept him with cold looks and were mumbling vague sounds that might have been dismissal or farewell, when he suddenly raised his voice in a loud, combative note:

" Oh, don't bother to be polite. There's no love between us and there needn't be any hypocrisies. You want to get rid of me and I want to go. But before I do, I'd like to say something." He drew a step nearer, his face suddenly suffused with a dark flush, his eyes set and narrowed. " You've done one thing to me that you're going to regret — stolen my child. Yes," in answer to a protesting sound from Mr. Janney, " stolen her — that's what I said. You think you can

hide behind your money bags and do what you like. Maybe you can nine times, but there's a tenth when things don't work the way you've expected. Watch out for it — it's due now."

His voice was raised, loud, furious, threatening. The dining room door flew open and Dixon appeared on the threshold in alarmed consternation. Mr. Janney stepped forward belligerently:

" Chapman, now look here —"

Mrs. Janney laid a hand on her husband's arm:

" Don't answer him, Sam," then to Chapman, her face stony in its controlled passion, " I want no more words with you. Our affairs are finished. Kindly leave the house as soon as possible." She turned to the butler who was staring at them with dropped jaw: " Shut that door, Dixon, and stay where you belong." The sound of footsteps at the stair-head caught her ear. "The other servants are coming: we'll have an audience for this pleasant scene. We'd better go, Sam, as Chapman doesn't seem to have heard my request for him to leave, the only thing for us is to leave ourselves."

She swept her husband off across the hall toward the balcony. Behind them the young man's voice rose:

" Oh don't have any fears. I'm going. But I may come back — that's what you want to remember — I may come back to settle the score."

The Parting of the Ways

Then they heard his footsteps mounting the stairs in a long, leaping run.

In his own room he found his valet, Willitts, a small, fair-haired young Englishman, closing the trunks. The door was open and he had a suspicion that the footsteps Mrs. Janney had heard were probably Willitts'. He didn't care, he didn't care what Willitts had heard. The man knew anyhow; they all knew. There wasn't a servant in the house or a soul in the village who wouldn't by to-morrow be telling how the Janneys had thrown him out and were planning to get possession of his child.

He strode about the room, tumbled the neat piles of cravats and handkerchiefs on the bureau, yanked up the blinds. In his still seething passion he muttered curses at everything, the clothes that lay across chair backs, the boots that he kicked as he walked, finally the valet who once got in his way. The man made no answer, did not appear to notice it, but went on with his work, silent, unobtrusive, competent. Presently Chapman became quieter; the storm was receding. He fell into a chair, sat sunk in moody reflection, and, after studying the shining toes of his shoes for some minutes, looked at the man and said, " Forget it, Willitts. I was mad straight through."

It may have been a capacity to make such amends that caused all servants to like Chapman Price. Wil-

litts, who had been in his service for nearly a year, was known to be devoted to him.

An hour later, when they left, the house had an air of desertion. The large lower hall, with vistas of stately rooms through arched doorways, was as silent as the Sleeping Beauty's palace. Chapman's glance swept it all — rich and still, gleams of parquette showing beyond the Persian rugs, curtains too heavily splendid for the breeze to stir, flowers in glowing masses, the big motor, visible through the wide-flung hall door, a finishing touch in the picture. It was the perfect expression of a carefully devised luxury, a luxury which for the last eight years had lapped him in slothful ease.

As he came out on the verandah steps a voice hailed him and he stopped, the sullen ill humor of his face breaking into a smile. Across the lawn, running with fleet steps, came his daughter Bebita. Laughing and gay with welcome, she was as fresh as a morning rose. Her hat, slipped to her neck, showed the glistening gold of her hair back-blown in ruffled curls; her rapid passage threw her dress up over her bare, sunburned knees, and her little feet in black-strapped slippers sped over the grass. Healthy, happy, surrounded by love which she returned with a child's sweet democracy, she was enchanting and Chapman adored her.

" Where are you going, Popsy ? " she cried and, 10

dodging round the back of the motor, came panting up the steps. Chapman sat down on the top, and drew her between his knees. Otto, the chauffeur, and Wil-litts with the bags, watched them with covert interest, ready to avert their eyes if Chapman should look their way. The nurse, an elderly woman, came slowly across the grass, also watching.

" To town," said the young man, scrutinizing the lovely, rosy face, with its deep blue eyes raised to his.

" For how long? " She was used to her father going to town and not reappearing for several days.

" Oh, I don't know; longer than usual, though, I guess. Going to miss me? "

" Um, I always miss you, Popsy. Will you bring me something when you come back? "

" Yes, or maybe I '11 send it. What do you want? "

" A 'lectric torch — one that shines. Polly's got one "— Polly was the little friend she had been visiting —" I want one like Polly's."

" All right. A 'lectric torch."

" I'm going to get one, Annie," she cried triumphantly to the nurse ; " Popsy's going to send me one." Then turning back to her father, " Take me to the station with you? "

Willitts and the chauffeur exchanged a glance. The nurse made a quick forward movement, suddenly gently authoritative:

" No, no, darling. You can't drive now. It's time to go in and take your rest."

Bebita looked mutinous, but her father, drawing her to him and kissing her, rose:

" I can't honey-bun. I'm in a hurry and there wouldn't be any fun just driving down to the village and back. You run along with Annie now and as soon as I get to town I'll buy you the torch and send it."

The nurse mounted the steps, took the child's hand, and together they stood watching Chapman as he got in. Willitts took the seat beside the chauffeur, adroitly disposing his legs among a pile of suitcases, golf bags, umbrellas and walking sticks. As the car started Chapman looked back at his daughter. She was regarding him with the intent, grave interest, a little wistful, with which children watch a departure. At the sight of his face, she smiled, pranced a little, and called:

" Good-by, Popsy dear. Don't forget the torch. Come back soon," and waved her free hand.

Chapman gave an answering wave and the big car rolled off with a cool crackle of gravel.

The village — the spotless, prosperous village of Berkeley enriched by the great estates about it — was a half mile from Grasslands' wrought-iron gates. The road passed through woods, opening here and there to afford glimpses of emerald lawns backed by large houses, with the slope of awnings above their balconies.

On either side of this highway ran a shady path, worn hard by the feet of pedestrians and the wheels of bicycles.

As the Janney motor turned out into the road a young woman was walking along one of these paths, returning to Grasslands. She appeared to be engrossed in thought, her step loitering, her eyes downcast, a slight line showing between her brows. Out of range of the sun she had let her parasol droop over her shoulder and its green disk made a charming background for her head. She wore no hat and against the taut silk her hair showed a glossy, burnished brown. It was beautiful hair, growing low on her forehead and waving backward in loose undulations to the thick knot at the nape of her neck. Her skin was pale, her eyes, under long brows that lifted slightly at the outer ends, deep-set, narrow and dark. She was hardly handsome, but people noticed her, wondered why they did, and then said she was " artistic-looking," or maybe it was just personality; anyway, say what you like, there was something about her that caught your eye. Dressed entirely in white, a slim, sunburned hand coiled round the parasol handle, her throat left bare by a sailor collar, she was as trim, as flecklessly dainty, graceful and comely as a picture-girl painted on the green canvas of the trees.

At the sight of her Chapman, who had been lounging

Miss Maitland Private Secretary

in the tonneau, started and his morose eye brightened. As the motor ran toward her, she looked up, saw who it was, and in the moment of passing, inclined her head in a grave salutation. Chapman leaned forward and touched the chauffeur on the shoulder.

" Just stop for a minute, Otto, I want to speak to Miss Maitland."

She did not see that the car had stopped or hear the footstep on the grass behind him. Chapman's voice was low:

" Hullo, Esther. Don't be in such a hurry. I'm going."

She wheeled, evidently startled, her face disturbed and unsmiling.

" Oh! Do you mean really going? "

" Yes. Parting of the ways — all that sort of thing."

He eyed her with a curious, watching interest and she returned the look, her own uneasily intent.

" Why do you stop to tell me that," was what she said. " Everybody knew it was coming."

He shrugged and then smiled, a smile full of meaning:

" I thought you'd like to hear it — from me, first hand. I'll be a free man in a year."

She stood for a moment looking at the ground, then lifting the parasol over her head, said:

The Parting of the Ways

" If you're going to catch the three forty-five you'd better hurry."

His smile deepened, showed a roguish malice, and as he turned from her, raising his hat, he murmured just loud enough for her to hear:

" Thanks for reminding me. I wouldn't miss that train for a farm — I'm devilish keen to get to the city."

He ran back to the waiting motor and the girl resumed her walk, her step even slower than before, her face down-drooped in frowning reverie.

There was no chair car on the three forty-five and Chapman had to travel in the common coach, Willitts and the luggage crowded into the seat behind him. It was an hour and a half run to the Pennsylvania Station and he spent the time thinking over the situation and arranging his future. His business — Long Island real estate — had been allowed to go to the dogs. He would have to get busy in earnest, and, with his friends and large acquaintance to throw things in his way, he could put it on a paying basis. His expenses would have to be cut down to the bone. He'd give up his chambers, a suite in a bachelor apartment — Willitts could find him a cheap room somewhere — and of course he'd give up Willitts. That had been already arranged and the faithful soul had asked leave to help him in the move and stay with him till a new job was

found. He would keep his car — it would be necessary in his business — and could be stored in the garage at Cedar Brook where he'd spend his week-ends with the Hartleys. Joe Hartley was one of his best friends, knew all about his marriage and had counseled a separation more than a year ago. He'd probably spend a good deal of his time at Cedar Brook, it was a growing place; unfortunate that it should be the next station after Berkeley, but it could not be helped. He was bound to run into the Janney outfit and he'd have to get used to it.

The train was entering the tunnel when he gave Wil-litts his instructions — go to the apartment and pack up, then see about a room. He himself would look up some places he knew of, and if he found anything suitable he'd come back to the apartment and the things could be moved to-morrow. They separated in the depot, Willitts and the luggage in a taxi, Chapman on foot. But that part of the city to which he took his way, dingy, unkempt, remote from the section where his kind dwelt, was not a place where Chapman Price, fallen from his high estate as he was, would have chosen to house himself.

CHAPTER II
MISS MAITLAXD GETS A LETTER

IT was Thursday morning, three days after her husband's departure, and Suzanne was sitting in the window seat of her room looking across the green distances to where the roof of Dick Ferguson's place, Council Oaks, rose above the tree tops. Council Oaks adjoined Grasslands, there was a short cut which connected them — a path through the woods. Before Mrs. Janney bought Grasslands the path had become moss-grown, almost obliterated. Then when she took possession the two households wore it bare again. The servants found it shortened the walk from kitchen to kitchen; Mr. Janney often footed its green windings; Dick Ferguson's father had been one of his cronies, and Dick Ferguson himself was the most constant traveler of them all.

Council Oaks was a very old place; it had been in the Ferguson family since the days when the British governors rolled over Long Island in their lumbering coaches. Before that the Indians had used it for a council ground, their tepees pitched under the shade of

the four giant oaks from which it took its name. The Fergusons had kept the farm house, built after the Revolution, adding wings to it, till it now extended in a long, sprawl of white buildings, with the original worn stone as a step to its knockered front door, and the low, raftered ceilings, plank floors, and deep-mouthed fireplaces of its early occupation.

There Dick Ferguson lived all summer, going to town at intervals to attend to the business of the Ferguson estate, for, like the young man in the Bible, he had great possessions. The dead and gone Fergusons had been canny and thrifty, bought land far beyond the city limits and sat in their offices and waited until the town grew round it. It was known among the present owner's intimates that he disapproved of this method of enrichment, and that his extensive charities and endowments were an attempt to pay back what he felt he owed. He was very silent about them, only a few knew of the many secret channels through which the Ferguson millions were being diverted to the relief of the people.

But none of this seriousness showed on the outside. If you didn't know him well Dick Ferguson was the last person you would suspect of a sense of responsibility or a view of life that was anything but easy-going and light-hearted. People described him as a nice chap, not a bit spoiled by his money, just a big, jolly boy, simple

and unaffected. He looked the part with his long, lank figure, leggy as a young colt, his shock of light brown hair that never would lie flat, his freckled, irregular face with gray eyes that had an engaging way of closing when he laughed. He did this a good deal and it may have been one of the reasons why so many people liked him. And he also had a capacity for listening to long-winded tales of trouble, which may have been another. He was twenty-nine years old and still unmarried, and that was his own fault as any one would tell you.

When Sam Janney married the Pittsburg widow Dick Ferguson became a friend of the family. He fitted in very well, for he was sympathetic and understanding and the Janneys had troubles to tell. He heard all about Chapman's shortcomings; a little from old Sam who was not expansive, more from Mrs. Janney, and most from Suzanne. He was very sorry for her and gave her good advice. " A poor little bit of bluff," he called her to himself, and then would stroll over to Grasslands and spend an hour with her trying to cheer her up.

He spent a good many hours this way and the time came when Suzanne began to wait and watch for his coming.

Sitting now in the cushioned window seat she was wondering if he would come that morning and she could

get him off in the garden and tell him that Chapman was gone. She saw herself saying it with lowered eyes and delicately demure phrases. She would frankly admit she was glad it was over, glad she would be free once more, for in the autumn she would go to Reno and begin proceedings for a divorce.

At this thought she subsided against the cushions, and closed her eyes smiling softly. Seen thus, the bright sunlight tempered by filmy curtains, she was a pretty woman, looking very girlish for her twenty-eight years. This was partly due to her extreme slenderness and partly to her blonde coloring. Both had been preserved with sedulous care: the one matter in which she exercised self-restraint was her food, the one occasion on which she showed patience was when her maid was washing her hair with a solution of peroxide.

Every window in the large, luxurious room was open and through them drifted a flow of air, scented with the sea and the breath of flowers. Then rising on the stillness came the sound of voices — a man's and a woman's — from the balcony below. They were Mr. Janney's and Miss Maitland's — the secretary was preparing to read the morning papers to her employer.

Suzanne opened her eyes and sat up, the smile dying from her lips. The dreamy complacence left her face and was replaced by a look of brooding irritation. It

changed her so completely that she ceased to be pretty — suddenly showed her years, and was revealed as a woman, already fading, preyed upon by secret vexations.

She rose adjusting her dress, a marvelous creation of thin white material with floating edges of lace. She went to the mirror, powdered her face and touched her lips with a stick of red salve, then studied her reflection. It should have been satisfying, delicate, fragile, a lovely, ethereal creature, with baby blue eyes and silky, maize-colored hair. It was not to be believed that any man could look at Esther Maitland when she was by — and yet — and yet —! She turned from the mirror with an angry mutter and went downstairs.

On the balcony Miss Maitland was looking over the papers with Mr. Janney opposite waiting to be read to. Suzanne sat down near them where she could command the place in the woods where the path from Council Oaks struck into the lawn. With a sidelong eye she noted the Secretary's hand on the edge of the paper — narrow, satin-skinned, with fingers finely tapering and pink-tipped. Her fingers were short and spatulate, showing her common blood, and all the pink on them had to be applied with a chamois. Miss Maitland began to read — the war news first was the rule

— and her voice was a pleasure to hear, cultivated, soft, musical. Suzanne, for all her expensive education

Miss Maitland Private Secretary

and subsequent efforts, had never been able to refine hers; the ugly Pittsburg burr would crop out.

A gnawing fancy that she had been fighting against for weeks rose suddenly into jealous conviction. This girl — a penniless nobody — had a quality, an air, a distinction, that she with all her advantages had never been able to acquire, could never acquire. It was something innate, something you were born with, something that made you fitted for any sphere. Immovable, apparently absorbed in the reading, Suzanne began to think how she could induce her mother to dispense with the services of the Social Secretary.

When the war news was finished Miss Maitland passed on to the news of the day. On this particular morning it was varied and interesting: A Western senator had attacked the President's policy with unseemly vigor; the mysterious murder of a woman in Chicago had developed a new suspect; a California mob had nearly killed a Japanese student; and in the New York loft district a strike of shirtwaist makers had attained the proportions of a riot in which one of the pickets had stabbed a policeman with a hatpin.

Mr. Janney was shocked at these horrors, but he always liked to hear them. Miss Maitland had to stop reading and listen to a theory he had evolved about the Chicago murder — it was the woman's husband and he demonstrated how this was possible. Then he took

Miss Maitland Gets a Letter

up the shirtwaist strike with a fussy disapproval — they got nothing by violence, only set the public against them and their cause. Miss Maitland was inclined to argue about it; thought there was something to say for their methods and said it.

Suzanne listened uncomprehending, unable to join in or to follow. She had heard such arguments before and had to sit silent, feeling a fool. The girl didn't know her place, talked as if she were their equal, talked to Dick that way, and DkV had been interested, giving her an attention he never gave Suzanne. Mr. Janney was doing it now, leaning out of his chair, voicing his hope that a speedy vengeance would overtake the picket who had made her escape in the melee.

The conversation was brought to an end by the appearance of Mrs. Janney. It was time for the mail; Otto had gone for it an hour ago. Before its arrival Mrs. Janney wanted their answers about two dinner invitations which had just come by telephone. One was for herself and Sam — Sunday night at the Dela-valles — and the other was from Dick Ferguson for tonight — all of them, very informally — just himself and Ham Lorimer who was staying there.

Mr. Janney agreed to both and in answer to her mother's glance Suzanne said languidly, " Yes, she'd go to-night — there was nothing else to do."

" And he wants you too, Miss Maitland," said Mrs.

Miss MMand Private Secretary

Janney, turning to the Secretary. " You'll come, won't you?"

Miss Maitland said she would and that it was very kind of Mr. Ferguson to ask her. Mr. and Mrs. Janney exchanged a gratified glance; they were much attached to the Secretary and felt that their lordly circle ignored her existence more than was necessary or kindly. Suzanne said nothing, but the edges of her small upper teeth set close on her under lip, and her nostrils quivered with a deep-drawn breath.

Mrs. Janney gave orders for messages of acceptance to be sent, then sank into a chair, remarking to her husband :

" I'm glad you'll go to the Delavalles. It's to be a large dinner. I'll wear my emeralds."

To which Mr. Janney murmured :

" By all means, my dear. The Delavalles will like to see them."

Mrs. Janney's emeralds were famous; they had once belonged to Maria Theresa. As old Sam thought of them he smiled, for he knew why his wife had decided to wear them. In her climbing days, before her marriage to him had secured her position, the Delavalles had snubbed her. Now she was going to snub them, not in any obvious, vulgar way, but finely as was her wont, with the assistance of himself and Maria Theresa.

The motor came into view gliding up the long drive

Miss Mcdtland Gets a Letter

and the waiting group roused into expectant animation. Mr. Janney rose, kicking his trouser legs into shape, Miss Maitland gathered up the papers, and Mrs. Janney went to the top of the steps. In the tonneau, her body encircled by Annie's restraining arm, Bebita stood, waving an electric torch and caroling joyfully:

" It's come — it's come. It was sent to me, in a box, with my name on it."

She leaped out, rushing up the steps to display her treasure, Annie following with the mail. There was quite a bunch of it which Mrs. Janney distributed — several for Sam, a pile for herself, one for Suzanne and one for Miss Maitland. They settled down to it amid a crackling of torn envelopes, Bebita darting from one to the other.

She tried her mother first:

" Mummy, look. You just press this and the light comes out at the other end."

Suzanne's eyes on her letter did not lift, and Bebita laid a soft little hand on the tinted cheek:

'* Mummy, do please look."

Suzanne pushed the hand away with an angry movement.

" Let me alone, Bebita," she said sharply and, getting up, thrust the child out of her way and went into the house.

For a moment Bebita was astonished. Her mother,

Miss Mcdtland Private Secretary

who was so often cross to other people, was rarely so to her. But the torch was too enthralling for any other subject to occupy her thoughts and she turned to her grandfather, reading a business communication held out in front of his nose for he had on the wrong glasses. She crowded in under his arm and sparked the torch at him waiting to see his delighted surprise. But he only drew her close, kissed her cheek and murmured without moving his eyes:

" Yes, darling. It's wonderful."

That was not what she wanted so she tried her grandmother :

*' Gran, do look at my torch."

Gran looked, not at the torch at all but at Bebita's face, smiled into it, said, " Dearest, it's lovely and I'm go glad it's come," and went back to her reading.

It was all disappointing, and Bebita, as a last resource, had to try Miss Maitland, who, if not a relation, was always sympathetic and responsive. The Secretary was reading too, holding her letter up high, almost in front of her face. Bebita laid a sly finger on the top of it, drew it down and sparked the torch right at Miss Maitland.

In the shoot of brilliant light the Secretary's face was like that of a stranger — hard and thin, the mouth slightly open, the eyes staring blankly at Bebita as if they had never seen her before. For a second the child

was dumb, held in a scared amazement, then backing away she faltered:

" Why — why — how funny you look! "

The words seemed to bring Miss Maitland back to her usual, pleasant aspect. She drew a deep breath, smiled and said:

" I was thinking, that was all — something I was reading here. The torch is beautiful; you must let me try it, but not now, I have to go. I've read the papers to Gramp and I've work to do in my study."

Any one who knew Miss Maitland well might have noticed a forced sprightliness in her voice. But no one was listening; Suzanne had gone and Mr. and Mrs. Janney were engrossed in their correspondence. She stole a look at them, saw them unheeding and, with a farewell nod to Bebita, rose and crossed the balcony. As she entered the house, the will that had made her smile, maintained her voice at its clear, fresh note, relaxed. Her face sharpened, its soft curves grew rigid, her lips closed in a narrow line. With noiseless steps she ran through the wide foyer hall and down a passage that led to the room, reserved for her use and called her study. Here, locking the door, she came to a stand, her hands clasped against her breast, her eyes fixed and tragic, a figure of consternation.

CHAPTER III

ANOTHER LETTEB AND WHAT FOLLOWED IT

SUZANNE, her letter crumpled in her hand, had gone directly to her own room. There she read it for the second time, its baleful import sinking deeper into her consciousness with every sentence. It was in typewriting and bore the Berkeley postmark:

"DEAR Mas. PRICE:

This is just a line to give your memory and your conscience a jog. Your bridge debts are accumulating. Also, I hear, there are dressmakers and milliners in town who are growing restive. If there was insufficient means I wouldn't bother you, but any one who dresses and spends as you do hasn't that excuse. Perhaps you don't know what is being said and felt. Believe me you wouldn't like it; neither would Mrs. Janney. It is for her sake that I am warning you. I don't want to see her hurt and humiliated as she would be if this comes out in The Eavesdropper, and it will unless you act quickly. 'There's a chiel among you takin' notes ' and that chiel's had a line on you for some time. So take these words to heart and as the boys say, ' Come across.'

A FRIEXD."

Ever since the opening of the season the summer colony of which Berkeley was the hub had been the subject of paragraphs — more or less scandalous — appearing in The Eavesdropper. The paper, a scurrilous

weekly, had evidently some inside informer, for most of the disclosures were true and could only have been obtained by a member of the community. Suzanne, whose debts would make racy reading, had quaked every time she opened it. So far she had been spared, and she had hoped to escape by a gradual clearing off of her obligations. But she had not been able to do it — unforeseen things had happened. And now the dreaded had come to pass — she would be written up in The Eavesdropper.

Though her allowance had been princely she had kept on going over it ever since her marriage and her mother had kept on covering the deficit. But last autumn Mrs. Janney had lost both patience and temper and put her foot down with a final stamp. Then the winter had come, a feverish, crowded winter of endless parties and endless card playing, and Suzanne had somehow gone over it again, gone over — she didn't dare to think of what she owed. Tradespeople had threatened her, she was afraid to go to her mother, she told lies and made promises, and at that juncture a woman friend acquainted her with the mystery of stocks — easy money to be made in speculation. She had tried that and made a good deal — almost cleared her score — and then in April all her stocks suddenly went down. Inquiries revealed the fact that stocks did not always stay down and reassured she set forth on

Another Letter and What Followed It

a zestful orgy of renewed bridge and summer outfitting. But the stocks never came up, they remained down, as far down as they could get, against the bottom.

She felt as if she was there herself as she reviewed her position.

She couldn't let it be known. She would be ruined, called dishonest ; the yellow papers might get it — they were always writing things against the rich. Dick Ferguson would see it, and he despised people who didn't pay their bills ; she had heard him say so to Mr. Janney, remembered his tone of contempt. There would be no use lying to him for she felt bitterly certain that Mr. Janney had told him what her mother gave her. There was nothing for it but to go to Mrs. Janney and she quailed at the thought, for her mother, forgiving unto seventy times seven, at seventy times eight could be resolute and relentless. But it was the one way out and she had to take it.

When no engagements claimed her afternoons Mrs. Janney went for a drive at four. At lunch she announced her intention of going out in the open car and asked if any of the others wanted to come. All refused: Mr. Janney was contemplating a ride, Suzanne would rest, Miss Maitland had some sewing to do on her dress for that evening. Both Suzanne and Miss Maitland were very quiet and appeared to suffer from a

Another Letter and What Followed It

loss of appetite. After the meal the Secretary went upstairs and Suzanne followed.

She waited until Mr. Janney was safely started^ on his ride, then, feeling sick and wan, crossed the hall to her mother's boudoir. Mrs. Janney was at her desk writing letters, with Elspeth, her maid, a gray-haired, sturdy Scotch woman, standing by the table opening packages that had just arrived from town. Elspeth, like most of Mrs. Janney's servants, had been in her employ for years, entering her service in the old Pitts-burg days and being promoted to the post of personal attendant. She knew a good deal about the household, more even than Dixon, admired and respected her mistress and disliked Suzanne.

The young woman's first remark was addressed to her, and, curtly imperious, was of a kind that fed the dislike:

" Go. I want to talk to Mrs. Janney."

" That'll do, Elspeth," said Mrs. Janney quietly. " Thank you very much. I'll finish the others myself." Then as the woman withdrew into the bedroom beyond, " I wish you wouldn't speak to Elspeth that way, Suzanne. It's bad taste and bad manners."

Suzanne was in no state to consider Elspeth's feelings or her own manners. She was so nervous that she blundered into her subject without diplomatic preliminaries, gaining no encouragement from her mother's

face, which, at first startled, gradually hardened into stern indignation.

It was a hateful scene, degenerated — anyway on Suzanne's part — into a quarrel, a bitter arraignment of her mother as unloving and ungenerous. For Mrs. Janney refused the money, put her foot down with a stamp that carried conviction. She was even grimmer and more determined than her daughter had expected, the girl's anger and upbraidings ineffectual to gain their purpose as spray to soften a rock. Her decision was ruthless; Suzanne must pay her own debts, out of her own allowance. Yes, even if she was written up in the papers. That was her affair: if she did things that were disgraceful she must bear the disgrace. The interview ended by Suzanne rushing out of the room, a trail of loud, clamorous sobs marking her passage to her own door.

When she had gone Mrs. Janney broke down and cried a little. She had thought the girl improved of late, less selfish, more tender. And now she had been so cruel; the charge of a lack in love had pierced the mother's heart. Mr. Janney, returned from his ride, found her there, looking old, her eyes reddened, her voice husky. When he heard the story, he took her hand and stroked it. His tact prevented him from saying what he felt; what he did say was:

" That bridge money'U have to be paid."

" It will all have to be paid," Mrs. Janney sighed, " and I'll have to pay it as I always have. But I'm going to frighten her — let her think I won't — for a few days anyway. It's all I can do and it may have some effect."

Her husband agreed that it might but his thoughts were not hopeful. There always had to be a crumpled rose leaf and Suzanne was theirs.

He accompanied his wife on her drive and was so understanding, so unobtrusively soothing and sympathetic, that when they returned she was once more her masterful, competent self. Noting a bank of storm clouds rising from the east, she told Otto to bring the limousine when he came for them at a quarter to eight. Inside the house she summoned Dixon and said as the family would be out " the help "— it was part of her beneficent policy to call her retinue by this name when speaking to any of its members — could go out that night if they so willed. Dixon admitted that they had already planned a general sortie on " the movies " in the village. All but Hannah, the cook, who had " something like shooting pains in her feet, and Delia, the second housemaid, who'd got an insect in her eyes, Madam. But it wasn't the hurt of it that kept her in, only the look which she didn't want seen."

At seven the storm drove up, black and lowering, and the rain fell in a torrent. It was still falling

when Mr. and Mrs. Janney descended the stairs, a little in advance of the time set, for, while dressing, Mrs. Janney had decided that her costume needed a brightening touch, which would be suitably imparted by her opal necklace. This, being rarely worn, was kept with the more valuable jewels in the safe of which Elspeth did not know the combination. Of course Mrs. Janney did, and at the foot of the stairs she turned into a passage which led from the foyer hall into the kitchen wing. It was a short connecting artery of the great house, lit by two windows that gave on rear lawns, and at present encumbered by a chair standing near the first window. Mrs. Janney recognized the chair as one from her sitting room which had been broken and which Isaac, the footman, had said he could repair. She gave it a proprietor's inspecting glance, touched the wounded spot, and encountering wet varnish, warned Mr. Janney away.

In the wall opposite the windows the safe door rose black and uncompromising as a prison entrance. It was large and old fashioned — put in by the former owner of Grasslands. Mrs. Janney talked of having a more modern one substituted but hadn't " got round to it," and anyway Mr. Janney thought it was all right — burglaries were rare in Berkeley. The silver had already been stored for the night, the bosses of great bowls, flowered rims, and filagree edgings shining from

darkling recesses. The electric light across the hallway did not penetrate to the side shelves and Mr. Jan-ney had to assist with matches while his wife felt round among the jewel cases, opening several in her search. Finally they emerged, Mrs. Janney with the opals which after some straining she clasped round her neck, while Sam closed the door.

As they reentered the main hall Suzanne came down the stairs, tripping daintily with small pointed feet. She was very splendid, her slenderness accentuated by the length of satin swathed about her, from which her shoulders emerged, girlishly fragile. She was also very much made up, of a pink and white too dazzlingly pure. With her blushing delicacy of tint, her angry eyes and sulkily drooping mouth, Mr. Janney thought she looked exactly like a crumpled rose leaf.

" Where's Miss Maitland? " she said to him, ostentatiously ignoring her mother.

Before he could answer Esther's voice came from the hall above:

" Coming — coming. I hope I haven't kept you," and she appeared at the stair-head.

The dress she wore, green trimmed with a design of small, pink chiffon rosebuds and leaves, was the realized dream of a great Parisian faiseur. It had been Mrs. Janney's who, considering it too youthful, had given it to her Secretary. Its vivid hue was singularly be-

Miss Maitland Private Secretary

coming, lending a warm whiteness to the girl's pale skin, bringing out the rich darkness of her burnished hair. Her bare neck was as smooth as curds, not a bone rippled its gracious contours; the little rosebuds and leaves that edged the corsage looked like a garland painted on ivory.

It was a good dinner, but it was not as jolly as Dick Ferguson's dinners usually were. Before it was over the rain stopped and a full moon shone through the dining room windows. Suzanne had hoped she and Dick could saunter off into the rose garden and have that talk about Chapman, but he showed no desire to do so. They sat about in long chairs on the balcony and she had to listen to Ham Lorimer's opinions on the war.

As soon as the motor came she wanted to go — she was tired, she had a headache. It was early, only a quarter past ten, and the night was now superb, the sky a clear, starless blue with the great moon queening it alone. Mr. Janney would have liked to linger — he always enjoyed an evening with Dick — but she was petulantly perverse, and they moved to the waiting car with Ferguson in attendance.

Mrs. Janney settled herself in the back seat, Suzanne, lifting shimmering skirts, prepared to follow, while Miss Maitland waited humbly to take what room was left among their assembled knees. She was close to

Ferguson who was helping Suzanne in, and looking up at the sky murmured low to herself:

" What a glorious night! "

Ferguson heard her and dropped Suzanne's arm.

" Isn't it? Too good to waste. Does any one want to walk back to Grasslands? "

Suzanne, one foot on the step, stopped and turned to him. Her lips opened to speak, and then she saw the back of his head and heard him address Esther:

"How about it, Miss Maitland? You're a walker, and it's only a step by the wood path. We can be there almost as soon as the car."

" You'll get wet," said Mrs. Janney, " the woods will be dripping."

Mr. Janney remembered his youth and egged them on:

" Only underfoot and they can change their shoes. Dick's right — it's too good to waste. I'd go myself but I'm afraid of my rheumatism. Hurry up, Suzanne, and get in. They want to start."

Miss Maitland said she wasn't afraid of the wet and that it would not hurt her slippers. Suzanne entered the car and sunk into her corner. As it rolled away Mr. and Mrs. Janney looked back at the two figures in the moonlight and waved good-byes. Suzanne sat motionless ; all the way home she said nothing.

THE CIGAR BAND

ESTHER and Ferguson walked across the open spaces of lawn and then entered the woods. Ferguson had set the pace as slow, but he noticed that she quickened it, faring along beside him with a light, swift step. He also noticed that she was quiet, as she had been at dinner; as if she was abstracted, not like herself.

He had seen a good deal of her lately and thought of her a good deal — thought many things. One was that she was interesting, provocative in her quiet reserve, not as easy to see through as most women. She was clever, used her brains; he had formed a habit of talking to her on matters that he never spoke of with other girls. And he admired her looks, nothing cheap about them; " thoroughbred " was the word that always rose to his mind as he greeted her. It seemed to him all wrong that she should be working for a wage as the Janneys' hireling, for, though he was " advanced " in his opinions, when it came to women there was a strain of sentimentality in his make-up.

The Cigar Band

On the wood path he let her go ahead, seeing her figure spattered with white lights that ran across her shoulders and up and down her back. They had walked in silence for some minutes when he suddenly said:

"What's amiss?"

She slackened her gait so that he came up beside her.

" Amiss ? With what, with whom ? "

"You. What's wrong? What's on your mind?"

A shaft of moonlight fell through a break in the branches and struck across her shoulder. It caught the little rosebuds that lay against her neck and he saw them move as if lifted by a quick breath.

" There's nothing on my mind. Why do you think there is? "

" Because at dinner you didn't eat anything and were as quiet as if there was an embargo on the English language."

" Couldn't I be just stupid? "

He turned to her, seeing her face a pale oval against the silver-moted background:

" No. Not if you tried your darndest."

Dick Ferguson's tongue did not lend itself readily to compliments. He gave forth this one with a seriousness that was almost solemn.

She laughed, the sound suggesting embarrassment, and looked away from him her eyes on the ground.

Just in front of them the woodland roof showed a gap, and through it the light fell across the path in a glittering pool. As they advanced upon it she gave an exclamation, stayed him with an outflung arm, and bent to the moss at her feet:

"Oh, wait a minute — How exciting! I've found something."

She raised herself, illumined by the radiance, a small object that showed a golden glint in her hand. Then her voice came deprecating, disappointed:

" Oh, what a fraud! I thought it was a ring."

On her palm lay what looked like a heavy enameled ring. Ferguson took it up; it was of paper, a cigar band embossed in red and gold.

" Umph," he said, dropping it back, " I don't wonder you were fooled."

" It was right there on the moss shining in the moonlight. I thought I'd found something wonderful." She touched it with a careful finger. "It's new and perfectly dry. It's only been here since the storm."

" Some man taking a short cut through the woods. Better not tell Mrs. Janney, she doesn't like trespassers."

She held it up, moving it about so that the thick gold tracery shone:

" It's really very pretty. A ring like that wouldn't 40

The Cigar Band

be at all bad. Look! " she slipped it on her finger and held the hand out studying it critically. It was a beautiful hand, like marble against the blackness of tha trees, the band encircling the third finger. Ferguson looked and then said slowly: " You've got it on your engagement finger." " Oh, so I have." Her laugh came quick as if to cover confusion and she drew the band off, saying, as she cast it daintily from her finger-tips, " There — away with it. I hate to be fooled," and started on at a brisk pace.

Ferguson bent and picked it up, then followed her. He said nothing for quite suddenly, at the sight of the ring on her finger, he had been invaded by a curious agitation, a gripping, upsetting, disturbing agitation. It was so sharp, so unexpected, so compelling in its rapid attack, that his outside consciousness seemed submerged by it and he trod the path unaware of his surroundings.

He had never thought of Esther Maitland being engaged, of ever marrying. He had accepted her as some one who would always be close at hand, always accessible, always in town or country to be found at the Janneys'. And the ring had brought to his mind with a startling clearness that some day she might marry. Some day a man would put a ring on that finger, put it on with vows and kisses, put it on as a

sign and symbol of his ownership. Ferguson felt as if he had been shaken from an agreeable lethargy. He was filled with a surge of indignation, at what he could not exactly tell. He felt so many things that he did not know which he felt the most acutely, but a sense of grievance was mixed with jealousy and both were dominated by an angry certainty that any man who aspired to her would be unworthy.

When they emerged into the open he looked at her with a new expression — questioning, almost fierce and yet humble. Sauntering at her side across the lawn he was so obsessed with these conflicting emotions that he said not a word, and hardly heard hers. The Jan-neys were awaiting them on the balcony steps and after an exchange of good-nights he turned back to the wood trail and went home. In his room he threw himself on the sofa and lay there, his hands clasped behind his head, staring at the ceiling. It was long after midnight when he went to bed, and before he did so he put the cigar band in the jewel box with the crystal lid that stood on the bureau.

The Janney party trailed into the house, Sam stopping to lock the door as the ladies moved to the stair foot. Suzanne went up with a curt " good-night" to her mother, and no word or look for the Secretary. Esther did not appear to notice it and, pausing with her hand on the balustrade, proffered a request — could

The Cigar Band

she have to-morrow, Saturday, to go to town? She was very apologetic; her day off was Thursday and she had no right to ask for another, but a friend had unexpectedly arrived in the city, would be there for a very short time and she was extremely anxious to see her. Mrs. Janney granted the favor with sleepy goodnature and Miss Maitland, very grateful, passed up the stairs, the old people dragging slowly in her wake, dropping remarks to one another between yawns.

A long hall crossed the upper floor, one side of which was given over to the Price household. Here were Suzanne's rooms, Chapman's empty habitation, and opposite them Bebita's nurseries. The other side was occupied on the front by Mrs. Janney and the Secretary with a line of guest chambers across the passage. In a small room between his wife's and his step-daughter's Mr. Janney had ensconced himself. He liked the compact space, also his own little balcony where he had his steamer chair and could read and sun himself. As the place was much narrower than the apartments on either side a short branch of hall connected it with the main corridor. His door, at the end of this hall, commanded the head of the stairway.

Mr. Janney had a restless night; he knew he would have for he had taken champagne and coffee and the combination was always disturbing. When he heard the clocks strike twelve he resigned himself to a nuit

Miss Maitland Private Secretary

blanche and lay wide awake listening to the queer sounds that a house gives out in the silent hours. They were of all kinds, gurglings and creaks coming out of the walls, a series of small imperative taps which seemed to emerge from his chest of drawers, thrum-mings and thrillings as if winged things were shut in the closets.

Half-past twelve and one struck and he thought he was going off when he heard a new sound that made him listen — the creaking of a door. He craned up his old tousled head and gave ear, his eyes absently fixed on the strips and spots of moonlight that lay white on the carpet. It was very still, not a whisper, and then suddenly the dogs began to bark, a trail of yaps and yelps that advanced across the lawn. Close to the house they subsided, settling down into growls and conversational snufflings, and he sank back on his pillow. But he was full of nerves, and the idea suddenly occurred to him that Bebita might be sick, it might have been the nursery door that had opened — Annie going to fetch Mrs. Janney. He'd take a look to be sure — if anything was wrong there would be a light.

He climbed out of bed and stole into the hall. No light but the moon, throwing silvery slants across the passage and the stair-head, and relieved, he tiptoed back. It was while he was noiselessly closing his door that he heard something which made him stop, still as

The Cigar Band

a statue, his faculties on the qui vive, his eye glued to the crack — a footstep was ascending the stairs. It was as soft as the fall of snow, so light, so stealthy that no one, unless attentive as he was, would have caught it. Yet it was there, now and then a muffled creak of the boards emphasizing its advance. The corridor at the head of the stairs was as bright as day and with his eye to the crack he waited, his heart beating high and hard.

Rising into the white wash of moonlight came Suzanne, moving with careful softness, her eyes sending piercing glances up and down the hall. Her expression was singular, slightly smiling, with something sly in its sharpened cautiousness. As she rose into full view he saw that she held her wrapper bunched against her waist with one hand and in the other carried Bebita's torch. He was so relieved that he made no move or sound, but, as she disappeared in the direction of her room, softly closed his door and went back to bed.

She had evidently left something downstairs, a book probably — he could not see what she had in the folds of the wrapper — and had gone to get it. If she was wakeful it was a good sign, indicated the condition of distressful unease her mother had hoped to create. Such alarm might lead to a salutory reform, a change, if not of heart, of behavior. Comforted by the thought, he turned on his pillow and at last slept.

CHAPTER V

ROBBERY IN HIGH PLACES

THE next morning Mr. Janney had to read the papers to himself for Miss Maitland went to town on the 8:45. He sat on the balcony and missed her, for the Chicago murder had developed several new features and he had no one to talk them over with. Suzanne, who never came down to breakfast, appeared at twelve and said she was going to the Fairfax's to lunch with bridge afterward. Though she was not yet aware of Mrs. Janney's intention to once more come to her aid, her gloom and ill-humor had disappeared. She looked bright, almost buoyant, her eyes showing a lively gleam, her lips parting in ready smiles. She was going to the beach before lunch, and left with a large knitting bag slung from her arm, and a parasol tilted over her shoulder. It was not until she was half way across the lawn that old Sam remembered her nocturnal appearance which he had intended asking her about.

She was hardly out of sight when Bebita and Annie came into view on the drive, returning from the morn-

'Robbery in High Places

ing bath. Bebita had a trouble and raced up the steps to tell him — she had lost her torch. She was quite disconsolate over it; Annie had said they'd surely find it, but it wasn't anywhere, and she knew she'd left it on the nursery table when she went to bed. In the light of subsequent events Mr. Janney thought his answer to the child had been dictated by Providence. Why he didn't say, " Your mother knows; she had it last night," he never could explain; nor what prompted the words, " Ask your mother; she's probably seen it somewhere." Bebita accepted the suggestion with some hope and then, hearing that her mother would not be home until the afternoon, fell into momentary dejection.

Mrs. Janney was to take her accustomed drive at four and her husband said he would go with her. Some time before the hour he appeared on the balcony, cool and calm, his poise restored after the trials of the previous day and the disturbed night, and sat down to wait. Inside the house his wife was busy. Several important papers had come on the morning mail and these, with the opals, she decided to put in the safe before starting. After they were stored in their shelves and the opals back in their box she could not resist a look at her emeralds, of all her material possessions the dearest. She lifted the purple velvet case and opened it — the emeralds were not there.

She stood motionless, experiencing an inner sense

Miss Maitland Private Secretary

of upheaval, her heart leaping and then sinking down, her body shaken by a tremor such as the earth feels when rocked by a seismic throe. She tried to hold herself steady and opened the other cases — the two pearl necklaces, the sapphire riviere, the diamond and ruby tiara. As each revealed its emptiness her hands began to tremble until, when she reached the white suede box of the black pearl pendant, they shook so she could hardly find the clasp. Everything was gone — a clean sweep had been made of the Janney jewels.

Moving with a firm step, she went to the balcony. In the doorway she came to a halt and said quietly to her husband:

" Sam, my jewels have been stolen."

Air. Janney squared round, stared at her, and ejaculated in feeble denial:

" Oh no! "

" Oh yes," she answered with the same note of grim control, " Come and see."

When he saw, his old veined hands shaking as they dropped the rifled cases, he turned and blankly faced his wife who was watching him with a level scrutiny.

" Mary! " was all he could falter. " Mary, my dear! "

" Last night," she nodded, " when we were out. The place was almost empty. I '11 call the servants."

She went to the foot of the stairs and called Elspeth, 48

Robbery in High Places

old Sam, bewildered by this sudden catastrophe, emerging from the safe, as pale and shaken as if he was the burglar.

" Last night, of course last night," he murmured, trying to think. " They were here at eight. I saw them, we saw them, anybody could have seen them."

Elspeth appeared on the stairs and came running down, Mrs. Janney's orders delivered like pistol shots upon her advance: ,

" I've been robbed. The safe's been opened and all the jewels are gone. Go and call the servants, every one of them. Tell them to come here at once."

Elspeth knew enough to make no reply, and, with a terrified face, scudded past her mistress to the kitchen. Mrs. Janney, her attention attracted by sounds of distracted amazement from her husband, mobilized him:

" Go and get Miss Maitland. We'll have to send for detectives. She can do it — she doesn't lose her head."

Mr. Janney, too stunned to be anything but meekly obedient, trotted off down the hall to Miss Maitland's study, then stopped and came back:

" She's in town; she hasn't got back yet."

" Teh! " Mrs. Janney gave a sound of exasperation. "I'd forgotten it. How maddening 1 You'll have to do it. Go in there to the 'phone "— she indicated the telephone closet at the end of the hall. " Call up the Kissam Agency — that's the best. We had

Miss Mcdiland Private Secretary

them when the bell boy at Atlantic City stole my sables. Get Kissam himself and tell him what's happened and to take hold at once — to come now, not to waste a minute. And don't you either — hurry ! —"

Mr. Janncy hasted away and shut himself in the telephone closet, as the servants, marshaled by Dixon and Elspeth, entered in a scared group. They had been taking tea in their own dining room when Elspeth burst in with the direful news. Eight of them were old employees — had been years in Mrs. Janney's service. Hannah, the cook, had been with her nearly as long as Dixon; Isaac, the footman, was her nephew. Dixon's large, heavy-jowled face was stamped with aghast concern; the kitchen maid was in tears.

Mrs. Janney addressed them like what she was — a general in command of her forces:

" My jewels have been stolen. Some time last night the safe was opened and they were taken. It is my order that every one of you stay in the house, not holding communication with any one outside, until the police have been here and made a thorough investigation. Your rooms and your trunks will have to be searched and I expect you to submit to it willingly with no grumbling."

Dixon answered her:

" It's what we'd expect, Madam. Me and Isaac both know the combination and we'd want to have our own

characters cleared as much as we'd want you to get back your valuables."

Hannah spoke:

" We'd welcome it, Mrs. Janney. There's none of us wants any suspicion restin' on 'em."

Delia, the housemaid with the inflamed eye, took it up. She was a newcomer in the household, and in her fright her brogue acquired an unaccustomed richness:

*' God knows I was in my room at nine, and not a move out of me till sivin the nixt mornin' and that's to-day."

Mr. Janney, issuing from the telephone closet, here interrupted them. He addressed his wife:

" It's all right. I got Kissam himself. He'll be here on the 5:30."

She answered with a nod and was turning for further instructions to Dixon when Suzanne entered from the balcony. Up to that moment Mr. Janney had forgotten all about his nocturnal vision; now it came back upon him with a shattering impact.

He felt his knees turn to water and his heart sink down to inner, unplumbed depths in his anatomy. He grasped at the back of a chair and for once his manners deserted him, for he dropped into it though his wife was standing.

" What's all this ? " said Suzanne, coming to a halt, her glance shifting from her mother to the group of

solemn servants. She looked very pretty, her face flushed, the blue tint of her linen dress harmonizing graciously with her pink cheeks and corn-colored hair.

Mrs. Janney explained. As she did so old Sam, his face as gray as his beard, watched his stepdaughter with a furtive eye. Suzanne appeared amazed, quite horror-stricken. She too sank into a chair, and listened, open-mouthed, her feet thrust out before her, the high heels planted on the rug.

" Why, what an awful thing! " was her final comment. Then as if seized by a sudden thought she turned on Dixon.

" Were all the windows and doors locked last night? "

" All on the lower floor, Mrs. Price. Me and Isaac went round them before we started for the village, and there's not a night —"

Suzanne cut him off brusquely:

" Then how could any one get in to do it? "

There was a curious, surging movement among the servants, a mutter of protest. Mr. Janney intervened:

'* You'd better let matters alone, Suzanne. Detectives are coming and they'll inquire into all that sort of thing."

" I suppose I can ask a question if I like," she said pertly, then suddenly ; looking about the hall, " Where's Miss Maitland?"

" In town," said her mother. 52

"Oh— she went in, did she? I thought her day off was Thursday."

"She asked for to-day — what does it matter?" Mrs. Janney was irritated by these irrelevancies and turned to the servants: " Now I've instructed you and for your own sakes obey what I've said. Not a man or woman leaves the house till after the police have made their search. That applies to the garage men and the gardeners. Dixon, you can tell them —" she stopped, the crunch of motor wheels on the gravel had caught her ear. " There's some one coming. I'm not at home, Dixon."

The servants huddled out to their own domain and Dixon, with a resumption of his best hall-door manner, went to ward off the visitor. But it was only Miss Maitland returning from town. She had several small packages in her hands and looked pale and tired.

The news that greeted her — Mrs. Janney was her informant — left her as blankly amazed as it had the others. She was shocked, asked questions, could hardly believe it. Old Sam found the opportunity a good one to study Suzanne, who appeared extremely interested in the Secretary's remarks. Once, when Miss Maitland spoke of keeping some of her books and the house-money in the safe, he saw his stepdaughter's eyelids flutter and droop over the bird-bright fixity of her glance.

It was at this stage that Bebita ran into the hall and made a joyous rush for her mother:

" Oh, Mummy, I've waited and waited for you,"— she flung herself against Suzanne's side in soft collison. " I've lost my torch and I've asked everybody and nobody's seen it. Do you know where it is? "

Suzanne arched her eyebrows in playful surprise, then putting a finger under the rounded chin, lifted her daughter's face and kissed her, softly, sweetly, tenderly ;

" Darling, I'm so sorry, but I haven't seen it anywhere. If you can't find it I'll buy you another."

CHAPTER VI
POOR MR. JANNEY!

THE peace and aristocratic calm of the Janney household was disrupted. Into its dignified quietude burnt an irruption of alien activity and the great white light of publicity. Kissam with his minions came that evening and reporters followed like bloodhounds on the scent. Scenes were enacted similar to those Mr. Janney had read in novels and witnessed at the theater, but which, in his most fevered imaginings, he had never thought could transpire in his own home. It was unreal, like a nightmare, a phantasmagoria of interviews with terrified servants, trampings up and down stairs, strange men all over the place, reporters on the steps, the telephone bell and the front door bell ringing ceaselessly. Everybody was in a state of tense excitement except Mr. Janney whose condition was that of still, frozen misery. There were moments when he was almost sorry he'd married again.

After introductory parleys with the heads of the house the searchlight of inquiry was turned on the servants. Their movements on the fateful night were subject of special attention. When Kissam elicited the fact that they had not returned from the village till nearly midnight he fell on it with ominous avidity. Dixon, however, had a satisfactory explanation, which he offered with a martyred air of forbearance. Mr. Price's man, Willitts, had that morning come up from town to Cedar Brook, the next station along the line. In the afternoon he had biked over to see them and, hearing of their plan to visit the movies, had arranged to meet them there. This he did, afterward taking them to the Mermaid Ice Cream Parlors where he had treated them to supper. They had left there about half past eleven, Willitts going back to Cedar Brook and the rest of them walking home to Grasslands.

From the women left in the house little was to be gathered. This was unfortunate as the natural supposition was that the burglary had been committed during the hours when they were alone there. Both, feeling ill, had retired early, Delia at about half-past eight, going immediately to bed and quickly falling asleep. Hannah was later; about nine, she thought. It was very quiet, not a sound, except that after she got to her room she heard the dogs barking. They made a great row at first, running down across the lawn, then they quieted, " easing off with sort of whines and yaps, like it was somebody they knew." She had

Poor Mr. Janneyl

not bothered to look out of the window because she thought it was one of the work people from the neighborhood, making a short cut through the grounds.

In the matter of the safe all was incomprehensible and mysterious. Five people in the house knew the combination — Mr. and Mrs. Janney, Dixon and Isaac and Miss Maitland. Mrs. Janney was as certain of the honesty of her servants and her Secretary as she was of her own. She rather resented the detectives' close questioning of the latter. But Miss Maitland showed no hesitation or annoyance, replying clearly and promptly to everything they asked. She kept the house money and some of her account books in the safe and on the second of the month — five days before the robbery — had taken out such money as she had there to pay the working people who did not receive checks. She managed the financial side of the establishment, she explained, paying the wages and bills and drawing the checks for Mrs. Janney's signature.

Questioned about her movements that afternoon, her answers showed the same intelligent frankness. She had spent the two hours after lunch altering the dress she was to wear that evening. As it was very warm in her room she had taken part of it to her study on the ground floor. When she had finished her work — about four — she had gone for a walk returning just before the storm. After that she had retired to

Miss Maitland Private Secretary

her room and stayed there until she came down to go to Mr. Ferguson's dinner.

The safe and its surroundings were subjected to a minute inspection which revealed nothing. Neither window had been tampered with, the locks were intact, the sills unscratched, the floor showed no foot-mark. There were no traces of finger prints either upon the door or the metal-clamped boxes in which the jewel cases were kept. The mended chair was just as Mrs. Janney remembered it, set between the safe and the window, in the way of any one passing along the hall.

It was on Sunday afternoon — twenty-four hours after the discovery — that Dick Ferguson appeared with one of his gardeners, who had a story to tell. On Friday night the man had been to a card party in the garage of a neighboring estate and had come home late " across lots." His final short cut had been through Grasslands, where he had passed round by the back of the house. He thought the time would be on toward one-thirty. Skirting the kitchen wing he had seen a light in a ground floor window, a window which he was able to indicate. He described the light as not very strong and white, not yellow like a lamp or candle. As he looked at it he noticed that it diminished in brightness as if it was withdrawn, moved away down a hall or into a room. He could see no figure, simply the lit oblong of the window, with the pattern

of a lace curtain over it, and anyway he hadn't noticed much, supposing it to be one of the servants coming home late like himself.

This settled the hour of the robbery. It had not been committed when the place was almost deserted, but when all its occupants were housed and sleeping. The window, pointed out by the man, was directly opposite the safe door, the light as he described it could only have been made by an electric lantern or torch, its gradual diminishment caused by its removal into the recess of the safe.

If before this Mr. Janney's mental state was painful, it now became agonized. He was afraid to be with the detectives for fear of what he would hear, and he was afraid to leave them alone, for fear of what he might miss. When Mrs. Janney conferred with Kissam he sat by her side, swallowing on a dry throat, and trying to control the inner trembling that attacked him every time the man opened his lips. He gave way to secret, futile cursings of the jewels, distracted prayers that they never might be found. For if they were, the theft might be traced to its author — and then what? It would be the end of his wife, her proud head would be lowered forever, her strong heart broken. Sleep entirely forsook him and the people who came to call treated him with a soothing gentleness as if they thought he was dying.

His misery reached a climax when something he remembered, and every one else had forgotten, came to light. It was one day in the library when Kissam asked Mrs. Janney if there had ever been any one else in the house — a discharged employee or relation — who had known the combination. Mrs. Janney said no and then recollected that Chapman Price did, he had kept his tobacco in the safe as the damp spoiled it. Kissam showed no interest — he knew Chapman Price was her son-in-law and was no longer an inmate — and then suddenly asked what had been done with the written combination.

At that question Mr. Janney felt like a shipwrecked mariner deprived of the spar to which he has been clinging. He saw his wife's face charged with aroused interest — she'd forgotten it, it was in Mr. Janney's desk, had always been kept there. They went to the desk and found it under a sheaf of papers in a drawer that was unlocked. Kissam looked at it, felt and studied the papers, then put it back in a silence that made Mr. Janney feel sick.

After that he was prepared for anything to happen, but nothing did. He got some comfort from the papers, which assumed the robbery to have been an " outside job "; no one in the house fitting the character of a suspect. It was the work of experts, who had entered by the second story, and were of that class of

burglar known as " tumblers." Mr. Janney, who had never heard of a " tumbler" save as a vessel from which to drink, now learned that it was a crackman, who from a sensitive touch and long training, could manipulate the locks and work out the combination. He found himself thanking heaven that such men existed.

When a week passed and nothing of moment came to the surface, the Janney jewel robbery slipped back to the inside page, and, save in the environs of Berkeley, ceased to occupy the public mind. Mr. Janney could once more walk in his own grounds without fear of reporters leaping on him from the shrubberies or emerging from behind statues and garden benches. His tense state relaxed, he began to breathe freely, and, in this restoration to the normal, he was able to think of what he ought to do. Somehow, some day, he would have to face Suzanne with his knowledge and get the jewels back. It would be a day of fearful reckoning; it was so appalling to contemplate that he shrank from it even in thought. He said he wasn't strong enough yet, would work up to it, get some more sleep and his nerves in better shape. And she might — there was always the hope — she might get frightened and return them herself.

So he rested in a sort of breathing spell between the first, grinding agony and the formidably looming fu-

ture. But it was not to last — events were shaping to an end that he had never suspected and that came upon him like a bolt from the blue.

It happened one afternoon eight days after the robbery. Mrs. Janney and Suzanne had gone for a drive and he was alone in the library, listlessly going over the morning papers. His zest in the news had left him — the Chicago murder offered no interest, the stabbed policeman in desperate case from blood poisoning, his assailant still at large, could not conjure away his dark anxieties. With his glasses dangling from his finger, his eyes on the green sweep of the lawn, he was roused by a knock on the door. It was Dixon announcing Mr. Kissam, who had walked up from the village and wanted to see him.

Kissam, with a brief phrase of greeting, closed the door and sat down. Mr. Janney thought his manner, which was always hard and brusque, was softened by a suggestion of confidence, something of intimacy as one who speaks man to man. It made him nervous and his uneasiness was not relieved in the least by the detective's words.

" I'm glad to find you alone, Mr. Janney. I 'phoned up and heard from Dixon that the ladies were out and that's why I came. I want to consult you before I say anything to Mrs. Janney."

" That's quite right," said Mr. Janney, then added 62

Poor Mr. Janney!

with a feeble attempt at lightness, " Are you, as the children say, getting any warmer f "

" We're very warm. In fact I think we've almost got there. But it's rather a ticklish situation."

Mr. Janney did not answer; he glanced at his shoes, then at the silver on the desk. For the moment he was too perturbed to look at Kissam's shrewd, attentive face.

" It's so out of the ordinary run," the man went on, " and so much is involved that I decided not to move without first telling you. The family being so prominent —"

" The family!" Mr. Janney spoke before he thought, his limp hands suddenly clenching on the arms of the chair.

The detective's eyes steadied on the gripped fingers.

"What do you mean? Let me have it straight," said the old man huskily.

Kiss am put his hand in his hip pocket and drew out an electric torch which he put on the desk.

" This torch I myself found two days ago in a desk in Mrs. Price's room. It was pushed back in a drawer which was full of letters and papers. It fits the description of the torch that was lost by Mrs. Price's little girl."

Mr. Janney's head sunk forward on his breast, and Kissam knew now that his suspicions were correct and that the old man had known all along. He was sorry for him:

" Mrs. Price not being your daughter, Mr. Janney, I decided to come to you. I suspected her after the second day and I'll tell you why. I had a private interview with that woman Elspeth, Mrs. Janney's maid, and she told me of a quarrel she had overheard between Mrs. Janney and her daughter. The subject of the quarrel was money, Mrs. Price asldng for a large sum to meet certain debts and losses in the stock market which Mrs. Janney refused to give her. That supplied the motive and gave me the lead. The loss of the torch was also significant. The child was confident — and children are very accurate — that she had left it on the table in her nursery when she went to bed. The proximity of the two rooms made the theft of the torch an easy matter. What puzzled me was how Mrs. Price had gained access to the safe, but that was cleared up when the written combination was found in your desk here; and finally I ran across what I should call perfectly conclusive evidence in Mrs. Price's room. I don't refer only to the torch, but to the fact that a wrapper that was hanging in the back of one of the closets showed a smudge of varnish on the skirt."

Mr. Janney leaned forward over his clasped hands, feeling wan and shriveled.

Poor Mr. Janney!

" If your surmise is right," he said, " where has she put them?"

" If! " echoed the other. " I don't see any if about it. You can't suspect either of the men servants — reliable people of established character — nor Miss Maitland. A girl in her position — even if she happened to be dishonest, which I don't for a moment think she is — wouldn't tackle a job as big as that. Come, Mr. Jannej, -we don't need to dodge around the stump. As soon as I'd spoken I saw you thought Mrs. Price had done it."

The old man nodded and said sadly:

" I did."

" Would you mind telling me why you did? "

There was nothing for it but to tell, and he told, the detective suppressing a grin of triumph. It cleared up everything, was as conclusive as if they'd seen her commit the act.

" As for where she put them," he said, " she may have a hiding place in the house that we haven't discovered, or cached them outside. In matters like this women sometimes show a remarkable cunning. I've looked up her movements on the Saturday and it's possible she hid them somewhere in the woods. She left the house at twelve, carrying a silk work bag, walked past Ferguson's place and talked there with him in the garden for about fifteen minutes, went on to

the beach, sat there a while, and then walked to the Fairfax house on the bluff, where she stayed to lunch, coming back here about half-past four. She had ample opportunity during that time and in the places she passed through to find a cache for them."

Mr. Janney raised a gray, pitiful face:

" Mr. Kissam, if Mrs. Janney knew this it would kill her."

Kissam gave back an understanding look:

" That's why I came to you."

" Then it must stop here — with me." The old man spoke with a sudden, fierce vehemence. " It can't go further. The girl's been a torment and a trouble for years. I won't let her end by breaking her mother's heart, bringing her gray hairs with sorrow to the grave. Good God, I'd rather say I did it myself."

" There's no need for that. We can let it fizzle out, die down gradually." He gave a slight, sardonic smile. " I've happened on this sort of thing before, Mr. Janney. The rich have their skeletons in the closet, and I've helped to keep 'em there, shut in tight."

" Then for heaven's sake do it in this case — help me hide this skeleton. Keep up the search for a while so that Mrs. Janney won't suspect anything; play your part. Mr. Kissam, if you'll aid me in keeping this dark there's nothing I wouldn't do to repay you."

Kissam disclaimed all desire for reward. His pro-

fessional pride was justified; he had made good to his own satisfaction. And, as he had said, the case presented no startling novelty to his seasoned experience. Many times he had helped distracted families to suppress ugly revelations, presented an impregnable front to the press, and seen, with a cynical amusement, columns shrink to paragraphs and the public's curiosity fade to the vanishing point. He promised he would aid in the slow quenching of the Janney sensation, gradually let it flicker out, ke'ep his men on the job for a while longer for Mrs. Janney's benefit, and finally let the matter decline to the status of an " unsolved mystery."

As to the restoration of the jewels he gave advice. Say nothing for a time, sit quiet and give no sign. If she was as thoroughly scared as she ought to be, she would probably return them — they would wake one fine morning and find everything back in the safe. If, however, she tried to realize on them it would be easy to trace them — he would be on the watch — and then Mr. Janney could confront her with his knowledge and have her under his thumb forever.

Mr. Janney was extremely grateful — not at the prospect of having Suzanne under his thumb, that was too complete a reversal of positions to be comfortable — but at the detective's kindly comprehension and aid. With tears in his eyes he wrung Kissam's hand and honored him by a personal escort to the front door.

CHAPTER VII

CONCEENING DETECTIVES

KISSAM kept his word and the interest in the Janney robbery began to languish. Detectives still came and went, morning trains still disgorged reporters, but it was not as it had been. The first, fine careless rapture of the chase was over; nothing new was discovered, nothing old developed. The house settled back to its methodical regime, the faces of its inmates lost their looks of harassed distress.

Mr. Janney, though much pacified, was not yet restored to his normal poise. His wife was now the object of his secret attention, for he knew her to be a very sharp and observant person, and the fear that she might " catch on " haunted him. It was therefore very upsetting when she remarked one morning at breakfast that " those men didn't seem to be doing much. They were just where they had been ten days ago."

He tried to reassure her — it would be a long slow affair — didn't she remember the James case, where a year after the theft the jewels were found under the

skin of a ham hanging in the cellar? Mrs. Janney was not appeased, she scoffed at the ham, and said the detectives were the stupidest body of men in the country outside Congress. She was going to offer a reward, ten thousand dollars — and then she muttered something about " taking a hand herself." In answer to Mr. Jan-ney's alarmed questions she quieted down, laughed, and said she didn't mean anything.

She did, however, and had Mr. Janney known it wakeful nights would again have been his portion. But she had no intention of telling him. She had seen that he was worn out, a mere bundle of nerves, and what she intended to do would be done without his knowledge or connivance. This was to start a private inquiry of her own. The written combination, loose in an unlocked drawer, had influenced her; it was possible some one in the house had found it. She felt that she owed it to her dependents and herself to make sure. And the best way to do this was to have a detective on the spot —but a detective whose profession would be unknown. Fortunately the plan was workable; there was a vacancy in the household staff. For the past month she had been advocating the engagement of a nursery governess for Bebita.

Two days after her slip to Mr. Janney an opportunity came for broaching the subject. They were at lunch when Suzanne announced that she intended going

to town the next morning. It was about Bebita — the child's eyes, which had troubled her in the spring, were again inflamed and she had complained of pain in them. Suzanne wanted to consult the oculist; she hoped a prescription would be sufficient, but of course if he insisted on seeing the child she would have to be taken in for an examination.

Mrs. Janney thought it the right thing to do and said she would accompany her daughter. Suzanne, who was eating her lunch, paused with suspended fork and sidelong eye; — why was that necessary, she was perfectly competent to attend to the matter. Mrs. Janney agreed and said she was going on another errand — to see about the nursery governess they had spoken of so often. It was time something was done, Bebita was running wild, forgetting all she had learned last winter. Mrs. Janney had heard of several women who might answer and would spend the day looking them up and interviewing them. Suzanne returned to her food. " Oh, very well, it might be a good thing, only please get some one young and cheerful who didn't put on airs and want to be a member of the family."

One of Suzanne's fads was a fear of the Pennsylvania Tunnel. Whether it was a pose or genuine she absolutely refused to go through it, declaring that on her one trip she had nearly died of fright and the pressure on her ears. Since that alarming experience she

always went to the city either by the old Long Island Ferry route, or by motor across the Queensborough Bridge.

It being a fine morning they decided to drive in — about an hour's run — and at ten they started forth. They chatted amicably, for Suzanne, since the robbery and the knowledge that her debts were paid, had been unusually gay and good-humored. They separated at Altman's, Mrs. Janney keeping the motor, Suzanne taking a taxi. At four they would meet at a tea room and drive home together.

Mrs. Janney's first point of call was a strange place in which to look for a nursery governess. It was the office of Whitney & Whitney, her lawyers, far downtown near Wall Street. She was at once conducted into Mr. Whitney's sanctum, for besides being an important client she was a personal friend. He moved forward to meet her — a large, slightly stooped, heavily built man with a shock of thick gray hair, and eyes, singularly clear and piercing, overshadowed by bushy brows. His son, George, was sent for, and after greetings, jolly and intimate, they settled down to talk over Mrs. Janney's business.

She told them the situation and her needs — could they find the sort of person she wanted. She knew they employed detectives of all sorts and Kissam's men had been so lacking in energy and so stupid that she wanted

no more of that kind. She had to have a woman of whose character they were assured, and sufficiently presentable to pass muster with the master and the servants. Mr. Whitney gave a look at his son and they exchanged a smile.

" Go and see if you can get her on the wire, George," he said, " and if she's willing tell her to come down right now." Then as the young man left the room he turned to Mrs. Janney. " I know the very person, the best in New York, if she'll undertake it."

" Some one who's thoroughly reliable and can fit into the place? "

" My dear friend, she's as reliable as you are and that's saying a good deal. As to fitting in, leave that to her. In her natural state there are still some rough edges, but when she's playing a part they don't show. She's smart enough to hide them."

" Who is she — a detective ? "

" Not a real one, not a professional. She was a telephone girl and then she made a good marriage — fellow named Babbitts, star reporter on the Despatch. She's in love and happy and prosperous, but now and again she'll do work for us. It's partly for old sakes' sake and partly because she has the passion of the artist — can't resist if the call comes to her. She came to our notice during the Hesketh case — did some of the cleverest work I ever saw and got Reddy out of

Concerning Detectives

prison. The Reddys are among her best friends — can't do too much for her."

Mrs. Janney, who knew the beautiful Mrs. Reddy, was impressed.

" Do you think she'll come? " she asked anxiously.

He gave her a meaning look and nodded;

" Yes. It's an unusually interesting case."

Half an hour later Mrs. Janney met Molly Morgen-thau Babbitts and laid the situation before her. She found the much-vaunted young woman, a pretty, slender girl, with crisply curly black hair, honest brown eyes, and a pleasantly simple manner. Mrs. Janney liked what she said and liked her. There was no doubt about her intelligence and as to rousing any suspicions in the household — she would have deceived Mr. Janney — she even would have deceived Dixon. As the case was outlined she could not hide her kindling interest and, when she agreed to undertake the work, Mrs. Janney felt that the nursery governess idea had been an inspiration. The interview ended with practical details: Mrs. Babbitts would make her reports to the Whitneys, who would figure as her employers and would hand on her findings to Mrs. Janney. She would arrive by the twelve-thirty train on the following day and be known at Grasslands as Miss Rodgers. As they were separating she asked if there was a branch telephone on the upper floor and, being told that there was in an alcove

Miss Maitland Private Secretary

off the main hall, requested that her room might be near it as the telephone played an important part in her work.

Suzanne's course had a curious resemblance to her mother's, though her plan of procedure was different.

From the day after the robbery she had developed an interest in the telephone " Red Book." She had taken it to her room and turning to the D's studied the list of detective agencies. After much comparison and cogitation she had copied down the name of one Horace Larkin, who appeared to be in business by himself and whose office was in a central and accessible part of the city.

After she had parted from her mother she went to a department store, shut herself in a telephone booth, and called up Mr. Larkin. A masculine voice, that of Larkin himself, had answered, and explaining her desire to see him on important business, he had made an appointment to meet her that afternoon at the Janney house on Fifth Avenue.

This was an excellent place for Suzanne's purpose, closed for the summer, its porch boarded up, its blue-blinded windows proclaiming its desertion. An ancient caretaker occupied the basement with her niece, Aggie McGee, to help and be company. Mrs. Janney never went there, but now and then Suzanne did, generally

on a quest for some needed garment, so that her presence in the house was in no way remarkable.

The appointment was for two and, after telling Aggie McGee that a gentleman would call and to show him into the reception room, she retired to the long Louis Quinze salon and threw herself on a sofa. She was a little scared at what she had planned but she did not let her uneasiness interfere with her intention, for, her jnind once set on a goal, she was as determined as her mother. Stretched comfortably on the sofa, her glance traveling over the covered walls, the chandelier, a misshapen bulging whiteness below the frescoed ceiling, she carefully thought out what she would say to Mr. Larkin.

A ring of the bell brought her to a sitting position, her hands pushing in loosened hairpins. She waited listening, heard the opening and closing of doors and then Aggie McGee's head appeared between the shrouded portieres and announced, " The gentleman to see you, ma'am."

Her first impression of him was as a tall, broad-shouldered shape, detailless against the light of the window. Then, as she sunk into a chair, motioning him to one opposite, a nearer view showed him as a fine-looking man, on to forty, with a fresh-colored, rounded face, its expression smilingly good-humored. After the unkempt and slouchy detectives she had seen

Miss Maitland Private Secretary

at Grasslands his appearance, natty, smart, almost that of a man of fashion, surprised and pleased her. She had an instinctive distaste for all ungroomed and ill-dressed people and seeing him so like the members of her own world, she felt a rising confidence and reassurance. Also his manners were good, respectful, business-like. The one thing about him that suggested the wily sleuth were his eyes, very light colored in his ruddy face, small, shrewd and piercing.

He came to the matter of the moment without any preamble. Yes, he knew of the robbery and knew who she was; he supposed she had called him up to consult him about the case.

" Of course, Mr. Larkin," she said, " that's what I wanted. But before I say anything it must be understood between us that this — er — sending for you — is entirely my affair. I want to employ you myself in-depently of the others."

He nodded, showing no surprise;

" You want to put your own detective on the case."

" Exactly. You're to be employed by me but no one must know you are or know what you're doing."

He smothered a smile and said :

" I see."

" I don't think the men that are working over it now are very clever or interested. They just poke about and ask the same questions over and over. The way

they're going I should say we'd never get anything back. So I decided I'd start an inquiry of my own and in a direction no one else had thought of."

Mr. I ;irkin gave a slight movement an almost imper-ceptib' -jtraightening up of his body:

** D< ou mean that you suspect some one? "

Sux ne looked at the arm of her chair and then smoou ed its linen cover with delicate finger tips. A very .light color deepened the artificial rose of her cheel .

" V*K afraid I do," she murmured.

"Afraid?"

She nodded, closing her eyes with the movement. She had the appearance of a person distressed but resolute.

" I can't help suspecting some one that I don't like to suspect. And that's why I want your assistance."

" I don't quite understand, Mrs. Price."

" This is the explanation. If it were known that this person was guilty it would ruin and destroy them. My idea is to be sure that they did it — have evidence — and then tell my mother. We could keep quiet about it, get the jewels back and not have the thief disgraced and sent to jail."

" Oh, I see. You want to face the party with a, knowledge of their guilt, have them restore the jewels,, and let the matter drop."

Miss Maitland Private Secretary

" Precisely. And I don't want to say anything until I'm sure, can come out with everything all clear and proved. That's where I expect you to help, put things together, find out, work up the case."

" Who is the person? "

Her color burned to a deep flush; she leaned toward him, urgent, almost pleading:

" Mr. Larkin, I hardly like to say it even to you, but I must. It's my mother's secretary, Miss Maitland."

He looked stolidly unmoved:

" She lives in the house? "

" Yes, for over a year now. My mother thinks everything of her, wouldn't believe it unless it was proved past a doubt."

" What are your reasons for suspecting her? "

Suzanne was silent for a moment moving her glance from him to the window. Mr. Larkin had a good chance to look at her and took it. He noticed the feverish color, the line between the brows, the tightened muscles under the thin cheeks. He made a mental note of the fact that she was agitated.

" Well that night, the night of July the seventh," she said in a low voice, " I was wakeful. I often am, I've always been a nervous, restless sort of person. About half past one I thought I heard a noise — some one on the stairs — and I got up and looked out of my

Concerning Detectives

door. I can see the head of the stairs from there, and as it was very bright moonlight any one coming up would be perfectly plain — I couldn't make a mistake — what I saw was Miss Maitland. She was going very carefully, tiptoeing along as if she was trying to make no noise. At the top she turned and went down the passage to her own room which is just beyond my mother's."

She paused and shot a tentative look at him. He met it, teetered his head in quiet comprehension and murmured:

"She didn't see you?"

" Oh no, she was not looking that way. And I didn't say anything or think anything then — thought she'd gone downstairs for something she'd forgotten. The next day it had passed out of my mind; it wasn't until I heard that the jewels were gone that it came back and then I was too shocked to say a word. It all came upon me in a minute — I remembered how I'd seen her and remembered that she knew the combination of the safe."

" Oh," said Mr. Larkin, " she knew that, did she?"

" Yes, she keeps her account books and money in there, things she uses in her work. You see she's been thoroughly trusted — never looked upon as anything but perfectly honest and reliable."

Miss Maitland Private Secretary

" Then she's filled her position to Mrs. Janney's satisfaction? "

" Entirely. Of course we really don't know very much about her. She was highly recommended when she came, but people in her position if they do their work well — one doesn't bother much about them."

" Have you noticed anything in her conduct or manner of life lately that could — er — have any connection with or throw any light on such an action? "

Suzanne pondered for a moment then said:

" No — she's always been about the same. She's gone into the city more this summer than she did last year, on her holidays, I mean. And — oh yes, this may be important — that night, when we came home from dinner, she asked my mother if she could have the following day — Saturday — in town. Mrs. Janney said she might and she went in before any of the family were up."

" Um," murmured Mr. Larkin and then fell into a silence in which he appeared to be digesting this last item. When he spoke again it was to propound a question that ruffled Suzanne's composure and caused her blue eyes to give out a sudden spark:

" Do you happen to know if she has any admirer — lover or fiance or anything of that sort? "

" I know nothing whatever about it, but I should say not. Certainly I never heard of such a person. I

Concerning Detectives

never saw any man in the least attracted by her and I should imagine she was a girl who had no charm for the other sex."

Mr. Larkin stirred in a slow, large way and said:

" Such a robbery is a pretty big thing for a girl like that to attempt. She must know — any one would — that jewels like Mrs. Janney's are hard to dispose of without detection."

Suzanne shrugged, her tone showing an edge of irritation :

" That may be the case, I suppose it is. But couldn't she have been employed by some one — aren't there gangs who put people on the spot to rob for them?"

" Certainly there are. And that would be the most plausible explanation. Not necessarily a gang, however, an individual might be behind her. At this stage, knowing what I do, that would be my idea. But, of course, I can say nothing until I'm better informed. What I'll do now will be to look up her record and then I think I'll take a run down to Berkeley and see if I can pick up anything there."

Suzanne looked uneasy:

" But you'll be careful, and not let any one guess what you're doing or that you have any business with me? "

He smiled openly at that:

" Mrs. Price, you can trust me. This is not ray first case."

After that there was talk of financial arrangements and future plans. Mr. Larkin thought he would come out to Berkeley in a day or two and take a lodging in the village. When he had anything of moment to impart he would drop a note to Mrs. Price and she could designate a rendezvous. They parted amicably, Suzanne feeling that she had found the right man and Mr. Larkin secretly elated, for this was the first case of real magnitude that had come his way.

At the appointed time Suzanne met Mrs. Janney at the tea room and on the way home they exchanged their news. The nursery governess had been found, approved and engaged, and the oculist had said to go on with the lotion and if Bebita's eyes did not improve to bring her in to see him. Both ladies agreed that their labors had exhausted them, but each looked unusually vivacious and mettlesome.

CHAPTER VIII

MOLLY'S STORY

I'VE been asked to tell the part of this story in which I figure. I've done that kind of work before, so I'm not as shy as I was that first time, and since then I've studied some, and come up against fine people, and I'm older — twenty-seven on my last birthday. But as I said then, so I'll say now — don't expect any stylish writing from me. At the switchboard there's still ginger in me, but with the pen I'm one of the " also rans."

Fortunately for me, I was always a good one to throw a bluff and, having made a few excursions into the halls of the rich and great, I felt I could be safely featured as a nursery governess. She belongs in the layer between the top and bottom and doesn't mix with either. I wouldn't have to play down to the kitchen standards or up to the parlor ones, just move along, sort of lonesome, in the neutral ground between. As for teaching the child, I knew I could do that as well as the girls who are marking time until they marry, or the decayed ladies who employ their declining years and intellects that way.

It didn't seem to me hard to size up the family. Mrs. Janney was the head of it, the middle and both ends — a real queen who didn't need a crown or a throne to make people bow the knee. Mr. Janney was a good, kind old»gentleman who was too law-abiding to get ricli any way but the way he did. Mrs. Price wasn't up to their measure — an only child, born with a silver lining. She was one of those slimp'sy, thin women that a man would be afraid to hug for fear she'd crack in his arms or snap in the middle. She was very cordial and pleasant to me and I will say she was fond of her little girl.

When I came to the servants I couldn't see but what every one of them registered honesty. If it had been printed on their foreheads with a rubber stamp it couldn't have been plainer. There were only two new ones in the outfit — girls, one of them my chambermaid — and no one, not even a sleuth desperate for glory, could have considered them. Outside there were gardeners and chauffeurs — in all there were twenty-one people employed — but it was the same with them. They were a decent, well-paid lot, the garage men and head gardener living on the place, the laborers lodged in the village.

The one person my eye lingered on was Miss Maitland the Secretary. Not that there was anything suspicious about her, but that she wasn't as simple and

easy to see into as the others. She was a handsome girl, tall and well made, sticking close to her job and not having much to do with any one. Her study was just under the day nursery where we had lessons and had its own door on to the piazza. When she wasn't at work, she'd either sit there reading or go off walking by herself and there was something solitary and serious about her that interested me. The nursery window was a good look-out, commanding the lawns and garden and with the tennis court to one side. After lessons I'd let the blinds down and coil up there on a cushion, and I saw her several times coming in and going out, always alone, and always looking thoughtful and depressed.

To get any information about her I had to be very careful for Mrs. Janney thought the world of her, but I managed to worm out some facts, though nothing of any importance. She had come to Mrs. Janney from a friend who had had her as secretary for two years. She was entirely dependent on her work for her living, was an orphan, and had no followers. The only thing the least degree out of line was that several times during the spring and the early summer she had asked for more days and afternoons off than formerly. Mrs. Janney didn't seem to think anything of this and I didn't either. The girl — settled down in her place

Miss Maitland Private Secretary

and knowing it secure — was slackening up on her first speed.

There were a lot of people coming and going in the house — oftenest, Mr. Richard Ferguson. I'd heard of him — everybody has — millions, unmarried, and so forth and so on. I hadn't been there thirty-six hours before I saw that Mrs. Price had an eye for him. That's putting it in a considerate, refined way. If I was the cat some women are, I'd say she was camped on his trail, with her lassoo ready in her hand. Of course she'd work it the way ladies do, very genteel, pretend to be lazy if he wanted to play tennis and when he was off for a swim wonder if she had the energy to walk to the beach. But she always got there; every time, rain or shine, she'd be awake at the switch. I didn't know whether he responded — you couldn't tell. He was the kind who was jolly and affable to everybody; even if he was a plutocrat you had to like him.

I had a good deal of time to myself — lessons only lasted two hours — and I roamed round the neighborhood studying it. The second afternoon I went into the woods, where there's a short-cut that goes past Council Oaks to the beach. Off the path, branching to the right, I found two smaller trails both leading to the same place — a pond, surrounded by trees, and with a wharf, a rustic bench, and two bathing

Molly's Story

houses, where the trails ended. In ray room that evening I asked Ellen, my chambermaid, about the pond and she told me it was called Little Fresh and that the bathing houses and wharf had been built by the former owner of Grasslands. But the first year of Mrs. Janney's occupation a boy from the village had been drowned there, since when Mrs. Janney had forbidden any one to go near or bathe in Little Fresh. She had put up trespassing signs and locked the bath houses, and no one ever went there now, because, anyway if you didn't go in and get drowned, folks said you might catch malaria.

A few days after that Bebita asked me to go into the woods with her and look for lady-slippers; the kitchen maid had found two and Bebita had to see if there weren't any left for her. Everybody said it was too late for them, but that didn't faze Bebita who had the kitchen maid's word for it and was set upon going.

The woods were lovely, all green and shimmery with sunlight. We took the trail I've spoken of, I strolling along the path, and Bebita hunting about in the underbrush for the flowers. I was some little distance ahead of her when I saw a figure moving behind the screen of trees toward the right. I could only catch it in broken bits through the leaves, hear the footsteps soft on the moss, and I didn't know whether it was a man or a woman. Then it came into view, out of the trail that

led to Little Fresh Pond, and I saw it was a man, who stopped short at the sight of me.

He was good-looking, the dark kind, naturally brown, and sunburned on top of it until he was as swarthy as an Indian, the little mustache on his upper lip as black as if it was painted on with ink. Now I'm not one that thinks men ought to be stunned by my beauty, but also I don't expect to be stared at as if the sight of me was an unpleasant shock. And that's the way that piratical guy acted, standing rooted, glaring angry from under his eyebrows.

I was going to pass on haughty, when Bebita's voice came from behind in a joyful cry of " Popsy." She rushed by me, her arms spread out, and fairly jumped at him. The ugly look went from his face as if you'd wiped it off with a sponge, and the one that took its place made him another man. He caught her up and held her against him, and she locked her feet behind his waist and her hands behind his neck swinging off from him and laughing out:

" Oh, Popsy, I was looking for lady-slippers and I found you"

" Well," he said, gazing at her like he couldn't look enough, " would you rather have found a lady-slipper? "

She hugged up against him, awful sweet and cunning.

Molly's Story

"Oh, Popsy, that's a joke. I like you better than all the lady-slippers in the world. Where have you been?"

" Over on the bluff, calling on some people. I'm taking a short cut through the woods."

" Where are you going now ? "

" To Cedar Brook. My car's out there on the road at the end of the path."

I knew Bebita had been told not to speak of her father. I'd heard it from Annie and Mrs. Janney had cautioned me, if she asked any questions, to say that he had gone away and was not coming back. Children are queer, take in more than you think, and I believe the little thing felt something of the tragedy of it. Anyway she said nothing more on that subject, but loosing one hand, waved it at me;

" That's my new governess, Miss Rogers. I'm studying lessons with her."

He looked at me, and having no free hand, just nodded. Though his expression wasn't as unfriendly as it had been, it didn't suggest any desire to know me better. He turned back to Bebita.

" Dearie, you'll have to let go for I must jog along. I've a date to play tennis at Cedar Brook and I'm late now."

He kissed her and she loosened her hold sliding through his arms to the ground. Then with a few last

words of good-by he swung off down the path. Bebita looked after him till the trees hid him, gave a sigh, and without a word pushed her little hand into mine and walked along beside me. She seemed sobered for a while, then picked up heart, began to look about her, and was soon back at her hunt for the flowers.

I was nearing the second path to Little Fresh, when again I saw a figure coming behind the trees. This time it showed in a moving pattern of lilac and the sight made me brisk up for I'd seen Miss Maitland that morning in a lilac linen dress. I quickened my step until I came to a turning from which I could look up the branch trail, and sure enough, there she was, walking very lightly and spying out ahead. At the sight of me she too stopped and looked annoyed. But women are a good deal quicker than men — in a minute the look was gone and she was all smiles of welcome.

" Oh, Miss Rogers, and Bebita too ! How nice to meet you. Are you going to the beach? "

Bebita explained our quest and said she was going to give it up — there wasn't a single lady-slipper left.

Miss Maitland's smile was kind and consoling:

" I could have told you that. They're gone for this year."

"Have you been looking for them?" Bebita asked.

No, Miss Maitland had been to the beach for a bath, and as the closed season for lady-slippers had begun,

Molly's Story

we turned back, Bebita and the Secretary in front, I meekly following. In answer to the child's questions Miss Maitland said she had taken a long swim, out beyond the raft.

Suddenly Bebita popped out with:

" Did you see my Daddy? "

There was a slight pause before she answered; when she did her voice was full of surprise:

" Mr. Price! Was he on the beach ? "

" No, in the woods. We met him. He was taking a short cut."

Miss Maitland said she hadn't seen him, that he must have been some distance in front of her, and changed the subject.

While they were talking I was thinking and absently looking at her back. They'd both come out of the branch trails that led to Little Fresh; they had taken different paths and not come at the same time; they had each got a jar when they saw me. As I thought, my eyes went wandering over her back and finally stopped at the nape of her neck. The hair was drawn up from it and hidden under her hat. I could see the roots and the little curly locks that drooped down against the white skin. And suddenly I noticed something — they were perfectly dry, not a damp spot, not a wet hair. The best bathing cap in the world couldn't keep the water out like that. She had not been

Miss Maitland Private Secretary

bathing at all, she had been with Chapman Price at Little Fresh Pond. And they wanted no one to know; were sufficiently anxious to lie about it.

The next day in a conference with Mrs. Janney, I asked her if Mr. Price had ever shown any interest in Miss Maitland. She was amazed, as shocked as if I'd asked if Mr. Janney had ever been in love with the cook. Chapman Price had taken no more notice of Miss Maitland than common politeness demanded, in fact, she thought that of late he had rather shunned her. She was curious to know why I asked such a question, and when I said I had to ask any and every sort of question or she'd be paying a detective's salary to a nursery governess, she saw the sense of it and quieted down.

That was more than I did. The way things were opening up, I was getting that small, inner thrill, that feeling like your nerves are tingling that comes to me when the darkness begins to break. I didn't see much, just the first, faint glimmer, but it was the right kind.

Two days later a thing happened that changed the glimmer to a wide bright ray. It was this way:

In the afternoon the family, unless they had a party of their own, were always out. The only person who stayed around was Miss Maitland, sometimes working over her books, sometimes sitting about sewing or reading. That day — about four — I'd seen her as I passed the study window writing at her desk. I'd

gone on into the big central hall where I wasn't supposed to belong, but feeling safe with everybody scattered, I thought I'd make myself comfortable and take a look at the morning papers. I'd just cuddled down in the corner of the sofa with my favorite daily when I heard the telephone ring.

Now the bell of the telephone is to me like the trumpet to the old war horse. And hearing it that way, tingling in the quiet of the big, deserted house, I got a flash that any one wanting to talk to Miss Maitland and knowing the habits of the family would choose that hour. There was a 'phone in the lower story — in a closet at the end of the hall — and the extension one was upstairs in a sort of curtained recess off the main corridor just outside my door. I rose off the sofa as if lifted by a charge of dynamite and slid for the stairs. As I sprinted up I heard the door of Miss Maitland's study open.

The upper hall was deserted and I dashed noiseless into that alcove place, one hand lifting off the receiver as soft as a feather, the other pressed against my mouth to smother the sound of my breathing. On the floor below Esther Maitland had just connected; I got her first sentence, quiet and clear as if she was in the room with me:

" Yes. This is Grasslands."

A man's voice answered:

Miss Maitland Private Secretary

"That you, Esther?"

I could tell she recognized it, for instantly hers changed, showed fear and a sort of pleading:

" Oh, why do you call me up here ? I told you not to."

" My dear girl, it's all right — I know they're all out at this hour."

" The servants — I'm afraid of them — and there's a new nursery governess come."

" I know. I met her in the woods that day. Did you?"

"Of course I did. How could I help it? I said I'd been bathing. We mustn't go there again — it's much better to write."

The man gave a laugh that was good-humored and easy:

" Don't take it so hard. There's not the slightest need to be worried. I called you up to say everything was O. K."

Her answer came with a deep, sighing breath:

"It may be now — but how can we tell? The first excitement's dying down but that doesn't mean they're not doing anything. Don't think for a moment, because it's worked right so far, that we're out of the woods."

" I'm wise to all that, I know them better than you do. And the fellow that knows has got it all over

the fellow that doesn't. Watchful waiting — that's out motto."

" Very well, then let it be watchful. And don't call me up unless it's urgent. I can see you in town when I go in. I won't talk any more. Good-by."

I heard the stillness of a dead wire and then before I let myself think, flew into my room, found a pad and pencil and wrote it down word for word.

CHAPTER IX

GOOD HUNTING IN BERKELEY

TWO days after his interview with Suzanne, Mr. Larkin came to Berkeley and took a room at the Berkeley Arms. He registered as Henry Childs, and described himself to the clerk as a plumber, who, having had a prosperous year, was looking for a bit of land upon which to build a bungalow.

Berkeley was much too exclusive to permit a hotel within its exclusive limits and the Berkeley Arms was allowed to exist in a small, subdued way as a convenience. It was an unassuming, gray-shingled building, withdrawn behind a lilac hedge, and too near the station to mar the smart and shining elegance of the main street. In it dwelt the shop-keepers who plied a temporary summer trade in the village, and the chauffeurs of the less wealthy cottagers. Here the detective heard much talk of the Janney robbery, and, after he had extended his field of observation to the post-office lobby and Bennett's drug store, Berkeley had no secrets from him.

The public mind was still occupied with all that per-

Good Hunting in Berkeley

tained to Grasslands. He heard of the separation of the Prices, the scene lie had made on leaving, and that slie hadn't treated him right. Berkeley was on Chapman's side, said she wanted to get rid of him to marry Ferguson. It was hoped that Ferguson — highly esteemed — wasn't going to fall for it; but you couldn't tell, the best men made mistakes. Gossips, who professed an intimacy with the Grasslands kitchens, hinted that Ferguson was " taken with " the secretary. But Berkeley, fattened by prosperity to a gross snobbishness, rejected the idea as vulgar and unfitting.

All this had its value for Mr. Larkin, but it was by accident that he acquired the most illuminating piece of intelligence. Late one afternoon he wandered forth into a road that threaded the woods near Grasslands. The day being warm, the way dusty, he seated himself on a rock to cool off and ponder. While there, concealed by the surrounding trees, he had seen two small boys padding toward him down the road, their heads together in animated debate. Unaware of his presence their voices were loud and his listening ear caught interesting matter. They had been in the forbidden area of Grasslands, had gone to Little Fresh for a bathe, and had almost been caught in the act by a lady and gentleman.

Mr. Larkin made his presence known, and a dime gassed into each grubby palm won their confidence.

Miss Maitland Private Secretary

They were on the wharf slipping off their clothes when they heard footsteps and had only time to rush to cover in the underbrush when Mr. Chapman Price appeared. He waited round a bit and then Miss Maitland came and they sat on the bench and talked. The boys had not been able to hear what they said, but that it was serious they gathered from Mr. Price's manner and the fact that Miss Maitland had cried for a spell. Mr. Price went away first, and as he was going he said loud, standing in the path, " Take the upper trail and if you meet anybody say you've been at the beach bathing." Then he'd gone and Miss Maitland had waited a while, and then she'd gone too, by the upper trail, the way he'd said.

Mr. Larkin had been very sympathetic and friendly, swore he'd keep his mouth shut, and cautioned the boys to do the same, for he'd heard that Mrs. Janney wouldn't stand for any one bathing in Little Fresh and you couldn't tell but what she might have them arrested.

The next day he had a meeting with Suzanne in a summer-house on the Setons' grounds, the Setons being in California for the season. He gave his report of Miss Maitland's career — entirely worthy and respectable — and then asked the question Molly had asked Mrs. Janney:

had Mr. Price ever exhibited any special interest in the secretary? Mrs. Price's surprise and

denial were as genuine and emphatic as her mother's had been and Mr. Larkin arrived at the same conclusion as Molly — here started the path that led to the heart of the maze.

He did not say this to Mrs. Price. What he did say was that he would leave Berkeley shortly and when he had anything of importance to tell make an appointment with her by letter. It was not necessary to inform her that his next move would be to Cedar Brook where he had heard that Chapman Price spent a good deal of his time.

Cedar Brook, six miles above Berkeley on the main line, had none of the prestige of its aristocratic neighbor. It was in the process of development, new houses rising round its outskirts, fields being turned into lawns. Mr. Larkin took a room in a clapboarded cottage which stared at other clapboarded cottages through the foliage of locust trees. Announcing his intention of buying a piece of land, he was soon an object of general attention and added to his store of knowledge. He heard a good deal of Chapman Price, who was there off and on with the Hartleys, and of his man Willitts. It was understood that Willitts was staying with Price till he got a job, and, as the Hartley house was small, lodged in the village; in fact, Mr. Larkin learned to his satisfaction, was living in one of the clapboarded cottages close to his own.

Professing a desire to study the environs of Cedar Brook he hired a wheel, and the third afternoon of his stay peddled out into the country. It was while passing the private hedge of a large estate, that he came upon a young man engaged over a disabled bicycle.

The day was warm, the salt air of the Sound shut out by forest and hill, the road bathed in a hot glow of sun. The man had taken off his coat, and, as Mr. Larkin drew near, looked up displaying a smooth-shaven, rosy face, beaded with perspiration.

Mr. Larkin, being by nature and profession curious, drew up and made friendly inquiries. The man answered them, explained the nature of the damage, his speech marked by the crisp, clipped enunciation of the Briton. His costume — negligee shirt, knickerbockers and golf stockings — did not suggest the country house guest, nor was his accent quite that of the English gentleman. The detective, who had some knowledge of these delicate distinctions, laid his bicycle against the bank and proffered his assistance. Together they repaired the stranger's wheel, and, when it was done, rested from their labors in the shade of the hedge, and engaged in conversation. This at first was of the war — the young man explaining that he was English and had volunteered at once, but been rejected on the ground of his eyes — very near-sighted, couldn't read the chart at all — touching with an indicating finger

the glasses that spanned his nose. After that he'd come to America; he could make good money then and had people dependent on him. At this stage Mr. Larkin asked his profession and learned that he was a valet, by name James Willitts, just now looking for a place. He had been in the employ of Mr. Chapman Price and was still staying with him until he got a new " situation." Mr. Larkin in return recited his little lay about the plumbing business and the bungalow, and, the introductions accomplished, they passed to more general topics and soon reached the Janney robbery.

It was a propitious meeting for the detective, for Willitts proved himself a free and expansive talker. He launched forth into the subject with an artless zest, not needing any prompting from his attentive listener. Mr. Larkin was grateful for it all, but especially so for an account of the movements of Mr. Price the day before the robbery. He had sent his valet to Cedar

Brook on the morning train, he to follow later in the afternoon. Willitts, after the unpacking and settling was done, had biked over to Grasslands to see " the help," and then made the engagement to meet them that night at the movies. Of course he had to go back, as part of his work was to lay out Mr. Price's dinner clothes and help him dress, and it was most unfortunate, because, when he went up to Mr. Price's room, Mr. Price said he

wouldn't change, would keep on the clothes he had and go motoring.

" Motoring," observed Mr. Larkin, mildly interested, " did he motor in the evening? "

" Not usually — but I don't know if you remember that night. After a heavy rain it cleared and the moon came out as bright as day."

Mr. Larkin didn't remember himself but he had a vague recollection of having read it in some of the papers.

" It was a wonderful night, and if it hadn't been I'd never have kept my date. For I got side-tracked — had to fetch the doctor for my landlady's little girl who was taken bad with the croup. And what with that and the long distance I'd have given it up if it hadn't been for the moon."

The detective did not find these details particularly pertinent, and edged nearer to vital matters:

" Pretty unpleasant position for those two men, Dixon and Isaac. I was in Berkeley before I came here and there was a lot of talk."

The valet looked at him with sharp surprise:

" But no suspicion rests on them, I'll be bound. I lived in that house since last October and I'll swear that there's not an honester pair in the whole coun-try."

Mr. Larkin, as a stranger to the parties, had no 102

need to display a corresponding warmth, merely remarking that Berkeley was convinced of their innocence.

The young man appeased, felt in his coat for a pipe and drew a tobacco pouch from his pocket. As he filled the bowl, his profile was presented to the detective's vigilant eye, which dwelt thoughtfully on the neat outline, almost handsome except that the chin receded slightly. A good looking fellow, Mr. Larkin thought, and smart — somehow as the conversation had progressed he was beginning to think him smarter than he had at the start.

" How about that Miss Maitland," he said, " the young lady secretary ? "

Willitts had the pipe in his mouth and was pressing the tobacco down with his thumb. He spoke through closed teeth:

"What about her?"

"Well, what sort is she? You needn't tell me she's good looking, for I saw her once in the post office and she's a peach."

The valet leaned forward and felt in his coat pocket for matches. The movement presented his face in full to Mr. Larkin's glance, and the detective noticed that its bright alertness had diminished, that a slight film of stolidity had formed over it like ice over a running stream. The man had removed his pipe and held

it in one hand while he scrabbled round in his coat with the other.

" She's a very fine young lady ; nothing but good's ever been said of her in my hearing. And very competent in her work — they say — and she would be, or Mrs. Janney wouldn't ^eep her."

He found the matches and, sitting upright, lit one and applied it to the pipe bowl. The detective, with his eyes ready to swerve to the landscape, hazarded a shot at the bull's-eye.

" They were saying — or more hinting I guess you'd call it — that Mr. Price was — er — getting to look her way too often."

Willitts was very still. The watching eyes noticed that the flame of the match burned steady over the pipe bowl; for a moment the valet's breath was held. Then, without moving, his voice peculiarly quiet, he said:

" Now I'd like to know who told you that? "

The other gave a lazy laugh:

" Oh, I can't tell — every kind of rumor was flying about. They were ready to say anything."

'* Yes, that's it. Say anything to get listened to and not care whose character they were taking away."

" Then there's nothing in it? "

" Tommyrot !" he snorted out the word with intense irritation. " The silly fools! Mr. Price is no more in

Good Hunting in Berkeley

love with her than I am. He's not that kind; he's an honorable gentleman. And, believe me, the wrong's not all on his side. It's not for me to tell tales of the family, but I will say that there's not many men could have put up with what he did."

His face was flushed, he was openly exasperated. Mr. Larkin remembered what he had heard of the man's affection for the master, and his thoughts formed into an unspoken sentence, " He knows something and won't tell."

" Well, well," he said cheerfulty, " when a big thing happens there's bound to be all sorts of scandal and surmise. People work off their excitement that way; you can't muzzle 'em —"

Willitts grunted a scornful assent and rose. It was time to go; Mr. Price would be coining up from town that night and he would be on duty. The detective, lifting his bicycle from the grass, casually inquired if Mr. Price motored from the city.

" Oh, dear no. He keeps his car here in Sommers' garage — he needs it, taking people about to see the country. He made a tidy bit of money here last week."

" Talking of money," said the other, " did you know that ten thousand dollars' reward has been offered for those jewels? "

Willitts, astride his wheel, stretched a feeling foot for the pedal:

Miss Maitland Private Secretary

" Yes, I saw it in the papers."

" Easy money for somebody."

" Yes, but is there somebody beside the thief — or thieves — who knows? That's the question."

They pedaled back side by side talking amicably, mutually pleased to find they were neighbors. On the outskirts of the village they parted with promises for a speedy reunion, Willitts to go to the Hartleys, and Mr. Larkin to Sommers' garage to ask the price of a flivver for an excursion beyond the reach of his bicycle.

When he arrived at the garage a large touring car, packed full of veiled females, was drawn up at the entrance. The driver, with Sommers and his assistant beside him, had opened the hood and the three of them were peering into the inner depths with the anxious concentration of doctors studying the anatomy of a patient. Mr. Larkin walked by them and went into the garage. He cast a rapid look about him, over the lined-up motors in the back, and then through the doorway into the small office. The place was empty. With a stealthy glance at the party round the touring car, he strolled in to where the time card rack hung on the wall. He ran his eye down the list of names until he came to " Price " and drew out the card. The second entry was dated July seventh and showed that that night Price had taken out his car at eight-thirty and not returned it until five minutes to two.

CHAPTER X

MOLLY'S STOKY

AS soon as I had the notes of that 'phone message down I wrote a report for the Whitney office — just an outline — and posted it myself in the village. The answer with instructions came the following evening. The next time Miss Maitland went into town I was to come with her. In the concourse of the Pennsylvania station I'd see O'Malley (the Whitneys' detective) and it would be my business to point her out to him. He was to follow her and I to come to the office and make my full report. Say nothing of what I'd heard to Mrs. Janney.

That was Tuesday; Thursday was Miss Maitland's holiday and right along she'd been going into town. Wednesday afternoon I heard her say she'd go in as usual on the eight forty-five, tipped off the office by 'phone, and told Mrs. Janney I'd need that day to make a report to Mr. Whitney — a business formality that had to be observed.

Miss Maitland and I went in together, looking very sociable on the outside, and talking about the weather, the new style in skirts, how flat Long Island was, and

Miss Maitland Private Secretary

other such lady-like topics. Coming off the train I stuck to her like a burr, was almost arm in arm going up the stairs, and then in the concourse broke myself loose and faded away toward the news stand. Right there, leaning against the magazine end, I'd seen a large, fat, sloppy-looking man, with a tired panama hat back from his forehead, and a masonic emblem on his watch chain.

O'Malley was a first class worker in his line, and his appearance was worth rubies. He'd a small-town, corner-grocery look that would have fooled any one unless they'd a scent for a sleuth like a dog for a bone. As I edged up near him, reaching out for a magazine, he cast a cold, disdainful glance at me like the rube that's wise to the dangers of the great city. I dragged a magazine out from behind his back and whispered, " In the lavender dress and the white hat with the grapes round it." And dreamy, as if his thoughts were back with mother on the farm, he heaved himself up from the stand and took the trail.

The Chief — that's my name for Mr. Whitney — and Mr. George were waiting for me in the old man's office. Gee, it was great to be there again, like times in the past when we'd meet together and thrash out the last findings. Of course the Chief had to have his joke, holding me by the shoulders and cocking.his head to one side as he looked into my face:

Molly's Story

" My, my, Molly, but the country's put a bloom on you! What a pity it is you're married or you might get one of those millionaires down there."

And I couldn't help answering fresh — he just sort of dares you to it:

" I won't say but what I might, Chief. But it's poor sort. Seeing what they've got to choose from it would be a shame to take the money."

Mr. George was impatient — he always gets bristly when things are moving — and cut us off from our fooling when a sharp:

" Come on, Molly, sit down and let's hear the whole of this."

So I took up the white man's burden, told them all I'd seen and heard and picked up, ending off with the full notes of the 'phone talk. Then I laid the paper on the table and looked at them. The Chief was gazing thoughtfully at the floor, and Mr. George's face was puckered with a frown like he'd eaten a persimmon.

" It's the queerest thing I ever heard in my life," he said. " Chapman and that girl! Why, it's impossible. Are you sure the man on the 'phone was Chapman? "

" It must have been. He spoke of meeting me in the woods and Mr. Price is the only man I ever met there."

The Chief looked up, glowering at me from under his big eyebrows:

Miss Maitland Private Secretary

"What's your opinion of this Maitland woman?"

" Well, I don't think there's anything wrong about her — I mean I'd never get that impression from her general make-up. But before I tapped that message, I did get a hunch that she was sort of abstracted and shut away in herself. She'd lonesome habits and she'd look downhearted when she thought no one saw her. I'd size her up roughly as some one who wasn't easy in her mind."

" Have you ever heard anything of her having any sort of affair or friendship with Price? "

" Not a hint of it. That's what made me sit up and take notice. Under everybody's eye the way they were and yet not a soul suspecting anything — you're not as secret as that for nothing."

" While they were talking on the 'phone did you notice anything in their voices — it certainly wasn't in the words — that suggested tenderness or love?"

" No, it was more as if they knew each other well. He sounded as if he was trying to jolly her along, keep up her spirits; and she as if she was scared, not at him but at what he might do."

" They'd be careful," said Mr. George. " A man and a woman who were Jnvolved in some dangerous scheme wouldn't coo at each other over the wire like two turtle doves."

" Love's hard to hide," said the old man, " betrays 110

Molly's Story

itself in small ways. And Molly's got a fine, trained ear."

" Well, it caught no love there, Chief. The only person at Grasslands who's got that complaint is Mrs. Price. She's in love with Mr. Ferguson."

Mr. George was very much surprised.

" The deuce you say! — Old Dick fallen at last."

The Chief gave a sort of sarcastic grunt.

" Ferguson can take care of himself. He's not as big a fool as he looks or pretends to be. Now these extra holidays of Miss Maitland's you've spoken of — how long has that been going on? "

" Since April. Before that she never wanted time off and often spent her Thursdays in the house. At Grasslands this summer she's gone into town every Thursday and three times asked for extra days. The last was July the eighth, the day after the robbery."

" Umph! " muttered the old man. " I guess we'll know something about that when we hear from O'Mal-ley."

Mr. George, slumped down in his chair, with his hands thrust in his pockets, his chin pressed on his collar, said gloomily:

" I confess I'm dazed. It's perfectly possible that Chapman, who didn't like his wife, should have fallen in love with the girl, it's perfectly natural that they should have kept it dark; but that he's joined with her

Miss Maitland Private Secretary

in a plan to steal Mrs. Janney's jewels! "— he shook his head staring in front of him —" I can't get the focus. Price wouldn't qualify for a Sunday school superintendent, but I can't seem to see him as a gentleman burglar."

" He was mad when he left," I said. " He made a sort of scene."

"What's that?" growled the old man, looking up quick.

" He got angry and threatened them. I don't know just in what way because I've only caught it in bits and scraps. But Dixon heard him and told in the village where I picked up an echo of it. He said they'd stolen his child."

" Sounds like him — and ugly temper. Try and get exactly what he said if you can."

We talked on a while, going back and forth over it like a lawn mower over grass. Then a knock on the door stopped us ; a boy put in his head and announced:

" Mr. O'Malley's outside and wants to see Mr. Whitney."

Mr. George and I squared round in our chairs with our eyes glued on the doorway. The Chief, slouched down comfortable with his shirt-bosom bulging, looked like a sleepy old bear, but from under the jut of his eyebrows his glance shone as keen as a razor. O'Mal-ley entered, hot and red, his panama in his hand, and

that air about him I've seen before — a suppressed triumph gleaming out through the cracks.

" Well ? " says Mr. George, curt and sharp.

O'Malley took a chair and mopped his forehead:

" There's no mistake she's got something up her sleeve. She took the Seventh Avenue car and went downtown until she came to Jefferson Court house, got out there, went a few blocks into the Greenwich Village section and stopped at a house on a small sort of thoroughfare called Ga\'7d r le Street. I think she let herself in with a key, bat I'm not sure. The place is a shady-looking rookery, no porch or steps, door opening right on the sidewalk, three windows to each floor, mansard roof. About ten minutes after she went in, a man came down the street, walking quick, hat low over his eyes — it was Mr. Chapman Price."

Mr. George stirred and gave a matter. The old man, stretching his hand to the cigar box at his elbow, took out a large fat cigar and said:

"Price, eh? —Go on."

" I thought the lady'd used a key, and I saw plain that he did. The door opened and he went in. I crossed over and looked at the bells. There were nine of them, all with names underneath except the top floor ones. These, the last three of the line, had no names, showing the top floor was vacant.

" There was a drug store right opposite and I 113

went in, took a soda, and asked the clerk about the locality — said I was looking for lodgings in that section.* I got him round to the house, where I heard I might get a room cheap. He said maybe I could — being summer there'd be vacancies — that the place was decent enough, but he'd heard pretty poor and mean. Just as I got through talking to him and was leaving I saw the door across the street open, and Mr. Price come out. He came quick, on the slant, and was among the folks on the sidewalk before you could notice. It was the way a man acts when he doesn't want to be seen. He walked off toward Seventh Avenue, his head down, keeping close to the houses. I didn't wait for Miss Maitland — thought I'd better come back here and report."

"Well!" said Mr. George. "I'm jiggered if I can make head or tail of it."

The Chief took the cigar out of his mouth and addressed O'Malley:

" Find out Price's movements on the night of July seventh, everything he did, everywhere he went." He turned to me. " And you want to remember not a hint of this gets to Mrs. Janney. She hates Price and when her blood's up she's a red Indian. We don't want the family drawn in until we know something."

CHAPTER XI

FERGUSON'S IDEA

DURING these days Dick Ferguson thought a good deal and said very little. Like the rest of his world he wondered over the unsolved mystery of the Janney robbery, but his won-derings contained an element of discomfort. He heard the subject discussed everywhere and often the name of Esther Maitland came up in the discussions. Not that any one ever suggested she might be involved; — it was more a sympathetic appreciation of her position. Every one spoke very feelingly about it: — poor girl, so uncomfortable for her, knowing the combination and all that sort of thing — the Janneys had stood by her splendidly, but still it was trying.

It tried him a good deal, made inroads on his temper, until it lost its sunny evenness and he was sometimes short and surly. The day after Molly and Esther went to town he had been called to a conference in the Fairfax house on the bluff. A gang of motor boat thieves had been operating along the Sound, had already stolen two launches, and the owners of water-

front property had convened to decide on a course. Ferguson, with a small fleet to his credit, had taken rather a high hand, and shown an unwonted irritation at the indecision of his associates. If they wanted their boats protected it was up to them to do it, establish a shore police patrol financed by themselves. That was what he intended to do and they could join with him or not as they pleased. He left them, ruffled by his brusqueness and remarking grumpily that "

Ferguson was beginning to feel his money."

He went from the meeting to his own beach and on the way met Suzanne returning with Bebita from the morning bath. They stopped for a chat in the course of which Suzanne made a series of remarks not calculated to soothe his perturbed spirit. They were apropos of Miss Maitland, who had taken an early morning swim, all alone, refusing to wait and go in with them. Suzanne said it was a pity Miss Maitland kept so much to herself — the girl seemed depressed and out of spirits lately, didn't he think so? Quite different to what she had been earlier in the season, seemed to be troubled about something. Too bad — every one liked her so much, and people did talk so. Then with an artless smile she went off under her white parasol.

There was no smile on Ferguson's face as he walked to his boat houses. He told his men of the police patrol

Ferguson's Idea

— to operate along the shore after nightfall — gave a few gruff orders and disappeared into a bath house. When he emerged, stripped for a swim, he stalked silently by them and dove from the end of the wharf. They were surprised at his manner, usually so genial, and wondered among themselves watching his head, sleek as a wet seal's, receding over the shining water.

The head was full of what Suzanne had said. Though he had offered no agreement to her suggestions, he had noticed the change in Esther. He had noticed it soon after the robbery, in fact before that, for it had dated from the evening when she dined at his house, the night the jewels were taken. Disturbance grew in him as he thought: — if so shallow a creature as Suzanne could see it, others could. And Suzanne had no sense, no realization of the weight of words. She might go round chattering like a fool and get the girl talked about. It would be the decent thing to give Esther a hint, put her wise to the fact that she ought to brighten up — not give any one a chance to say she was not as she had been.

As his long, muscular body slid through the water he decided to go over and have a talk with her. The decision cheered him, for to be with Esther Maitland was the keenest pleasure he knew.

Suzanne had told him she and her mother would be out that afternoon, so at three — the hour they were

Miss Maitland Private Secretary

to leave — he set out for Grasslands by the wood path. As he crossed the garden his questing glance met an encouraging sight — Esther Maitland sitting under a group of maples at the end of the terrace. She was alone, an empty chair beside her, her head bowed over a book.

Her welcoming smile was very sweet; his eye noticed a faint color rise in her cheeks as he came up. These signs were so agreeable that he would like to have sat there, placidly enjoying her presence, but he was a person who once possessed by an idea " had to get it out of his system." This he proceeded to do, advancing on his subject with what he thought was a crafty indirectness:

" You know, Miss Maitland, you're not a credit to Long Island."

She raised her brows, deprecating, also amused:

"What have I done?"

" It's what you haven't done. We expect people to come here worn and weary and then blossom like the rose. You've gone back on the tradition."

She stretched a hand for a bundle of knitting — a soldier's muffler — on the table beside her:

" I don't feel worn or weary and I'm sorry I look so."

" Oh, you always look lovely," he hastily assured her. " I didn't mean that it wasn't becoming. But —

er — er — what I wanted to say was — er — why is it? "

Miss Maitland began to knit, her face bent over the work, her dark head backed by the green distances of the lawn. Ferguson thought she had the most beautifully shaped head he had ever seen. He would like to have leaned back in his chair studying its classic outline. But he was there for a purpose and he held himself sternly to it, looking at her profile and trying to forget that it was as fine as her head.

" I don't know why it is," she answered, " but I do know that you're not very complimentary."

" If you give me a dare like that I'll show you how complimentary I can be. But I'll put that off until later. What I think is that you're worrying — that the robbery has got on your nerves."

" Why should it get on my nerves ? "

He was aware of her eyes — diverted from the knitting — looking curiously at him:

" Why, it's been so — so — unpleasant, all this fuss and publicity. It's been a shock."

Her hands with the knitting dropped into her lap. She was now staring fixedly at him:

" Do you mean that I'm worrying because I think I may be suspected of it?"

He was shocked to angry repudiation.

" Good Lord, no! What a thing to say 1" 119

She took up her work, and answered with cool composure :

" Nevertheless I have wondered if anybody ever thought it. You see I'm the only one in the house — the only one who knows the combination — who is a sort of stranger. Dixon and Isaac are like members of the family."

" Don't talk such rubbish," he protested, then leaning nearer, " Have you had that on your mind all this time? Is that what's made the change? "

She looked up at him, startled:

" Change — what change? "

" Change in you. Yes," in answer to the disturbed inquiry of her glance, " there is one. I've noticed it ; other people have."

" What do you mean ? "

" Why, you're different, you've lost your good spirits. You're not like you were before this happened."

Her response came with something combative in its countering quickness:

" I'm busier than I used to be. Since the robbery I've taken over a good deal of the housekeeping. Mrs. Janney has been much more upset than you guess."

" And you're so withdrawn, keep more to yourself. I used to find you about when I came over; now I almost never see you."

The interview had taken on the character of a verbal duel, he thrusting, she parrying, both earnest and insistent.

" I've just told you; I have more work, I've not the leisure I used to have."

" So busy you have to shun people? "

" That's absurd, you imagine it. I've never shunned any one and there's no reason why I should."

" I agree with you but let me ask one more question. You say your work is harder and you do look tired and worn out. Why don't you take a decent rest on your holidays? Last year you spent them here, out of doors, loafing about. Now you go to town. I've been over twice on Thursdays and when I ask for you, always hear you're in the city. And you've been at other times too — Mrs. Janney told me so. It's the most fatiguing thing you can do in this hot weather. Why do you go ? "

He saw her color suddenly deepen. She had let the knitting drop to her lap and now she took it up again and began to work, very fast, the needles flashing in her white hands. She smiled as she answered:

" You seem to have kept rather a sharp lookout on me, Mr. Ferguson. Did it never occur to you that a woman might need clothes, or might want to see a friend who happened to be staying in town for the summer? "

Miss Maitland Private Secretary

The young man had been admiring the white hands. As she spoke something in their movements caught and held his eye — they were trembling. He was so surprised that he made no answer, his glance riveted on them trying to hold the needles steady to their task. Miss Maitland made an effort to go on, then dropped the knitting in a bunch on her knees and clasped the hands over it. Neither speaking, their eyes met. The expression of hers, furtively apprehensive like a scared child's pierced his heart and he leaned toward her, his sunburned face full of concern:

"Miss Maitland, what's wrong? Something is — tell me."

Without answering she shook her head, her lips tightly compressed. He could see that she was shaken, that the clasped hands on her knee were clenched together to control their trembling. He could see that, for a moment, taken unawares, she did not trust herself to speak.

" Look here," he said, low and urgent, " be frank with me. I've seen for some time something was troubling you — I told you so that night at my place. Why not let me lend a hand? That's what I want to do — that's what I'm for."

She had found her voice and it came with a high, light hardness, in curious contrast to the feeling in his:

Ferguson's Idea

" You're all wrong, Mr. Ferguson. You're seeing what doesn't exist." She started to her feet, making a grab at her knitting as it slid toward the ground. " Oh, my needle! I almost pulled it out. That would have been a calamity." She carefully pushed the stitches on to the needle as if her whole interest lay in preserving the woven fabric. " There I've picked them up, not lost one." Then she looked at them, smiling, her expression showing a veiled defiance, " You ought to have been a novelist — your imagination's wasted. Here you are seeing me as a distressed damsel, while I'm only a perfectly normal, perfectly commonplace person. Romantic fiction would have been your line."

She gave a laugh that brought the blood to the young man's face, for its musical ripple contained a note of derision:

" But for my sake please curb your fancy. Don't suggest to my employers that I'm weighted down by a secret sorrow. They mightn't like a blighted being for a secretary and I might lose my job, and then I really would be worried."

He stood it unflinching, only the dark flush betraying his mortification. He assured her of his reticence and ended by asking her pardon. She granted it, even thanked him for his concern in her behalf and with a smile that was still mocking, said she had notes to write, gathered up her work, and bade him good-by.

Dick Ferguson walked back through the woods to Council Oaks. When the first discomfort of the rebuff had passed he pondered deeply. He was sure now beyond the peradventure of a doubt that Esther Maitland was in trouble of some kind, and was ready to use all the weapons at her command to keep him from finding it out.

Two nights after that he dined at Grasslands. It was just a family party, and, being such, Miss Maitland was present. She met him with the subdued quietness that he was beginning to recognize as her " social secretary manner "— the manner of the lady employee, politely colorless and self-effacing.

In the dining room, with its clustered lights along the walls, where long windows framed the deep blue night, they looked a gay and goodly party. To the unenlightened observer they might have stood for a typical group of the care-free rich, waited on by obsequious menials, feeding sumptuously in sumptuous surroundings. Yet each one of them was preyed upon by secret anxieties.

When the ladies withdrew Mr. Janney and Ferguson sat on smoking and sipping their coffee. If every member of the party had his hidden distress, Mr. Jan-ney's was by no means the least. His problem was still unsolved, still menacing. Kissam's suggestion and

Ferguson's Idea

his own fond hope, that the jewels would be restored had not been realized, and he was contemplating the day when he would have to face Suzanne with his knowledge. Damocles beneath the suspended sword was not more uncomfortable than he. Any allusion to the robbery made his heart sink, and, as the allusions were frequent, conversation had become a thing harkened to with held breath and sick anticipation.

Alone with Ferguson he was experiencing the usual qualms, but the young man, instead of the customary questions, asked him his opinion of Willitts, Chapman's valet, whom he thought of engaging. Mr. Janney brightened up, told Dixon to bring some of his own especial cigars, and relapsed into tranquillity. He could recommend Willitts highly, smart, capable and honest, but he thought he'd heard Dick say he couldn't stand a valet fussing about him. Dick had said it and was still of the same mind, but most of his guests were men and he needed some one to look after their clothes. They made a lot of bother, tl?e servants had kicked, and he'd thought of Willitts.

Mr. Janney could give no information as to Willitts' whereabouts, but Dixon, entering with the cigar box and lamp, could. Willitts was at Cedar Brook where Mr. Price spent a good deal of time; he was still disengaged and looking for a position, if Mr. Ferguson would like Dixon would get word to him. Mr. Ferguson

would like, and, the box presented at his elbow, he took out a cigar and held its tip to the lamp. Mr. Janney forgot Willitts and drew his guest's attention to the cigar, a special brand of rare excellence.

" We keep them in the safe," said the old man. " Only place that's secure against the damp. It was Chapman's idea — the one thing in my acquaintance with Chapman I'm grateful for."

It was an unfortunate remark, for Ferguson, leaning back in his chair with the cigar between his lips, 4 murmured dreamily:

" The safe — do you know I've been thinking over things lately. I can't understand one point. Why didn't the thief take those jewels when the house was virtually empty instead of waiting until it was full ? "

Mr. Janney's heart took a dizzying, downward dive. He had been looking forward to his smoke, now all his zest departed, his old, veined hand shaking as it felt in the box.

Ferguson we,nt on:

" The fellow may have come in early and hidden himself — not got down to business until every one was asleep."

Mr. Janney emitted an agreeing murmur and motioned Dixon to hold the lamp nearer. As he bent toward it the young man was silent and Mr. Janney began to hope that the obnoxious subject was aban-

doned. He sent a side glance at his guest and the hope was strengthened. Ferguson had taken his cigar from his lips and was looking at the paper band that encircled it. He was looking at it so intently that Mr. Janney felt sure his interest was diverted and sought to drive it into safer channels.

"Pretty fine cigar, eh?" he said. "This is the first of a new lot, just come."

Ferguson drew the band off and laid it beside his plate:

" Excellent. That's a good idea — keeping them in the safe. Do you always do it? "

" Yes, it's the only thing — much better than a humidor."

" I haven't got a safe or I'd try it. Did you have any there the night of the robbery? "

Mr. Janney felt that the gods had sought him out for a special vengeance and murmured drearily:

" I believe so — a few. Dixon knows."

Dixon who was on his way to the door turned:

" Yes, sir, only one box, the last we had."

Ferguson laughed:

" If the thief had had time to try one he'd have taken the box along too."

Dixon, who treated all allusions to the subject with a tragical seriousness, said:

" I don't think he touched them, sir. The box looked 127

Miss Maitland Private Secretary

just the same. Mr. Kissam was very particular to ask about it, but I told him I thought they was intact, as you might say. Though if it was the loss of one or two I couldn't be certain."

Dixon left the room and Mr. Janney looked dismally at his plate, having no spirit to fight against fate. Ferguson, with a glance at his down-drooped face, picked up the band and slipped it in his pocket.

He did not stay long after dinner. As soon as his car came he left, telling the chauffeur to hurry. At home he ran up the stairs to his room, switched on the light over the bureau and opened the box with the crystal lid. Under the studs and pins lay the band Esther had found the night he walked with her through the woods. He compared it with the one he took from his pocket and saw that they matched. The new one he threw into the fireplace, but put the other back in the box — it was something more than a souvenir. Then he sat down on the end of the sofa and thought.

Mr. Janney could not have dropped it for he had driven both to and from Council Oaks. Neither Dixon nor Isaac could have, for they had gone to the village by the main road and come back the same way at midnight. He had found it at half-past ten, untouched by the heavy shower, which had lasted from about seven till half-past eight. Therefore, whoever had thrown it there had passed that way between the time when

the rain stopped and the time when Esther had found it. It had been dropped either by a man who had one of the cigars in his possession and had been on the wood path between eight-thirty and ten-thirty, or by a man who had taken a cigar from the safe between those hours.

Ferguson sat staring at the wall with his brows knit. If it had not been for the light his own gardener had seen he would have felt that he had struck the right road.

CHAPTER XII

THE MAN WHO WOULDN'T TELL

MR. LARKIN had lingered on at Cedar Brook. He said that he needed a holiday, the prosperity of the last year had worn him out, also the bungalow sites were many and a decision difficult.

He saw a good deal of Willitts; they had become very friendly, almost chums. Their lodgings were but a few yards apart and of evenings they smoked neighborly pipes on the porch steps, and of afternoons took walks into the country. During these hours their talk ranged over many subjects, the valet proving himself a brightly loquacious companion. But upon a subject that Mr. Larkin introduced with delicate artfulness — Price and Esther Maitland — he maintained the evasive reticence that had marked him at their first meeting. For all the walks and talks Mr. Larkin learned no more, and as his curiosity remained unsatisfied his inclination for Willitts' society increased.

It was a few days after that first meeting that, strolling down Main Street toward Sommers' garage, the

detective stopped short, staring at two figures emerging from the garage entrance. One was Sommers, the other a fat, red-faced man with a sunburned Panama on the back of his head. A glance at this man and Mr. Larkin turned on his heel and made down a side lane at a swinging gait. Safe out of range behind a lilac hedge, he slowed up, lifted his hat from a perspiring brow and swore to himself, low and fiercely. He had recognized Gus O'Malley, private detective of Whitney & Whitney, and he knew that Whitney & Whitney were Mrs. Janney's lawyers. Another investigation was on foot, evidently following on the lines of his own.

After two days O'Malley left by the evening train and Mr. Larkin emerged from a temporary retirement, and sought coolness and solitude on the front porch. Here, when night had fallen, Willitts joined him taking a seat on the top step.

The house behind them was empty of all other tenants, its open front door letting a long gush of light down the steps and across the pebbled path to the gate. It was a warm night, heavy and breathless, and Mr. Larkin, in his shirt sleeves, lolled comfortably, his chair tilted back, his feet on the railing. The place where he sat was shaded with vines, and he was discernible as a long, out-stretched bulk, detailless in the shadow.

Willitts had good news to impart; that afternoon he had been to Council Oaks to see Mr. Ferguson who had engaged him as valet. It was an A1 place, the pay high, the duties light, Mr. Ferguson known to be generous and easy tempered. Congratulations were in order from Mr. Larkin, and if they lacked in warmth Willitts did not appear to notice it.

A pause fell, and his next remark caused the detective to deflect his gaze from the darkling street to the head of the steps:

" Did you notice a chap about here yesterday — a fat, untidy looking man in a Panama hat and a brown sack suit? "

Mr. Larkin had and wanted to know where Willitts had seen him.

" In Sommers' garage. He was hiring a motor, wanted to see the country — and Sommers telling him I knew it well, asked me to go with him."

"Did you go?"

" I did ; I had nothing else to do. We went a long way, through Berkeley and beyond. He's what you'd call here * some talker' and curious — I'd say very curious if you asked me."

" Curious about what ? "

" Everything in the neighborhood, but especially the robbery."

" Did he have any theories about it? "

" None that I hadn't heard before."

The detective laughed:

" That accounts for the drive — hoped he'd get some racy gossip about the family out of you."

" Maybe that was his idea."

" Of course it was. I'll bet he pumped you about Price."

" I don't know that I'd call it pumping — he did ask some questions."

Willitts was sitting with his elbows on his knees, his hands supporting his chin. The light from the open door behind him lay over his back, gilded the top of his smooth head and slanted across his cheek. He was not smoking and he was very still, facts noted by Mr. Larkin.

The detective stretched, yawned with a sleepy sound and said:

" So it's still a subject of popular curiosity, is it?"

" Yes, it is, but why should Mr. Price be? "

The valet's voice was low and quiet, holding a quality hard to define; the listener decided it was less uneasiness than resentment. After a moment's silence he spoke again, very softly, as if the words were self-communings:

" I'd like to know who the feller is."

Mr. Larkin's feet came down from the rail striking 133

the floor with a thud. He sat up and looked at his friend:

" I can tell you. He's a defective, Gus O'Malley, employed by Whitney & Whitney."

Willitts' hands dropped and he squared round:

"A detective! That's it, is it? That accounts for the milk in the cocoanut. I might have guessed it. And what's he after me for? "

" You lived at Grasslands. Something might be dug out of you."

" But tell me, why should he be curious about Mr. Price?"

He had dropped one hand on the flooring and supported by it leaned forward toward his companion. The boyish good humor had gone from his face; it looked sharp-set and pugnacious.

The other shrugged:

" Ask him. All I can tell you is that Whitney & Whitney are Mrs. Janney's lawyers."

Willitts pondered, and while he pondered his eyes stared past the shadowy shape that was Mr. Larkin into the vine-draped blackness of the porch. Then he said:

" Mrs. Janney's down on Mr. Price. She's all for her daughter. I think she 'ates J im."

The two h's dropped off with a simple unconsciousness that surprised Mr. Larkin. Never before in his

intercourse with Willitts had he heard the letter so much as slighted. He made a mental note of it and said dryly:

" So I've heard."

The man again relapsed into thought, his glance riveted on the darkness, his expression obviously perturbed. Suddenly he looked at the vague bulk of Mr. Larkin and said sharply:

" 'Ow do you know so much about 'im? "

Mr. Larkin's answer came out of the shadow with businesslike promptness:

" Because I'm a detective myself."

For a moment the valet's face seemed to set, lose its flesh and blood mobility and harden into something stony, its lines fixed, vitality suspended,— a vacuous, staring mask. Then life came back to it, broke its ici-ness and flooded it with a frank, almost ludicrous astonishment.

" You — you! " he stammered out, " and me never so much as thinking it! Would any one, I'm asking you? Would— " he stopped, his amazement gone, a sudden belligerent fierceness taking its place, " And are you after Mr. Price too?"

Mr. Larkin laughed:

" I'm after no one at this stage. I'm only assembling data. If O'Malley's got to the point of finding a suspect he's far ahead of me."

Miss Maitland Private Secretary

Willitts' excitement instantly subsided; his answer showed a hurried urgency:

" No, no — he didn't say anything one could take 'old of — only a few questions. And it's maybe all in my feelings. I couldn't bear a person to think evil of Mr. Price. It 'urts me; I'd be sensitive; I might see it if it wasn't there."

" If you got that impression I guess it was there."

This remark, delivered with a sardonic dryness, appeared to rekindle Willitts' anger. It flared up like the leap of a flame:

" Then to 'ell with 'im. If they're working up any dirty suspicions against my gentleman they've come to the wrong man. I've got nothing to say; there's no information to be wormed out of me for I 'ave none. Umph — lies, trickery — that's what / call it! "

He dropped back into his former position, his angry breathings loud on the silence, mutterings of rage breaking through them.

" Well," said Mr. Larkin, " now I've put you wise you can form your own conclusion as to what's in their minds."

"Is it in yours, too?"

The question came quick, shot out between the deep-drawn breaths. Mr. Larkin was ready for it:

" I told you I hadn't got as far as that; I'm just feeling my way. But let me say something to you."

The Man Who Wouldn't Tell

He rose and, going to the steps, sat down beside Wil-litts, dropping his voice to a confidential key. " I'll be frank with you — I'll show you how I stand. I didn't intend to tell you what I was, but this fellow coming up here has forced my hand. He knows me, he'll be after you again, and you'd have found it out. Now, here's my position: I want to get this case; it's my first big one and it'll make me every way — professionally and financially."

He looked at the man beside him who, gazing into the street, nodded without speaking.

" There's ten thousand dollars offered for the restoration of the jewels. If I could get them I'd share that money with the person who — who — er — helped."

Willitts repeated his silent nod.

" And even if I didn't get them I'd pay and pay •well for any information that would be useful."

" I see," said the other, " 'oever 'elps along in the good work gets 'is reward."

Mr. Larkin did not like the words or the tone, but went on, his confidential manner growing persuasive:

" I'm engaged on the side of law and order. All I'm trying to do is to restore stolen property to its owner. Any one that helps me is only doing his duty."

" A duty that gets its dues, as you might say." 137

" Exactly. The money made by such services is earned honestly and there's plenty of it to earn."

" Righto! When the Janneys want a thing they'll open the purse wide and generous."

"And here's a point worth noticing: What I'm hired for is to get the jewels, not the thief. The party behind me isn't out for vengeance or prosecution. If I could deliver the goods it would be all right and no questions asked. But the Whitneys wouldn't stop there — they're bloodhounds when it comes to the chase. If they got anything on Price they'd come down on him good and hard and Mrs. Janney'd stand in with them."

He was looking with anxious intentness at Willitts' profile. As he finished it turned slowly, until the face was offered in full to his watchful scrutiny. It was forbidding, the eyes sweeping him with a cold contempt:

" I can't 'elp understanding you, Larkin, and I'm sorry to 'ear you got your suspicions of my gentleman and of me. The first is too low to take notice of; the second is as bad, but I'll answer it to put us both straight. I'm not the kind you take me for; I'm not to be bought. Even if I did know anything that would be * useful' as you say, wild 'orses wouldn't drag it out of me. And no more will filthy lucre. Filthy — it's the right name for it, you couldn't get a better." He rose, not so much angry as hurt and haughty. " I can't find it in me to sit 'ere any longer. I could talk of insults, but I won't. All I'll say is that I've 'ad a bit too much, and not wanting to 'ear more I'll bid you good-night."

Before the detective could find words to answer he had gone down the path and vanished in the darkness.

CHAPTER XIII

MOLLY'S STORY

ONE of the chief features of detective work is that you must be able to change your mind. That may not sound hard — especially when the owner of the mind happens to be a female — but believe me it's some stunt. You get pointed one way, and to have to shift and face round in another is candy for a weather vane but bread for a sleuth.

Well, that's what happened to me. In the week that followed my visit to the Whitneys I had to start out fresh on a new line of thought. I'd left the office pretty certain, as the others were, that the bond between Esther Maitland and Chapman Price was love, and before those seven days were gone I'd thrown that theory into the discard, rolled up my sleeves, taken a cinch in my belt, and set forth to blaze a new trail.

I came round to it slow at first and I came round through Mr. Ferguson. It was fine weather and when Bebita would go off with Annie, I'd curl up in my conning tower in the school room window and take observations. As I said before, it was a convenient place, just

over Miss Maitland's study, deserted all afternoon, and with the Venetian blinds down against the sun, I could sit comfortable on my cushion and spy out between the slats.

The first thing that caught my attention was that Mr. Ferguson, who'd come over pretty nearly every day, wouldn't make straight for the front piazza which was the natural way to get there. Instead he'd take a slanting course across the garden, come up some steps to the terrace, and then walk slow past the study door. Sometimes he'd see Miss Maitland and stop for a chat, and sometimes she wouldn't be there and he'd go by. But each and every time, thinking no one was watching, he'd let a look come on his face that's common to the whole male sex when the one particular star is expected above the horizon. I guess the cave man got it when, club in hand, he was chasing the cave girl and Solomon with his six hundred wives must have had it stamped on his features so it came to be his habitual expression.

Though it was registered good and plain on Mr. Ferguson's countenance, I couldn't at first believe it. It was too like a novel, too like Cinderella and the Prince. Then, seeing it so frequent, I was convinced. I'd say to myself " Why not — a girl's a girl if she is a plutocrat's social secretary, and all men are free and equal when it comes to disposing of their young affec-

tions." The romance of it got me, gripped at my heart. I'd sit with my eye to the crack in the blinds staring down at him as he'd send that look out for her

— that wonderful look, that look which gives you chills and fever, blind staggers and heart failure and you'd rather have than a blank check drawn to your order and signed by John Rockefeller. Oh, gee — I was a girl once myself — don't I know! I'd have been interested if it was just an ordinary love story, but it wasn't. It was a love story with a mystery for good measure; it was a love story that had Mrs. Price thrown in to complicate the plot; it was a love story that was all tangled up with other elements ; and it was a love story that I only could see one side of.

For I couldn't get at her feelings at all. This was mostly because I hardly ever saw her with him. If she did happen to be there when he passed, she'd be either in her room or under the balcony roof and I couldn't see how she acted or hear what she said. Also she had such a hold on herself, had such a calm, reserved way with her, that you'd have to be a clairvoyant to get under her guard.

Any woman would have been thrilled but me, knowing what I did — can't you see my thoughts going round in wheels and whirligigs ? If she reciprocated — and there's few that wouldn't or I don't know my own sex

— what was she doing with Price? Was she a siren

playing the two of them? Was she Mrs. Price's secret rival with both men? Was she the kind of vampire heroine they have in plays who can break up a burglar-proof home with one hand tied behind her? You wouldn't think it to look at her — but the more I hit the high spots of society the more I feel you can't tell people by the ordinary trade-marks.

Then one afternoon toward the end of the week I saw a little scene right under my window that lightened up the darkness. It gave me what I call facts; what the Whitneys, anyway Mr. George — but that belongs farther on.

Mr. Ferguson came out of the wood path, Across the garden and on his usual beat, up the terrace steps. He had a spray of lemon verbena in his hand and as he walked over the grass with his long, light stride, he kept his eyes on the balcony keen and expectant, his face all eager and serious. Suddenly it changed, brightened, softened, glowed like the sunlight had fallen on it — you didn't need to be a detective to know she'd come out of the study.

This time she came down the steps and went toward him. They met under my window and stood there, he facing me, brushing his lips with the spray of lemon verbena and looking down at her, a lover if ever I saw one. He asked her what she was doing that afternoon, and she said going for a walk, and when he wanted to

know where, she said through the woods to the beach. "A solitary walk?" he asked and she said yes, her walks were always solitary.

" By preference ? "

She turned half away from him and I could see her profile. I'd hardly have known it for Miss Maitland's, soft, shy, the cheek pink. Her eyes were on the toe of her shoe, white against the green grass, and with her head drooping she was like a girl, bashful and blushing before her beau.

" It generally is by preference," she said.

" Would it exclude me," he asked, " if I tried to butt in? "

She didn't answer for a moment, then said very low:

" Not if you really wanted to come — didn't do it just to be kind to a lonesome lady."

"Lonesome lady be hanged," he exclaimed as joyful as if she'd given him a kiss, " it's just the other way round — kindness to a lonesome gentleman. I'm terribly lonesome this afternoon."

But he wasn't going to be long — far from it. Round the corner of the house, walking soft as a cat, came Mrs. Price. She made me think of a cat every way, stepping so stealthy, her body so slim and lithe, a small, secret smile on her face as if she'd come on two nice little helpless mice. She was all in white, shining and spotless, a tennis racket in one hand, a bunch of

letters in the other. They didn't see her and she got quite close, then said, sweet and smooth as treacle:

" Good afternoon, Dick."

They weren't doing anything but planning a walk, but they both started like it had been a murder.

" Oh," says Mr. Ferguson, looking blankly disconcerted, " oh, Suzanne, I didn't see you. How do you do — good afternoon."

She came to a halt and stood softly swinging her racket, looking at him with that mean, cold smile.

" I was in my room and saw you so I came down at once. It's a splendid afternoon for our game, not a breath of wind."

I saw, and she saw, and I guess any but a blind man could have seen, he'd a date to play tennis with her and had forgotten it. Of course a woman would have scrambled out, had something to offer that made a noise like an excuse; but that poor prune of a man — they're all alike when a quick lie's needed — couldn't think of a thing to say. He just stood between them, looking haunted and stammering out such gems of thought as, " Our game — of course our game — I hadn't noticed it but there is no wind."

She had him; he couldn't throw her down after he'd made the engagement, and with her there he couldn't say what he wanted to Esther Maitland. And neither of them helped him; Mrs. Price listened to his flounderings

with the little smile, light and cool on her painted lips, and Miss Maitland stood by, not a word out of her. I noticed that Mrs. Price never looked at her, acted as if she wasn't there, and presently Ferguson, getting desperate, turns to her and says:

" How about taking our walk later — after Mrs. Price and I have finished our game?"

The girl got red, burning; she started to answer, but Mrs. Price cut in, for the first time addressing her:

" Oh, Miss Maitland, that reminds me — I want these letters answered, if you'll be so kind. Just follow the notes on the edges, and please do it as soon as possible — they're rather important. They must go out on the evening mail."

She handed the letters to the girl and Esther Maitland took them with a murmur. I know that kind of answer — it's the agreeing response of the wage-earner. It comes soft and polite — it has to — but like the pleasant rippling of the ocean on the beach it's not the only sound that element can give forth.

Ferguson tried to say something; he was mad and mortified and everything else he ought to have been, but she wouldn't give him a chance.

" Come along, Dick," she says, bright and easy, " you've kept me waiting which is very rude, but I'm in a good humor and I'll forgive you. There's a racket at the court — we were playing there this morning.

You can walk with Miss Maitland some other day. I'm afraid she'll have to attend to my work this afternoon."

He got balky, lingered, looked at Miss Maitland, but she turned sharply away and moved toward the balcony. So there was nothing for him to do but to go off with his captor. I couldn't but look after them, both in beautiful white clothes, both rich, both young, he so tall, she so slim, for all the world like a picture of lovers on the cover of a magazine. Then I switched back to Miss Maitland. She's come to a halt, right below the window, and, standing there like a graven image, was watching them.

I never saw any one so still. You wouldn't have known she was alive except for her eyes which moved after them, moved and moved, until the pair disappeared behind the rose-covered trellis that hid the courts. Then she let out a sound, a smothered ejaculation that you couldn't spell with letters; but you didn't need to, it said more than printed pages. Rage was in it and pain and love. They were in her face, too, stamped and cut into it. I wouldn't have known it for hers, it was all marred and tragic, a pitiful, dreadful face.

She looked blankly at the letters in her hand, at first as if she didn't know what they were, then crumpled them, threw them on the ground and made a run for

Miss Maitland Private Secretary

the balcony. She was almost there, I craning my neck to keep her in sight, when she stopped, wheeled around, went back to the scattered papers and picked them up. " Oh, bread and butter," I thought, " bread and butter! Aren't you cursing it now?" Bad as I believed her to be I couldn't but be sorry for her, for I've been in that position myself. Take it from me, licking the hand that feeds you is a job that comes hard to the worst of us.

She pressed out the letters, smoothed away the creases slow and careful and came back to the balcony. Just before she disappeared under it she stopped and lifted her face, the eyes closed, the teeth pressed on her under lip. It quivered like a child's on the brink of tears, but she wasn't crying — fighting, I'd say, against something deeper than tears. I couldn't bear to look at it and shut my own eyes; when I opened them she was gone.

You didn't need to tell me any more after that. She was in love with Ferguson, not Price; she was in love and straining every nerve to hide it ; she was in love so she was jealous of Mrs. Price — and I'd bet a hat she was the kind who could love fierce and hard.

I had to get this into the office and the next day asked for time off from Mrs. Janney and went in. I found them different to what they had been on my first visit, taking it serious like they were warming to it. I'd

Molly's Story

hardly sat down before I heard the reason. O'Malley had been busy and turned up enough evidence to make them sure that Chapman Price and Miss Maitland were in deep in some sort of plot or conspiracy.

O'Malley's investigation of Price's movements on the night of July the seventh had revealed these facts: Price had taken his car from Sommers' garage at Cedar Brook at eight-thirty, not returning till five minutes before two. To one of the garage men he had said that the night being so fine he had gone for a long run over the island. No trace of his whereabouts during these hours had been found until O'Malley dropped on a policeman at the end of the Queensborough Bridge. This man said Price had crossed over to the city between nine-thirty and ten. He was positive of his identification, as early in June he had stopped the young man for exceeding the speed limit on the bridge, taken his name and address and had a heated altercation with him. From that time to his return to Cedar Brook Price had dropped out of sight. He had not been in the lodgings he kept in town or in any of the garages he patronized. Whatever his business had been in the city he had had plenty of time to return to Grasslands and participate in the theft of the jewels.

A continued watch of the house at 76 Gayle Street had shown that both Miss Maitland and Price had been there on the Thursday previous and Price on Sunday

Miss Maitland Private Secretary

afternoon. Each had entered with noiseless haste and each had used a latchkey. O'Malley in a search for a room had interviewed the janitor, a grouchy old chap living in the basement; and got a line on all the tenants, none of whom answered to the description of Price or Miss Maitland. Of their visits to the house the man was evidently ignorant, but he supplied some information which showed how they could come and go without his cognizance.

On July the eighth a lady, giving no name, had taken the right hand front room on the top floor for a friend, Miss Agnes Brown, an art student coming from the west but not yet arrived in the city. The lady paid a month's rent in advance, took the key, and said when Miss Brown arrived, the janitor would be informed, but that she might be delayed through illness in her family. This lady, as described by the janitor, was beyond a doubt Esther Maitland.

O'Malley was positive that the man honestly believed the room unused and awaiting its occupant. He had seen no signs of habitation, heard no sound from behind its closed door. Cooking was permitted in the house and it was part of his business to sweep down the halls every morning and empty the pails containing the food refuse which were placed outside the doors. He had seen no pail, no milk bottles, and never at night, when he went up to light the hall gas, had there

Molly's Story

been a gleam from the transom of Miss Brown's apartment.

The room had been engaged by Esther Maitland the day after the robbery, had been secured for a tenant who had not materialized. She had taken the key herself and had visited the place, as Chapman Price had done. Both had made their exits and entrances so carefully that the janitor had no idea any one had ever been inside the door since the day it was rented.

After I'd heard all this I opened up with what I'd collected. The Chief didn't say much, which is his way when you come in with a new " twist," but Mr. George wouldn't have it, got quite peevish and said my imagination had run away with me.

" Do you think a girl in love with another man would have embroiled herself with Price the way she has ? " he snapped out.

" I don't know, Mr. George. I'm not ready to say yet what she's done or hasn't done. No one can deny that things are dead against her. All I'm sure of now is that she is in love with Mr. Ferguson and, that being the case, I don't think she's the kind, guilty or innocent, who'd take up with another man."

" But you can't base a conviction on a moment's pantomime such as you overlooked. The girl was probably angry at Mrs. Price's manner. It can be a deuced disagreeable manner; I've seen it."

" She didn't act like that — it wasn't only anger — it was all sorts of feelings."

He couldn't see it any way but his own and hammered at me.

" But the whole structure's built on the assumption of an affair between her and Price. Do you think she'd steal for him, lie for him, hire a room to meet him in, unless she was so crazy about him she was clay in his hands ? "

" Mr. George," I said, dropping back in my chair sort of helpless but still as obstinate as a government mule, " every word you say sounds like sense and I'm not saying it isn't. But while I'm not passing any criticisms on you, in this kind of question, I'd back my own judgment against any man's that ever lived since Adam tried to throw the blame on Eve."

The Chief laughed like he was amused at the scrapping of two kids.

" That's right, Molly," he says, " don't let him browbeat you, stick to your own opinion."

"Well, what do you think?" Mr. George turned to him all red and ruffled up. " Isn't she building up theories on the flimsiest kind of foundation? "

The Chief wouldn't give him any satisfaction.

" I'll take a leaf out of her book," he said, " not pass any criticisms. And I think we're going on too fast. I expect to have Chapman here himself in a day

or two and ask some questions about that long ride on the night of July the seventh. After that we'll be on a firmer footing — or we ought to be. Meantime, Molly, you go back to Grasslands. Keep your eyes open and your mouth shut and if anything turns up let me know."

A CHAPTER ABOUT BAD TEMPERS

THINGS were not going Mr. Larkin's way. What had begun with such bright promise was declining to a twilight uncertainty. The morning after his ignominious failure with Willitts he had a letter from Suzanne, forwarded from his New York office, telling him that she would be in town on the following Monday and would like to see him. The letter disturbed him greatly. It was not alone that he had nothing to report; it was that the tone of the missive was irritated and impatient. It was the angrily imperious summons of a lady who is disappointed in her hireling.

He packed up his things and left Cedar Brook — the collapse of his endeavor there was complete — and at the hour appointed found Suzanne waiting in the shaded reception room. Her words and manner showed him how disagreeable a fine lady can be; they gave him a cold premonition that his fat salary would end unless something distinct and definite was soon forthcoming. In fact she hinted it; his assurances that interesting

developments were pending, that this sort of work was necessarily slow, kindled no responsive enthusiasm in the crossly accusing eye she fastened on him. His manner became almost pleading; he was on the edge of discoveries, unquestionably he would have something to tell her by the end of the week. At that she hung dubious, the angry eye less disconcerting, and said she would be in town on Friday as she was going to take her little girl to the oculist.

Mr. Larkin hailed the announcement with a sleuth-like eagerness, but, as if anxious to quench any little flicker of his spirit, she added blightingly that she didn't think it would be possible to see him as the child would be with her. He grappled with the difficulty, displaying both patience and resourcefulness, for Mrs. Price, in a bad temper, had a talent for creating obstacles.

Why, he suggested, couldn't the little girl go to the oculist with her nurse or companion and Mrs. Price be left, so to speak, free to roam? Mrs. Price's answer snapped with an angry click — that was of course what she would do — she always did. But , Mr. Larkin did not suppose she took the exhausting trip from Berkeley for nothing, did he? She had matters to attend to herself, shops to go to, people to see; when they came into town they were swamped, simply swamped, by what they had to do. She depicted with a lively irritation their harried progress, the party split into halves,

Miss Maitland Private Secretary

one in a hired vehicle, one in the family motor, passing through the marts of trade in a stampede of breatliless shopping. She rubbed it in, seemed to be intimating that he was attempting to frustrate an overtaxed and weary woman in the accomplishment of gigantic tasks.

Mr. Larkin met the difficulties and kept his patience. It took a good deal to finally reach a settlement which was obvious from the start. The child and her companion could go on their errands and Suzanne could go on hers, but be back before them. He could meet her at the house at any hour she named and would leave before the return of the other half of the party. He forced her to an admission that the plan was feasible, though she gave it grudgingly, her manner still suggesting that if he had conducted himself as a detective worthy of his hire she would not have been put to so much trouble. She arranged to be at the house at twelve which she calculated might give her half an hour alone with him. Should there be any change of plans she would let him know, and she hoped, with an accentuated glance, he would have something satisfactory to tell her.

His good temper unshaken, Mr. Larkin assured her he would and rose to go. On the doorstep he mopped his forehead though the day was not warm, also he swore softly as he descended the steps.

A day or two after this, Chapman Price went to the 156

Whitney office. He had received a communication from them asking for an interview, the ostensible subject of debate being Suzanne's divorce. The suit would be conducted at Reno where Mrs. Price would go in the autumn, but the Whitneys, as the Janney lawyers, wanted to talk the matter over with Mr. Price for the arranging of various financial details.

These were quickly opened up for his attention by Wilbur Whitney, who, with George, saw the young man in his private office. The ground of divorce — non-support — was touched on with a tactful lightness. Mrs. Price would of course ask for no alimony and so forth and so on. From that the elder Whitney passed to the subject of the child; it was the desire of its mother and grandparents that Chapman should relinquish all claim on it. The young man listened, gloomy and scowling, now and then muttering in angry repudiation. But the diplomatic arguments of the lawyer bore down his opposition; he had to give in. The child ought to remain with its mother, the natural guardian of its tender years; left entirely to the Jan-neys it would be the eventual heiress of their great wealth, but if Chapman antagonized them by a fight for its possession its prospects might suffer. It was a persuasive appeal, made to Chapman's parental affections, the welfare of his daughter before his own. It brought him to a sullen consent, and Wilbur Whitney, with a sound of approval, pushed back his chair, elated as by a good work done.

Price rose, his face flushed and frowning. That he was resentful was plain to be seen, but he had himself in hand, inquiring with a sardonic politeness if that was all they wanted of him. The elder Whitney with a hospitable gesture toward the empty chair, said no, there were some questions he'd like to ask, nothing of any especial moment and on an entirely different matter.

" Mrs. Janney," he explained, " has suggested that we make a separate, private investigation of the robbery. She's lost faith in Kissam, who hasn't done anything but draw his pay envelope and wants us to see what we can do. So we've been clearing up a lot of dead wood, looking into the movements of the people in the house and the neighborhood that night."

Price, who had remained standing, turned his eyes on the speaker in a gaze that had a quality of sudden fixed attention.

" Oh," he said, in a tone containing a note of hostile comprehension, " so you're in it, are you? "

' Yes; we're in it — only a little way so far. We've been rounding up every one that has, or has had, any dealings with the family and we've taken you in in the sweep."

" Me? " Price's voice showed an intense surprise. " What have I got to do with it? "

" Nothing, my dear boy, except that you "were a member of the household, and as I said, we're clearing up every one in sight. It's only a formality, a tagging and disposing of all unnecessary elements. You went for a motor ride that night — a long ride. You wouldn't mind telling us where, would you? It's just for the purpose of eliminating you along with the rest of the dead wood."

The young man's gaze dropped from Whitney's face to his own hat lying on the table. He looked at it with an absent stare.

" A motor ride? " he murmured.

" Yes, from eight-thirty till nearly two."

" Um," Price appeared to be considering. " Let me see — what was the date, I don't remember?"

George assisted his memory:

" July the seventh — a moonlight night."

" Ah," he had it now, nodding his head several times in restored recollection. " Of course, I remember perfectly. There was a heavy rain early in the evening and then a full moon." He turned to the elder man. " I'm rather fond of ranging about at night, and couldn't quite place what especial ride you referred to. I took a long spin up the Island."

" Up ? " said Whitney, " not being a Long Islander I don't know your directions. Would * up' mean toward the city ? "

" No, the other way, out along the Sound roads and on toward Peconic."

" Kept to the country, eh? Too fine a night to waste in town."

Price's face darkened. George watching him noticed a slight dilation of his nostrils, a slight squaring of the line of his jaw. His answer came in a tone hard and combative:

" Exactly. I get enough of town in the day. I rode, as I told you, out to the east, a long way — I can't give you the exact route if that's what you want." He suddenly leaned forward and snatched his hat from the table. Holding it against his side he made an ironical bow to his questioner said, " Does that eliminate me as a suspect? "

Whitney laughed, a sound of lazy good humor rich with the tolerance of a vast experience:

" My dear Chapman, why use such sensational terms? Suspect is a word we haven't reached yet. Take this as it's meant — a form, merely a form."

" The form might have included a questioning of me before you took the trouble to look up what I did. Evidently my word wasn't thought sufficient."

His glance, darkly threatening, moved from one man to the other. George started to protest, but he cut in, his words directed at old Whitney:

" It's all I have to offer you now. It's what I say 160

against what you've been told to believe. I can prove no alibi, for I was with no one, saw no one, started alone and stayed alone. That's all you'll get out of me, and you can take it or leave it as you d n please."

He turned and walked toward the door, the elder Whitney's conciliatory phrases delivered to his back. The door knob in his hand he wheeled round, the anger he had been struggling to subdue fierce in his face:

" Don't think for a moment you've fooled me. I was ignorant when I came in here, but I'm on to the whole dirty business now. I see through this pussy-footing round the divorce. It's the Janneys — the blow in the back I might have known was coming. They've got my child, set you on to wheedle her out of me. But that wasn't enough — they're going to try and finish the good work — put me out of business so there's no more trouble coming from me. Brand me as a thief — that's their game, is it ? Well — they've gone too far. I've held my hand up to this but now I'll let loose. They'll see! By God, they'll see that I can hit back blow for blow."

CHAPTER XV

WHAT HAPPENED ON FRIDAY

THE Friday morning when Suzanne was to go to town broke auspiciously bright and cloudless. As Annie was not the proper person to take Bebita to the oculist, and as Suzanne would be too busy to go herself, Miss Maitland had been impressed into the service. It had been decided two days earlier, and though she had received some instructions at the time, on the drive in, Mrs. Price went over her plans with a meticulous thoroughness. They would go first to the Fifth Avenue house, pick up there some clothes of Bebita's needing alteration, and then separate. Esther would take a cab from the rank on the side street, and go with Bebita to the oculist, to the dressmaker with the clothes, and execute several minor commissions in shops along the Avenue. Bebita begged for a box of caramels from Justin's, the French confectioner, a request which was graciously acceded to by her mother, Miss Maitland jotting it down on her list. Mrs. Price would take the motor and go about her own affairs, which would occupy probably an hour. She would then return to

What Happened on Friday

the house and wait for them — for she would have finished before they did — and afterward they would go out to lunch somewhere. She said she thought it would be fully an hour and a half before they got back and Miss Maitland, eyeing the long list, said it might be even longer.

Aggie McGee had the clothes tied up in a box and Suzanne and Bebita stood on the steps waiting while Miss Maitland went for the cab. The rank was just round the corner and in a few minutes she came back with a taxi running along the curb behind her.

" Quite a piece of luck to find one," she said, as she took the box. " They're not always there in the dead season."

Bebita jumped in, settling herself with joyful pranc-ings and waving a little white-gloved hand. Esther followed, snapped the door shut, and they glided away. Suzanne watched them go, then stepped into the big motor and was swept off in the opposite direction.

She came back before the hour was up. She had hurried as she wanted to have done with Larkin before they returned. It would be extremely uncomfortable if they found her in confab with the detective; it would necessitate boring explanations and the inventing of lies.

She sat down in the reception room close to the window, pulled up the blind and waited. Drawn back from

the eyes of passers-by she could command the sidewalk and the street for some distance and if, by any evil chance, Larkin should be late, she could see him coming and tell Aggie McGee to say she was not there.

Up to now Larkin had been punctual to the dot, but on this, the one occasion when punctuality was vital, he was not on time. Twelve passed, then the quarter, and the sun-swept length of the great avenue gave up no masculine figure that bore any resemblance to him. She was growing nervous, wondering what she had better do, when he hove in sight walking quickly toward the house. A glance at her wrist watch told her it was twenty minutes past twelve — Miss Maitland and Bebita might not be back for another half hour yet. She would chance it, for she was extremely anxious to see him, and anyway, if they should come in before he left, she could tell him to go into the drawing room and slip out after they had gone. Relieved by the decision she rose and was turning toward the mirror, when she caught sight of a taxi scudding up the street with Esther Maitland's face in the window.

A word not generally used by ladies escaped Suzanne. There was nothing for it but to send him away. She ran into the hall and pressed the bell, listening in a fever for Aggie McGee's step on the kitchen stairs. Simultaneously with its first heavy thud came the peal of the front door bell. Suzanne, who had noticed that

What Happencd on Friday

the taxi was moving fast and would make the steps before Larkin, called down on Aggie McGee's ascending head:

" That's Miss Maitland. A gentleman I expected is just behind her. I can't see him now, I haven't time. Tell him I've been here and gone."

She went back into the reception room and stood listening. She heard the door opening, Esther's step in the hall; it was all right, the detective would get his conge without being seen by any one but Aggie Mc-Gee. She drew a breath of relief and turned smiling to the girl in the doorway. Miss Maitland did not give back the smile; she sent a searching look over the room and said in a low, breathless voice as if she had been running:

"IsBebitahere?"

There was a moment of silence. Through it the heavy tread of Aggie McGee passing along the hall sounded unnaturally loud. As it went clump, clump, down the kitchen stairs Suzanne was aware of Miss Maitland's face, startlingly strange, ashen-colored. At first it was all she took in.

" Bebita — here ? " she stammered. " How could she be? She's with you."

Miss Maitland made a step into the room, her hands went up clenched to her chest, her voice came again through the broken gasps of a runner:

" No — she isn't. I thought I'd find her with you — I thought she'd come back. Oh, Mrs. Price—" she stopped, her eyes, telling a message of disaster, fixed on the other.

Suzanne's answer came from opened lips, dropped apart in a sudden horror:

" What do you mean ? Why should she be here ? "

" Mrs. Price, something's happened! "

Suzanne screamed out:

"Where is she?"

" I don't know — but — but — I haven't got her — she's gone. Mrs. Price —"

Suzanne screamed again, putting her hands against the sides of her head, her face, between them, a livid mask.

" Gone — gone where ? Is she dead ? "

The girl shook her head, swallowing on a throat dried to a leathern stiffness:

" No — no — nothing like that. But — the taxi — it went, disappeared while I was in Justin's. I was in there buying the candy and when I came out it was gone. I looked everywhere; I couldn't believe it; I thought she'd come back here — run away from me for a joke."

Suzanne, holding the sides of her head, stared like a mad woman, then gave a piercing cry, thin and high, a wild, dolorous sound. Only the solidity of the house prevented it from penetrating to the lower regions where

What Happened on Friday

Aggie McGee and her aunt were comfortably lunching. " Listen, Mrs. Price." Esther took her hands and drew them down. "The driver may have made a mistake, taken her somewhere else — he couldn't —" Suzanne shrieked in sudden frenzy: " She's been stolen — my baby's been stolen! " For a second they looked at one another, each pallid face confessing its conviction of the grisly thought. Esther tried to speak, the sentences dropping disconnected :

" If it's that then — then — it's some one who knorrs you're rich — some one — they'll want money. They'll give her up for money — Oh, Mrs. Price, I looked — I hunted —"

Suzanne's voice came in a suddenly strangled whisper: " It's you — It's your fault! You've let them steal my baby. You've done it! You'll be put in jail."

With the words issuing from her mouth she staggered and crumpled into a limpness of fiberless flesh and trailing garments. Esther put an arm about her and drew her to the sofa. Here she collapsed amid the cushions, her eyes open, moans coming from her shaking lips. Esther knelt beside her:

" Mrs. Price, it's horrible, but try to keep up, don't break down this way. No one would dare to do anything to her. If she's been stolen it's to the interest of the person who did it to keep her safe. We'll find

Miss Maitland Private Secretary

her in a day or two. Your mother, her position, her power — she'll do something, she'll get her back."

Suzanne rolling her head on the cushion, groaned:

" Oh, my baby! Oh, Bebita! " Then burst into wild tears and disjointed sentences. She was almost unintelligible, cries to heaven, wails for her child, accusations of the woman at her feet broke from her in a torrent. Once she struck at the girl with a feeble fist.

There was no help to be got from her and Esther rose. She spoke more to herself than the anguished creature on the sofa:

" We can't waste time this way. I'll call up Grasslands and ask what to do."

The telephone was in the hall and, as she waited for the connection, she could hear the sounds of the mother's misery beating on the house's rich silence. Then Dixon's voice brought her faculties into quick order. She wanted to speak to Mrs. Janney herself, at once, it was important. There followed what seemed an endless wait, and then Mrs. Janney. When she had mastered it, her voice came, sharp and incisive:

" Hold the wire, I have to speak to Mr. Janney."

Another wait, through which, faint as the shadows of sound, Esther could hear the tiny echo of voices, then the jar of an approaching step and a man answered:

" Hello, Miss Maitland, this is Ferguson. I've orders from Mrs. Janney — Go straight down to the

Whitney office, tell them what's happened and put the thing in their hands. Say nothing to anybody else. Mr. and Mrs. Janney are starting to go in. They'll be in town as quickly as they can get there and will meet you at the office. Got that straight? All right. Good-by."

She cogitated a moment, then called up the Whitney office getting George. She gave him a brief outline of what had occurred and told him she would be there with Mrs. Price within a half hour.

Back in the reception room she tried to arouse Suzanne, but the distracted woman did not seem to have sense left to take in anything. At the sound of Esther's voice her sobs and wails rose hysterical, and the girl, finding it impossible to make her understand, set about preparing her for the drive. Any word of hers appeared to make Suzanne's state worse, so silently, as if she were dressing a manikin, she pinned the hat to the disordered blonde hair, draped a motor veil over it, composed the rumpled skirts, gathered up her purse and gloves, and finally, an arm crooked round one of Suzanne's, got her out to the motor.

On the long drive downtown almost nothing was said. The roar of the surrounding traffic drowned the sounds of weeping that now and then rose from the veiled figure, which Esther held firm and upright by the pressure of her shoulder.

CHAPTER XVI

MOLLY'S STORY

THAT Friday — gee, shall I ever forget it! —-opening so quiet and natural and suddenly bang, in the middle of it, the sort of thing you read in the yellow press.

It was a holiday for me and I was sitting in the upper hall alcove making a blouse and handy to the extension 'phone. Now and then it would ring and I'd pull it over with a weary sigh and hear a female voice full of cultivation and airs ask if Mrs. Janney'd take a hand at bridge, or a male one want to know what Mr. Jan-ney thought about eighteen holes at golf.

It was on for one when it rang again and with a smothered groan — for I was putting on the collar — I jerked it over. Believe me, I forgot that blouse! Stiff, like I was turned to stone, I sat there listening, hearing them come, one after another, getting every word of it. When they were through I got up, feeling sort of gone in the middle, and lit out for the stairs. I couldn't have kept away — Bebita disappeared! " Kidnapped!" I said to myself as I ran along the

hall. " Kidnapped! that's what it is — it's only poor children that get lost."

On the stairs I met Mrs. Janney coming up on the run. It wasn't the speed that made her breath short; but she was on the job, the grand old Roman, with her mouth as straight as the slit in a post box and her face as hard as if it was cut out of granite.

" Go down there," she said, giving a jerk of her head toward the hall below. " Sit there and wait. Something's happened and you may be useful."

I went on down and took a seat. Outside on the balcony I could see Mr. Janney, wandering about with a hunted look. From the telephone closet came Ferguson's voice telling his chauffeur to bring his car to Grasslands, now, this minute, and enough gasoline for a long run. Then he came out, hooked an armful of coats off the hall rack, and ran past me on to the balcony. He gave the coats to Mr. Janney, who stood holding them, looking after Ferguson wherever he went and quavering questions at him. I don't think Ferguson answered them, but he pulled one of the coats out of the old man's arms and put him into it, quick and efficient. When the motor came up he tried to make Mr. Janney get in, but he wouldn't, standing there, helpless and pitiful, and calling out for Mrs. Janney.

" I'm here, Sam," came her voice from the stairs and she scudded by where I was sitting, tying her motor

Miss Maitland Private Secretary

veil over her hat. She seemed to have forgotten me and I followed her out on to the balcony, not knowing what she wanted me to do. As I stood there Ferguson's big car came shooting up the drive.

She climbed quickly into her own motor, waiting at the bottom of the steps, Mr. Janney scrambled in after her and Ferguson threw a rug over them. They were just starting when she looked up and saw me.

" Oh," she cried, leaning across the old man, " we'll want you — you must come."

Mr. Janney stared bewildered at her and said:

" Why — why should she come? "

" Keep quiet, Sam," then over her shoulder to Ferguson as the car began to move, " Bring Mrs. Babbitts, Dick. Take her with you."

The car glided off, Mr. Janney's voice floating back:

" But why, why — why do you want her? "

Ferguson's motor swung round the oval and came to a halt. The chauffeur jumped out, and, told he wasn't wanted, disappeared. The young man turned to me, not a smile out of him now.

" Come on, get in," he said and then giving a nod at one of the coats lying over a chair, " and bring that with you — it may blow up cold and it's a long run."

I did as I was told — there was something about him that made you do what he said — and jumped in. He came on my heels, snapped the door and we started.

Before we got to the gates he speeded the machine up and in a few minutes we were close on the Janney motor which was flying along the woody road at a pace that would have strained the heart of a bicycle cop. Their dust came over us in a cloud, and Mr. Ferguson slowed down, and, his hand resting easy on the wheel, said:

" What does Mrs. Janney want you for? "

I'd hoped he hadn't noticed that, but in case he had I'd an answer ready.

" Maybe she thought I might have noticed if any one was hanging round lately — hanging round to size up the habits of the family and Bebita's movements."

" Oh," he said, looking at me very pointed, " then you know what's happened to Bebita."

I hadn't any answer ready for that. I had to get hold of something quick and as you will do when you're taken off your guard, I got hold of a lie:

" I met Mrs. Janney on the stairs and she told me."

" That's funny," he says, sort of thoughtful. " Before she went she told both Mr. Janney and myself that no one in the house must hear a word of it."

I began to get red, and for a moment, stared at my feet pressed side by side on the wood in front of me. It didn't make it any pleasanter to know that Ferguson was looking at me, intent and narrow, out of the tail of his eye.

Miss Mattland Private Secretary

"I guess she was so excited she forgot and just blabbed it out."

It was the best I could do, but it was poor stuff. If you knew Mrs. Janney you'd see why.

" Um," said Ferguson, and took a look ahead at the cloud of dust that hid the other car. Then he comes out with another:

" I wonder if that was the reason she called you Mrs. Babbitts?"

I took a good breath from the bottom of my lungs and said:

" I shouldn't be surprised. Having your grandchild lost is enough to mix up any woman."

He didn't answer and we ran on some way, out of the woods on to a long straight stretch of road. The motor in front was going at a tremendous clip, Mrs. Janney's veil lashing out like a wild hand beckoning us on.

" Look here," says Ferguson, soft and gentle right into my ear, " what are you, anyway ? "

"Me?" I bounced round and gave him a baby stare. " I'm a governess. What do you think I am? "

" You may be a good governess but you're a poor liar. I was in the telephone closet and heard what Mrs. Janney said to you on the stairs. And I don't think you're a governess at all — you're a detective."

I thought a minute but what was the use, he had me. 174

Molly's Story

So I raised up my chin and met him, eye for eye:

" All right, I am. What of it? "

" Oh, lots of it. I've had my suspicions for some time. You tapped that 'phone message from New York? "

" I did — it's my job. I have to do it."

" Don't apologize — it wastes time and we haven't any to lose. Now just tell me Miss Rogers, or Mrs. Babbitts, what have you found out about the robbery; where were you getting to before this hideous mess to-day?"

" Well, you've got your nerve with you! " I snorted.

" I have, right here handy. I'm a friend of the Janneys, I'm a —" he stopped. His nerve was handy all right but he hadn't enough to tell me it was because of Esther Maitland he was so keen.

" Go on," I said sarcastic. " I'm interested to hear what you are now you've found out what I am."

" I'm almost a member of the household. I can help. I want to help — and I want to know."

" Maybe you do," I said. " We often want things in this world that we can't get. Don't think you have the monopoly of that complaint."

The motor rose over the crest of a hill, flashed by a farm and slid down an incline. Before us stretched a white line of road, with the forward car racing along it in a blur of dust.

Miss Mcdtland Private Secretary

"You mean you won't tell me? "

" You got me."

We suddenly began to slow up, the car swung off sideways from the roadbed, ran toward the bushes on the right, and came to a halt. Ferguson dropped against the back of the seat, stretched his legs and said:

" This is a nice shady place to stop in."

" Stop! " I cried. " Forget it! What do you want to stop for? "

" I don't — it's you. I'm going to rest here quietly while you tell me."

*' Young man," I said, fixing him with a cold eye, " this is no time to be funny."

" I entirely agree with you. Therefore as we're of the same mind it behooves you to get busy and give me the information I want."

The coolness of him would have riled a hen. It did me; I gave a stamp on the footboard and angrily said:

" Start up this machine. I was ordered to go to New York and I've got to get there."

" You will as soon as you tell me. But I won't move until you do. We'll stay here all day, all night if necessary. There's just one thing certain: we'll stay till I hear what I want to know."

I was beaten and it made me mad straight through. 176

Molly's Story

I was helpless too and that made me madder. If I'd had the least notion of how you started the dinged machine I was angry enough to have tried to do it, though it wouldn't have been any use with Ferguson there to frustrate me.

" You're losing time," said he. " There'll be trouble if you don't show up."

" Do you think it's a high class thing," I snapped out, " to put a girl in a position like this? "

" Don't you think you can trust me? " he answered very quiet.

I looked at him, a long, slow survey, and as I did it my anger simmered down. It's part of my business to read faces and what I saw in his made me say sort of reluctant:

"Well, maybe I can."

He leaned forward and put his hand on mine.

" Miss Rogers, if you'll stand in with me, trust me and let me help, you won't make any mistake. For I'll stand in with you, not now, not just for this thing, but for always. You've my word on it and I don't break my word."

That ended it — not what he said but the look of him while he said it. Almost without knowing it my hand turned under his and they clasped. Solemn as a pair of images we shook. Any one passing would have thought we were crazy, backed into the brushwood, side

Miss Maitland Private Secretary

by side on the front seat, shaking hands as if we'd just been introduced.

I told him the whole story and he never said a word. When I came to Miss Maitland's part in it, I couldn't but look at him. He drew his eyebrows down in a frown and fiddled with his fingers on the wheel. Even when I told him what they thought about her and Chapman Price he didn't made a sound, but he straightened up, and drew a deep breath like he wanted more air in his lungs. I got it some way then — I can't exactly say how — that he was a good deal more of a person than I'd guessed — a lot more iron in his make-up than I'd thought when I liked his laugh and his boyish, jolly ways.

When I finished he said, easy and cool:

" Thank you — that gives me just what I wanted. You won't regret having told me. As for Whitney & Whitney, they won't say anything. They're my lawyers — known 'em all my life. I'll take care of that."

He took hold of the wheel and the car backed out into the road.

" Can we ever catch them up? " I asked.

" I guess so — this car can make seventy-five miles an hour. Are you game for a race ? "

" I'm game for anything that'll land me where I belong."

" All right — hold on to your hat." 178

Molly's Story

I guess the Lord protects those who are bent on His own business. Anyway I don't know why else we weren't killed. We ate up that road like a dago eating macaroni; it ran under the car like a white ribbon fastened to a spindle somewhere behind us. The woods were two green streaks on either side, and now and then a chuck hole would send me bouncing, landing anywhere — on the floor once.

" Hold on to something," he shouted at me. " I don't want to lose you."

And I shouted back:

" You couldn't. I'm wished on to this motor till death do us part or it lands me somewhere alive."

Through the villages we had to slow up. Gliding dignified along the tree-shaded streets put me into a fever and I guess it wore on him for more than once I heard him muttering to himself, and believe me, he wasn't saying his prayers. I glimpsed sideways at him, and saw his tanned face, with the hair loose and tousled by the wind, looking changed, hardened and older, all the gay expression gone. The news he'd forced out of me had hit him a body blow, struck him in the heart. And I was sorry, awfully sorry. You can hurt a mean person or a criminal and not care, but it's no lady's job to have to wound a decent man. That's why I'd never make a good professional — the

Miss Maitland Private Secretary

people get as big as the case to me, and if you're the real thing it's only the case that counts.

We were almost in Long Island City when we caught up with the Janneys, Mrs. Janney's veil still waving like a hand beckoning us to hurry.

MISS MAITLAND IN A NEW LIGHT

AT the entrance of the great building which housed the Whitney office the two motors came to a halt. Ferguson went in with the others saying he would see if he could be of any use, and if he was not wanted would return to the street level and wait. In the elevator Mr. Janney, who had been informed en route of Molly's real status, eyed her morosely, but when the car stopped forgot everything but the urgencies of the moment, and crowded out, tremulous and stumbling, on his wife's heels.

They were met by Wilbur Whitney who in a large efficient way, distributed them: — Ferguson was sent back to the street to wait, Molly waved to a chair in the hall, and the old people conducted up the passage to his private office. In a room opening from it Suzanne lay stretched on a sofa, restoratives and stimulants at hand, and a girl stenographer to fan her. She had revolted against the presence of Esther, who had been removed from her sight and shut in the sanctum of a junior partner.

Miss Maitland Private Secretary

Mrs. Janney went in to see her and the old man fell upon Whitney. It was Price's doing — they were certain of it, his wife had said so at once. He was bound to get back at them some way, he'd said he would — he'd left Grasslands swearing vengeance, and had been only waiting his opportunity. The lawyer nodded in understanding agreement and, Mrs. Janney returning, they drew up to the table and conferred in low voices.

What Whitney said confirmed the Janneys' belief. He told of his interview with Price; the man's anger and threats. Nevertheless he was of the opinion that the plot to kidnap the child had not been undertaken in sudden passion, but had probably been for some time germinating in Chapman's mind. The news of Bebita's loss, telephoned to the office by Miss Maitland, while it had shocked, had not altogether surprised him, though he had hardly thought the young man's desire to get square would have carried him to such lengths. Immediately after Esther's communication, George had telephoned to Price's office receiving the answer that he was not there but could probably be found at the Hartleys' at Cedar Brook. From the Hartleys they had learned that Mr. Price was in town, and had sent word that morning he would not come out this week-end.

There were other circumstances which the lawyer 182

said pointed to Price. These they could hear from Mrs. Babbitts who had made some important discoveries. He rose to send for her, but Mrs. Janney stayed him with a gesture — before they went into that she would like to see Miss Maitland and hear from her exactly what had occurred. Mr. Whitney, suavely agreeable, sent a summons for Esther, then softly closed the door into the room where Suzanne lay.

" Mrs. Price is very bitter against her," he said in explanation.

Mrs. Janney, too wrought up for polite hypocrisies, said brusquely:

" Oh, that's exactly like Suzanne. She has no balance at all. Of course we can't blame Miss Maitland — it's not her fault."

Mr. Whitney dropped back into his revolving desk chair and swung it toward her with a lurch of his body:

" She tells a very clear story — extremely clear. I'll let you get your own impression of it and then we'll have a talk with Mrs. Babbitts and you can see —"

A knock on the door interrupted him; in answer to his " Come in," Esther entered. She halted a moment on the threshold, her eyes touching the faces of her employers questioningly, as if she was not sure of her reception. But Mrs. Janney's quick, " Oh, Miss Mait-

land) I want to see you," brought her across the sill. Though she looked harassed and distressed, her manner showed a restrained composure. She took a chair facing them, meeting their glances with a steady directness. Mrs. Janney's demand for information was promptly answered; indeed her narrative was so devoid of unnecessary detail, so confined to essentials, that it suggested something gone over and put in readiness for the telling.

She had taken Bebita to the dressmaker and the oculist, the child accompanying her into both places. At the third stop, Justin's, she had persuaded Bebita to stay in the taxi. She had left it at the curb and had not been more than ten minutes in the store. When she came out it was gone. She had spent some time looking for it, searched up and down the street, and, though she was frightened, she could not believe anything had happened. Her idea had been that Bebita, tired of waiting or wanting to play a joke on her, had prevailed on the driver to return to the Fifth Avenue house. She had hailed a cab and gone back there and it was not till she saw Mrs. Price that she realized the real extent of the calamity. Mrs. Price had been utterly overwhelmed, and, not knowing what else to do, she had called up Grasslands for instructions.

Mr. Janney, who had been twisting and turning on his chair, burst out with:

" The man — the driver — did you notice him ? "

She lifted her hands and dropped them in her lap.

" Oh, Mr. Janney, of course I didn't. Does any one erer look at those men? He never got off his seat, opened the door by stretching his arm round from the front. I have a sort of vague memory of his face when I called him off the stand, and I think — but I can't be sure — that he wore goggles."

" It's needless to ask if you remember the number," Mrs. Janney said.

The girl answered with a hopeless shake of the head.

" You say you ran about looking for the taxi "— it was Mr. Janney again —" Why did you waste that time? "

" Mr. Janney," she leaned toward him insistent, but with patience for his afflicted state, " I thought it had gone somewhere farther along. You know how they won't let the vehicles stand in Fifth Avenue. I supposed it was down the block or round the corner on a side street. I asked the door-man but he hadn't noticed. I looked in every direction and even when I finally gave up and went after her I hadn't an idea that she'd been stolen."

"Time lost —all that time lost!" wailed the old man and began to cry.

*' Come, come, Mr. Janney," said Whitney, " don't 185

Miss Maitland Private Secretary

despond. It's not as bad as all that, and I'm pretty confident we'll have her back all right before very long."

Mr. Janney, with his face in his handkerchief, emitted sounds that no one could understand. His wife silenced him with a peremptory, " Be quiet, Sam," and returned to Miss Maitland:

" You say you dissuaded her from going into Justin's. Why did you do that? "

For the first time the girl lost her even poise. As she answered her voice was unsteady: " We were so pressed for time and I knew I could get through much quicker without her. That's why I did it — begged her to stay in the taxi and she said she would,"— she stopped, biting on her under lip, evidently unable to go on.

There was a moment's silence broken by Mrs. Jah-ney's voice low and grim :

" The man heard you and knew that was his chance."

Miss Maitland, her eyes down, the bitten lip showing red against its fellow, said huskily:

" You must blame me — you can't help it — but I'd rather have died than had such a thing happen."

Mr. Janney began to give forth inarticulate sounds again and his wife said with a sort of dreary resignation:

"Oh, I don't blame you, Miss Maitland. Nobody 186

Miss Maitland in a New Light

does. Mrs. Price is not responsible; she doesn't know what she's saying."

" Of course, of course," came in Whitney's deep, bland voice, " we all understand Mrs. Price's feelings — quite natural under the circumstances. And Miss Maitland's too." He rose and pressed a bell near the door. " Now if you've heard all you want I'll call in George and we'll talk this over. And Miss Maitland," he turned to her, urbanely kind and courteous, " could I trouble you to go back to Mr. Quincy's office; just for a little while? We won't keep you waiting very long this time."

A very dapper young man had answered the summons and under his escort Esther withdrew. Whitney went to a third door connecting with his son's rooms, opened it and said in a low voice:

" George, go and get Molly. We're ready for her now."

Coming back, he stood for a moment by the desk, and swept the faces of his clients with a meaning look:

" What you're going to hear from Mrs. Babbitts will be something of a shock. She's unearthed several rather startling facts that in my opinion bear on this present event and what led up to it. It's a peculiar situation and involves not only Price but Miss Maitland."

Mrs. Janney stared:

Miss Maitland Private Secretary

" Miss Maitland and Chapman! What sort of a situation? "

" At this stage I'll simply say mysterious. But I'm afraid, my dear friend, that your confidence in the young woman has been misplaced. However, before I go any further I'll let you hear what Mrs. Babbitts has to say and draw your own conclusions."

What Mrs. Babbitts had to say came not as one shock but as a series. Mrs. Janney could not at first believe it; she had to be shown the notes of the telephone message, and dropped them in her lap, staring from her husband to Wilbur Whitney in aghast question. Mr. Janney seemed stunned, shrunk in his clothes like a turtle in its shell. It was not until the lawyer, alluding to the loss of the jewels, mentioned Miss Maitland's possible participation either as the actual thief or as an accomplice, that he displayed a suddenly vitalized interest. His body stretched forward, and his neck craned up from its collar gave him more than ever the appearance of a turtle reaching out of its shell, his voice coming with a stammering urgency :

" But — but — no one can be sure. We mustn't be too hasty. We can't condemn the girl without sufficient evidence. Some one else may have been there and—"

Mrs. Janney shut him off with an exasperated impatience :

Miss Maitland in a New Light

" Oh, Sam, don't go back over all that. I don't care who took them; I don't care if I never see them again. It's only the child that matters." Then to Whitney the inconsequential disposed of, " We must make a move at once, but we must do it quietly without anything getting into the papers."

Whitney nodded:

"That's my idea."

" What are you going to do — go directly to him ? "

" No, not yet. Our first step will be made as you suggest, very quietly. We're going to keep the matter out of the papers and away from the police. Keep it to ourselves — do it ourselves. And I think — I don't want to raise any false hopes — but I think we can lay our hands on Bebita to-night."

"How — where?" Mr. Janney's head was thrust forward, his blurred eyes alight.

" If you don't mind, I'm not going to tell you. I'm going to ask you to leave it to me and let me see if my surmises are correct. If Chapman has her where I think he has, I'll give her over to you by ten o'clock. If I'm mistaken it will only mean a short postponement. He can't keep her and he knows it."

" The blackguard! " groaned the old man in helpless wrath.

Mrs. Janney wasted neither time nor energy in futile passion. She attacked another side of the situation',

Miss Maitland Private Secretary

" What are we to do with Miss Maitland? You can't arrest her."

" Certainly not. She's a very important person and we must have her under our eye. You must treat her as if you entirely exonerated her from all blame — maintain the attitude you took just now when talking with her. If my immediate plan should fail our best chance of getting

Bebita without publicity and an ugly scandal will be through her. She must have no hint of what we think, must believe herself unsuspected, and free to come and go as she pleases."

" You mean she's to stay on with us ? ? ' Mr. Jan-ney's voice was high with indignant protest.

" Exactly — she remains the trusted employee with whose painful position you sympathize. It won't be difficult, for you won't see much of her. You'll naturally stay here in town till Bebita is found. What I intend to do with her is to send her back to Grasslands with a competent jailer—" he paused and pointed where Molly sat, silent and almost forgotten.

For a moment the Janneys eyed her, questioning and dubious, then Mrs. Janney voiced their mutual thought:

"Is Mrs. Babbitts, alone, a sufficient guard?"

The lawyer smiled.

" Quite. Miss Maitland doesn't want to run away. She knows too much for that. No position could be

Miss Maitland in a New Light

better for our purpose than to leave her — apparently unsuspected — alone in that big house. She will be confident, possibly take chances." He turned on Molly, glowering at her from under his overhanging brows. " The safest and quickest means of communication with Grasslands, when the family is in town and the servants ignorant of the situation, would be the telephone."

That ended the conference. Mrs. Janney went to get Suzanne and Molly received her final instructions. She was to return to Grasslands with Miss Maitland, Ferguson could take them in his motor. She was to sit in the back seat with the lady and casually drop the information that she had come to town in answer to a wire from the Whitney office. She might have seen suspicious characters lurking about the grounds or in the woods. On no account was she to let her companion guess that Price was suspected, and any remarks which might place the young woman more completely at her ease, allay all sense of danger, would be valuable.

They left the room and went into the entrance hall where Esther, and presently Mrs. Janney, joined them. Whitney struck the note of a reassuring friendliness in his manner to the girl, and the old people, rather reservedly chimed in. She seemed grateful, thanked them, reiterating her distress. In the elevator, going

Miss Maitland Private Secretary

down, Molly noticed that she fell into a staring abstraction, starting nervously as the iron gate swung back at the ground floor.

Ferguson, waiting on the curb, saw them as they emerged from the doorway. His eyes leaped at the girl, and, as she crossed the sidewalk, were riveted on her. Their expression was plain, yearning and passion no longer disguised. If she saw the look she gave no sign, nodded to him, and, leaving Molly to explain, climbed into the back seat and sunk in a corner. Though the afternoon was hot she picked up the cloak lying on the floor and drew it round her shoulders.

The drive home was very silent. Molly gave the prescribed reasons for her presence and heard them answered with the brief comments of inattention. She also touched on the other matters and found her companion so unresponsive that she desisted. It was evident that Esther Maitland wanted to be left to her own thoughts. Huddled in the cloak, her eyes fixed on the road in front, she sat as silent and enigmatic as a sphinx.

CHAPTER XVIII

THE HOUSE IN GAYLE STREET

THE Janney party left the office soon after Molly and Esther. They had decided to stay at the St. Boniface hotel where rooms had already been engaged, and, with Suzanne swathed in veils and clinging to her mother's arm, they were escorted to the elevator and cheered on their way by the two Whitneys. When the car slid out of sight the father and the son went back into the old man's room.

It was now late afternoon, the sun, sinking in a fiery glow, glazed the waters of the bay, seen from these high windows like a golden floor. The day, which had opened fresh and cool, had grown unbearably hot; even here, far above the street's stifling level, the air was breathless. The men, starting the electric fans, sat down to talk things over and wait. For the machinery of " the move " spoken of by Wilbur Whitney already had been set in motion.

Immediately after Esther's telephone message O'Mal-ley had been called up and, with an assistant, dis-

The House in Gayle Street

patched to watch the Gayle Street house. As Whitney had told his clients, the news of the child's disappearance had hardly surprised him. Chapman's anger and threats portended some violent action of reprisal, and, even as the lawyer had questioned what form it might take, came the answer. Chapman had stolen his own child and had a hiding place prepared and waiting for her reception. It was undoubtedly only a temporary refuge, he would hardly keep her in such sordid surroundings. The Whitneys saw it as a night's bivouac before a longer flight. And that flight would never take place; every exit was under surveillance, there was no possibility of escape. The two men, smoking tranquilly under the breath of the electric fans, were quietly confident. They would bring Chapman's vengeance to an abrupt end and avert an ignominious family scandal. Meantime they awaited O'Malley — who was to return to the office for George — and as they waited discussed the kidnapping, knowledge supplemented by deductions.

When Chapman had decided on it he had instructed Esther, telling her to inform him when the opportunity offered. This she could do by letter, or, if time pressed, by telephone from a booth in the village. The trip to New York had been planned several days in advance and he had been advised of it, its details probably telephoned in the day before. He — or some one in his

Miss Maitland Private Secretary

pay — had driven the taxi. It had been stationed in the rank near the house, where in the dead season there were few vehicles and from whence the extra one needed by Suzanne would naturally be taken. That Esther, with a long list of commissions to execute, should leave the child in the cab was an entirely natural proceeding. Her explanation of her subsequent actions was also disarmingly plausible, and the minutes thus expended gave the time necessary for the driver to make his get-away. Before she had acquainted Suzanne with the news, the child was hidden in the room at 76 Gayle Street.

Whether the room was taken for this purpose was a question. If it was then the idea had been in Chapman's mind for weeks — it was the " coming back " he had hinted at when he left Grasslands. If, however, it had been hired as a place of rendezvous with his confederate, it had assisted them in the carrying out of their plot — might indeed have suggested it. For as a lair in which to lie low it offered every advantage — secluded, inconspicuous, the rest of the floor untenanted. They could keep the child there without rousing a suspicion, for if Chapman was with her — and they took for granted that he was — she would be contented and make no outcry. She loved him and was happy in his society.

" Poor devil! " growled the old man. " You can't 195

help being sorry for him, even if he did do it to hit back. It's his child and he's fond of her."

George gave a short laugh:

" I fancy it's more the hitting back than the fondness. Chapman's not shown up lately in a very sentimental light. It wouldn't surprise me if he'd ransom in the back of his mind. But we'll put an end to his ambitions or parental longings or whatever's inspiring him." He looked at his watch, then rose. " It's a quarter past seven and O'Malley's due at the half hour. It's understood we're to bring the child here first? "

His father gave an assenting grunt and hitched his chair into the current of air from the fan.

George turned on the lights, their tempered radiance flooding the room, the windows starting out as black squares sewn with stars.

" I don't quite see what I'm going to say to him," he muttered, a sidelong eye on his father.

" Say nothing," came the answer. " Bring the child back here — that's your job. Leave him to me. Mrs. Janney and I'll have it out with him when the time comes."

On the tick of half-past seven O'Malley appeared. Trickles of perspiration ran down his red face, and his collar was melted to a sodden band.

" Gee," he panted as he ran a handkerchief round 196

The House in Gayle Street

his neck, " it's like a Turkish bath down there in the street."

" Well," said George, impatient of all but the main issue, " is it all right? "

" Yep — I've left two men in charge — every exit's covered. And there's only one they could use — no way out back except over the fences and through other houses."

" He could hardly tackle that with a child." " He couldn't tackle it alone and make it — not the way I've got things fixed. And I've worked out our line of action; Stebbins relieved me at half-past six and I went and had a seance with the janitor. Said I was coming round later with a man who was looking for a room — the room I'd been inquiring about. That'll let us in quiet; right up to the top floor and no questions asked."

" The only hitch possible can come from Chapman — he may be ugly and show his teeth." The old man answered:

" I guess he'll be tractable. If he's inclined to argue bring him along with you. It's after eight. I don't want to sit here half the night. Get busy and go."

O'Malley had a taxi waiting and they slid off up the deserted regions of Broadway. After a few blocks they swerved to the left, plunging into a congeries of mean streets where a network of fire-escapes encaged

the house fronts. The lights from small shops illumined the sidewalks, thick with sauntering people. The taxi moved slowly, children darting from its approach, swept round a corner and ran on through less animated lanes of travel, upper windows bright, disheveled figures leaning on the sills, vague groupings on front steps. At intervals, like the threatening voice of some advancing monster, came the roar of the elevated trains, sweeping across a vista with a rocking rush of light. O'Mal-ley drew himself to the edge of the sea and peered out ahead.

" We're not far off now," he muttered. " We'll stop at the corner of the block — there's a book-binding place there that's dark and quiet. If we go to the door they might catch on, get panicky, and make a row."

At one end of the street's length the lamp-spotted darkness of Washington Square showed like a spangled curtain. The cab turned from it and crossed a wide avenue over which the skeleton structure of the elevated straddled like a vast centipede. Beyond stretched a darkling perspective touched at recurring intervals with the white spheres of lamps. It was a propitious time, the evening overflow dispersed, the loneliness of the deep night hours, when a footfall echoes loud and a solitary figure looms mysterious, not yet come.

The cab drew up at the curb by the shuttered face of 198

the book bindery and the man alighted. With a low command to the driver, O'Malley, George beside him, walked up the block. From a shadowy doorway a figure detached itself, slunk by them with a whispered hail and vanished. Toward the street's far end they stopped at a door level with the sidewalk, and O'Malley, bending to scrutinize a line of push buttons, pressed one.

" Is this the place? " George whispered, in startled revulsion.

" This is the place. And a good one for Price's purpose as you'll see when you get in."

The young man noted the battered doorway, slightly out of plumb, then stepped back and glanced at the facade. Many of the windows, uncurtained and open, were lit up. Those of the top floor — dormers projecting from a mansard roof — were dark. He was about to call O'Malley's attention to this, when the sounds of footsteps within the house checked him.

There was a rattling of locks and bolts and the door swung open disclosing a man, grimy, old and bent, a lamp in his hand. He squinted uncertainly at them, then growled irritably as he recognized O'Malley:

" Oh, it's you. I thought you wasn't comin' ? If you'd been any later you wouldn't 'a got me up."

O'Malley explained that the gentleman was detained — couldn't get away any earlier, very sorry,

Miss Maitland Private Secretary

but they'd be quick and make no noise — just wanted to see the rooms and get out.

In single file, the janitor leading, they mounted the stairs. To the aristocratic senses of George the place seemed abominable. The staircase, narrow and without balustrade, ran up steeply between walls once painted green, now blotched and smeared. At the end of the first flight there was a small landing, a gas bracket holding aloft a tiny point of flame. It was as hot as an oven, the stifling atmosphere impregnated with mingled odors of cooking, stale cigar smoke, and the mustiness of close, unaired spaces.

On the second landing one of the doors was open, affording a glimpse of a squalid interior, and a man in his shirt sleeves bent over a table writing. He did not look up as they creaked by. From somewhere near, muffled by walls, came the thin, frail tinkling of guitar strings. As they ascended the temperature grew higher, the air held in the low attic story under the roof, baked to a sweltering heat. The janitor muttered an excuse — the top floor being vacant the windows were kept shut — it would be cool enough when they were opened.

He had gained the last landing, which broadened into a small square of hall cut by three doors. As he turned to one on the left, O'Malley slipped by him and drew away toward that on the right. There was a moment of silence, broken by the clinking of the man's keys.

He had trouble in finding the right one and set his lamp down on a chair, his head bent over the bunch. George was aware of O'Malley's figure casting a huge wavering shadow up the wall, edging closer to the right hand door.

The key was found and inserted in the lock and the janitor entered the room, his lamp diffusing a yellow aura in the midst of which he moved, a black, retreating shape. With his withdrawal the light in the hall, furnished by a bead of gas, faded to a flickering obscurity. O'Malley's shadow disappeared, and George could see him as a formless oblong, pressed against the panel. There was a moment of intense stillness, the guitar tinkling faint as if coming through illimitable distances. The detective's voice rose in a whisper, vital and intimate, against the music's spectral thinness:

" Queer. There's not a sound."

His hand stole to the handle, clasped it, turned it. Noiselessly the door opened upon darkness into which he slipped equally noiseless.

That slow opening was so surprising, so dream-like in its quality of the totally unexpected, that George stood rooted. He stared at the square of the door, waiting for voices, clamor, the anticipated in some form. Then he saw the darkness pierced by the white ray of an electric torch and heard a sound — a rumbled oath

from O'Malley. It brought him to the threshold. In the middle of the room, his torch sending its shaft over walls and floor, stood the detective alone, his face, the light shining upward on the chin and the tip of his nose, grotesque in its enraged dismay.

" Not here — d n them! " and his voice trailed

off into furious curses.

"Gone?" The surprise had made George forgetful.

" Gone — no! " The man almost shouted in his anger. " How could they go ? — Didn't I say every outlet was blocked. They ain't been here. They ain't had her here. Get a match, light the gas — I got to see the place anyway."

The torch's ray had touched a gas fixture on the wall and hung steady there. As the men fumbled for matches, the janitor came clumping across the hall, calling in querulous protest:

" Say — how'd you get in there ? That ain't the place — it's rented."

He stopped in the doorway, scowling at them under the glow of his upheld lamp. A match sputtered over the gas and a flame burst up with a whistling rush. In the combined illumination the room was revealed as bleak and hideous, the walls with blistered paper peeling off in shreds, the carpet worn in paths and patches, an iron bed, a bureau, by the one window, a table.

His face was ludicrous in its enraged enmity

The House in Gayle Street

The janitor continuing his expostulations, O'Malley turned on him and flashed his badge with a fierce :

" Shut up there. Keep still and get out. We've got a right here and if you make any trouble you'll hear from us."

The man shrank, scared.

" Police!" he faltered, then looking from one to the other. " But what for ? There's no one here, there ain't ever been any one — it's took but it's been empty ever since."

O'Malley who had sent aai exploring glance about him, made a dive for a newspaper lying crumpled on the floor by the bed. One look at it, and he was at the man's side, shaking it in his face:

" What do you say to this ? Yesterday's — how'd it get here? Blew in through the window maybe."

The janitor scanned the top of the page, then raised his eyes to the watching faces. His fright had given place to bewilderment and he began a stammering explanation^— if any one had been there he'd never known it, never seen no one come in or go out, never heard a sound from the inside.

" Did you see any one — any one that isn't a regular resident — come into the house yesterday or to-day? " It was George's question.

He didn't know as he'd seen anybody — not to notice. The tenants had friends, they was in and out

all day and part of the night. And anyway he wasn't around much after he'd swept the halls and taken down the pails. Yesterday and to-day he guessed he'd stayed in the basement most of the time. If anybody had been in the room — and it looked like they had — it was unbeknownst to him. The lady had the key; she could have come in without him seeing; it wasn't his business to keep tab on the tenants. He showed a tendency to diverge to the subject of his duties and George cut him off with a greenback pushed into his grimy claw and an order to keep their visit secret.

Meantime O'Malley had started on an examination of the room. There was more than the paper to prove the presence of a recent occupant. The bed showed the imprint of a body; pillow and counterpane were indented by the pressure of a recumbent form. On its foot lay a book, an unworn copy, as if newly bought, of " The Forest Lovers." The table held an ink bottle, the ink still moist round its uncorked mouth, some paper and envelopes and a pen. There was a scattering of pins on the bureau, two gilt hairpins and a black net veil, crumpled into a bunch. Pushed back toward the mirror was the cover of the soap dish containing ashes and the butts of four cigarettes.

O'Malley studied the bureau closely, ran the light of his torch back and forth across it, shook out the veil, sniffed it, and put it and the two hairpins care-

fully into his wallet. Then with the book and the paper in his hand he straightened up, turned to George, and said:

" That about cleans it up. There's nothing for it now but to go back."

The janitor, anxiously watchful, followed on their heels as they went down the stairs. Their clattering descent was followed by the strains of the guitar, thinly debonair and mocking as if exulting over their discomfiture. In the street the same shape emerged from the shadows and slouched toward them. A grunted phrase from O'Malley sent it drifting away, spiritless and without response, like a lonely ghost come in timid expectation and repelled by a rebuff.

O'Malley dropped into a corner of the taxi and as it glided off, said:

" That's the last of 76 Gayle Street as far as they're concerned."

" Why do you say that? "

In the darkness the detective permitted himself a sidelong glance of scorn.

" You don't leave the door unlocked in that sort of place unless you're done with it. They've got all they wanted out of it and quit."

"Abandoned it?"

" That's right — made a neat, quiet getaway. They didn't say they were going, didn't give up the key —

it was on the inside of the door. Just slid out and vanished."

" Some one was there yesterday."

" Um," O'Malley's voice showed a pondering concentration of thought. " Some one was lying on the bed reading; waiting or passing time."

" They couldn't have been there to-day — before your men were on the job? "

O'Malley drew himself to the edge of the seat, his chest inflated with a sudden breath:

" Why couldn't they? Why couldn't that have been the rendezvous? Why couldn't she have lost the child down here on Gayle. Street instead of opposite Justin's? Price was there beforehand: up she comes, tips him off that the taxi's in the street, sees him leave and goes herself, across to Fifth Avenue where she picks up a cab. It's safer than the other way — no cops round, janitor in the basement, if she's seen nothing to be remarked — a lady known to have a room on the top floor." He brought his fist down on his knee. " That's what they did and it explains what's been puzzling me."

"What?"

" There was no dust on the top of the bureau; it had been wiped off to-day. There was no dust on that veil; it hadn't been there since yesterday. A woman fixed herself at that glass not so long ago. Price had

a date with her to deliver the child and he was lying on the bed reading while he waited. When he heard her he threw down the book, got the good word and lit out. After he'd gone she took off her veil — what for? To get her face up to show to Mrs. Price — whiten it, make it look right for the news she was bringing. When she left she was made up for the part she was to play. And I take my hat off to her, for she played it like a star."

CHAPTER XIX

MOLLY'S STORY

IT was nearly seven when we got back to Grasslands. We alighted as silent as we started, and I was following Miss Maitland into the hall, Ferguson behind me, when she turned in the doorway and spoke. She had orders that the servants must know nothing; she was to tell them that the family would stay in town for a few days, and for me to be careful what I said before them. Then, before I could answer, she glanced at Ferguson and said good-by, her eyes just touching him for a moment and passing, cold and weary, back to me. She'd wish me good-night, she was going to her room and not coming down again — no, thanks, she'd take no dinner, she was very tired. She didn't need to say that. If I ever saw a person dead beat and at the end of her string she was it.

Ferguson stood looking after her. I think for the moment he forgot me, or maybe he wasn't conscious of what his face showed. Some way or other I didn't like to look at him; it was as if I was spying on something

I had no right to see. So I turned away and dropped into one of the balcony chairs, sunk down against the back and feeling limp as a rag.

Presently came his step and he was in front of me, his head bent down with the hair hanging loose on his forehead, and his eyes like they were hooks that would pull the words out of me:

" What happened up there at the Whitneys? "

" Mr. Ferguson," I answered solemn, *' I've told you more than I ought already. Is it the right thing for me to go on doing wrong? "

" Yes," he says, sharp and decided, " it's exactly the right thing. Keep on doing it and we'll get somewhere."

I set my lips tight and looked past him at the lawn. He waited a minute then said:

" I thought you agreed to trust me."

" There's a good deal more to it now than there was then."

" All the more reason for telling me. Of course I can get all I want from Mrs. Janney or either of the Whitneys; they don't let ladylike scruples stand in the way. But that means a trip to town and I'm not ready to take it."

It was surprising how that young man could make you feel like a worm who had a conscience in place of common sense.

Miss Maitland Private Secretary

" Have I got your word, sworn to on the Bible, if we had one here, not to give her a hint of it? "

"Good Lord!" he groaned. "Don't talk like the ingenue in a melodrama. Let me see why the Whit-neys think so much of you. You must have some intelligence — give me a sample of it."

That settled it.

" Take a seat," I said. " You make me nervous staring at me like the lion in the menagerie at the fat child."

He sat down and I told him — the whole business, what she had said, what they had thought — everything. When I'd finished he rose up and, with his hands burrowed deep in his pockets, began pacing up and down the balcony. I didn't give a peep, watching him cautious from under my eyelids.

After a bit he said in a low voice:

" Preposterous — crazy! She had no more to do with it than you have."

" They think different."

" I've gathered that. And Price had nothing to do with it either."

It was all very well for him to stand by her, but to sweep Price off the map! I couldn't sit still and let him rave on.

"Price hadn't? Take another guess. Price is the mainspring of it."

Molly's Story

" I'll leave guessing to you — it's your business, and you appear to do it very well."

" Say, drop me altogether. I'm only a paid servant. But you'll have to admit that Mr. Whitney and his son count pretty big in their line."

" Very big, Miss Rogers. But they've made a mistake this time — or possibly been misled. The Jan-neys have never been fair to Price. They're prejudiced and they've branded the prejudice on. He isn't an angel, neither is he a rascal. He didn't take his child, he never thought of it, he couldn't do it."

"Then who did?"

" That's what I want to find out."

" Jerusalem!" I said, sitting up, feeling like the peaceful scene around me was suddenly dark and strange. " You don't think she's really been kidnaped? "

" I can't think anything else." He stopped in front of me, looking at me hard and stern. " I'd like to find another solution but I'm unable to."

" But, gee-whizz! " I stared at him, all worried and mixed. " You can't get away from the facts. They're all there — there's hardly a break."

" I don't admit that. This man and woman have got characters and records that haven't been considered — but even if you had a hole-proof case against them I wouldn't believe it."

Miss Maitland Private Secretary

"Oh, pshaw!" I said, simmering down, "you just believe what you want to. I've seen people like that before."

" I daresay you have, I'm not a unique specimen in the human family. But I'll tell you what I am just at this juncture — the only one among you that's right." He drew back and gave a vengeful wag of his head at me. " You've all gone off at half-cock — doing your best to ruin a man who's harmless and a girl who's — who's —" he stopped, and wheeled away from me. " Teh — it makes me sick! Hate and anger and jealousy — that's what's at the bottom of it. I can't talk about it any longer — it's too beastly. Goodnight!"

He turned on his heel, ran down the steps and over the grass, clearing the terrace wall with a leap. I looked after him, fading into the early night, disturbed and with a sort of cold heaviness in my heart. He was no fool — suppose what he thought was true? Suppose that dear child whom I'd grown to love — but, rubbish ! I wouldn't think of it. It was easy to account for the way he felt. Every little movement has a meaning of its own — and the meaning in all his little movements was love. He had it bad, poor chap, out on him like the measles, and while you have to be gentle with the sick you don't pay much attention to what they say.

Molly's Story

That was a dreary evening. There being no one but me around they served my dinner in the dining room, and it added to the strain. Some of the food I didn't know whether to eat with a fork or a spoon, so I had to pass up a lot which was hard seeing I was hungry. But when you're born in an east side tenement you feel touchy that way — I wasn't going to be criticized by two corn-fed menials. I'm glad I'm not rich; it's grand all right, but it isn't comfortable.

The next day — Saturday — it rained and I sat round in the hall and my room where I could hear the 'phone and keep an eye on Miss Maitland. All she did was to go for a walk, and in the afternoon stay in her study. We saw each other at meals, our conversation specially edited for Dixon and Isaac.

Sunday was fine weather again and Ferguson came round at twelve. Miss Maitland had gone for another walk and he and I had the hall to ourselves. He'd been in town the day before, seen George Whitney and told him what he thought. When I asked how Mr. George took it, he gave a sarcastic smile and said, " He listened very politely but didn't seem much impressed." He also told me they'd hoped to find the child Friday night in the room at 76 Gayle Street and had been disappointed.

" Of course she wasn't there," and he ended with " it was only wasting valuable time, but there's a proverb

Miss Maitland Private Secretary

about none being so blind as those who won't see."

After that he dropped the subject — I think he wanted to get away from it — and pow-wowing together we worked around to the robbery, which had been sidetracked by the bigger matter. He said it had been in his mind to tell me a curious circumstance that he'd come on the night the jewels were taken and that he thought might be helpful to me. It was about a cigar band that Miss Maitland had found in the woods that evening when he and she had walked home together. Before he was half through I was listening attentive as a cat at a mouse hole, for it was a queer story and had possibilities. After I put some questions and had it all clear, we mulled it over — the way I love to do.

" A man dropped it," I said slowly, my thoughts chasing ahead of my words, " who went through the woods after the storm."

" Exactly — between eight-thirty and ten-thirty. And do you grasp the fact that those were the hours the house was vacated — the logical time to rob it?"

" Yes, I've thought of that often — wondered why they waited."

" And do you grasp another fact — that Hannah a little before nine heard the dogs barking and then quieting down as if they scented some one they knew? "

" It couldn't have been Price for he was on the way to town then."

"Oh, Price—" he gave an impatient jerk of his head —" of course it wasn't Price, but it was some one the dogs knew. That would have been just about the time a man, watching the house and seeing the ground floor dark, would have come across the lawn to make his entrance."

I pondered for a spell then said:

" Did you ever tell this to Mrs. Janney or any of them?"

" No, I didn't think of it myself until a little while ago — the night I dined here and saw it was one of Mr. Janney's cigars. And then what was the use — the light by the safe had fixed the time."

" Yes — if it wasn't for that light you'd have got a real lead. Too bad, for it's a bully starting point, and it would have let out those other two."

He stiffened up, suddenly haughty looking.

" There's no necessity of letting out people who never were in. But if that light was eliminated you could work on the theory that a professional thief — an expert safe opener — had done the business."

" How would the dogs know him? " I asked.

He leaned toward me, looking with a quiet sort of meaning into my face:

" Suppose you put that mind of yours, that Wilbur 215

Whitney values so highly and I'm beginning to see indications of, on that question."

"What's the sense of wasting it? My mind's my capital and I don't draw on it unless there's a need. You get rid of that light at one-thirty and I'll expend some of it."

I laughed, but he didn't, looking on the ground frowning and thoughtful. Then a step on the balcony made us both turn. It was Miss Maitland, back from her walk, looking much better, a smile at the sight of him, and a little color in her face. She joined us and, Dixon announcing lunch, Ferguson invited himself to stay. It was the first human meal I'd eaten since the doors of the dining room had opened to me.

After lunch I left them on the balcony and went upstairs to my room. I tried to read but the air, blowing in warm and sweet and the scent of the garden coming up, made the book seem dull, and I went to the window and leaned out.

A while passed that way and then I saw Ferguson going home, a long figure in white flannels striding across the lawn to the wood path. Then out from the kitchen come the servants, all togged up, six girls and Isaac, and away they go on their bikes to the beach. From what I've seen of the homes of the rich I'd rather be in the kitchen than the parlor — the help have it all over the quality for plain enjoyment. They went

off bawling gayly, and presently Dixon appears, looking like a parson on his day off, all brisk and cheerful. Last of all comes Hannah, her hair as slick as a seal's, a dinky little hat set on top of it, and a parasol held over it all. She waddled off, large and slow, in another direction, toward the woods — for a cup of tea and a neighborly gossip in Ferguson's kitchen, I guess. How I wished I was along with them!

There I was left, lolling back and forth on the sill, kicking with my toes on the floor, and wondering what my poor, deserted boy was doing in town. Then sudden, piercing the stillness with a sort of tingling thrill, comes the ring of the hall telephone.

I gave a soft jump, snatched up my pad and pencil, and was at the table and had the receiver off before she'd got to the closet downstairs. It was so quiet, not a sound in the house, that I could hear every catch in her breath and every tone in her voice. And what I heard was worth listening to. A man spoke first:

"Hello, who's this?"

" Esther Maitland. Is it — is it ? "

" Yes — C. P. I've waited until now as I knew there wouldn't be anybody around. It's all right."

" Truly. You're not saying it to keep me quiet? "

" Not a bit. There's no need for any worry. Everything's gone without a hitch."

Miss Maitland Private Secretary

" And you think it's safe — to — to — take the next step? "

" Perfectly. We're going to get her out of town on Tuesday night."

" Oh! " I could hear the relief in her voice. *' You don't know what this means to me? "

He gave a little, dry laugh:

" Me too — I'll admit it's been something of a strain. That's all I wanted to say. Good-by."

I scratched it on the pad, and tiptoed back to my room, short of breath a bit myself. What would Ferguson say to this? I stood by the window, thinking how to send it in, and things went right for out she came from the balcony and walked across to a place on the lawn where there were some chairs under a group of maples. She sat down and began to read, and I stole back to the hall and took a call for the Whitney house. Being Sunday they might be out, but that went right too, for I got the Chief himself. I told him and asked for instructions and they came straight and quick:

" Bring her into town to-morrow morning. There's a train at nine-thirty you can take. Get a taxi at the depot and come right up to the office. You'll have to tell her in what capacity you're serving the family. That'll be easy — you were engaged for the robbery. Don't let her think you have any interest in the kidnaping, and on no account let her guess we suspect her.

Molly's Story

Say you've had a message from me, that some new facts have come in and I want to ask her a few questions — see if the information tallies with what she saw. Keep her quiet and calm. Got that straight? All right — so long."

CHAPTER XX

MOLLY'S STORY

THE next morning, in the hall, right after breakfast I told her what I had to tell — I mean who I was. It gave her a start — held her listening with her eyes hard on mine — then when I explained it was for inside work on the robbery she eased up, got cool and nodded her head at me, politely agreeing. She understood perfectly and would go wherever she was wanted; she was glad to do anything that would be of assistance; no one was more anxious than she to help the family in their distress, and so forth and so on.

On the way in she was quiet, but I don't think as peaceful as she acted. She asked me some questions about my work. I answered brisk and bright and she said it must be a very interesting profession. I've seen nervy people in my time but no woman that beat her for cool sand, and the way I'm built I can't help but respect courage no matter what the person's like who has it. Before we reached town I was full of admiration for that girl who, as far as I could judge, was a crook from the ground up.

When we reached the office I was called into an inner room where the Chief and Mr. George were waiting. I gave them my paper with the 'phone message on it, and answered the few questions they had to ask. I learned then that they'd got hold of more evidence against her. O'Malley had snooped round the Gayle Street locality and heard that on Friday morning about half-past eleven a taxi, containing a child resembling Bebita, had been seen opposite a book bindery on the corner of the block. I didn't hear any particulars but I saw by the Chief's manner, quiet and sort of absorbed, and by Mr. George, like a blue-ribbon pup straining at the leash, that they had Esther Maitland dead to rights and the end was in sight.

After that I was sent back into the hall where I'd left her and told to bring her into the old man's private office. We went up the passage, a murmur of voices growing louder as we advanced. She was ahead and, as the door opened, she stopped for a moment on the threshold, quick, like a horse that wants to shy. Over her shoulder I could see in, and I don't wonder she pulled up — any one would. There, beside the Chief and Mr. George, were the two old Janneys and Mrs. Price, sitting stiff as statues, each of them with their eyes on her, gimlet-sharp and gimlet-hard. They said some sort of " How d'ye do " business and made bows like Chinese mandarins, but their faces would have made a chorus girl get thoughtful. I guessed then they knew about the tapped message and had come to see Miss Maitland get the third degree. She scented the trouble ahead too — I don't see how she could have helped it; there was thunder in the air. But she said good-morning to them, cordial and easy, and walked over to the chair Mr. George pushed forward for her.

Sitting there in the midst of them, she looked at the Chief, politely inquiring, and I couldn't help but think she was a winner. Mrs. Price, all weazened up and washed out, was like a cosmetic advertisement beside her. She held herself very straight, her hands folded together in her lap, her head up cool and proud. She had on the white hat with the wreath of grapes and a wash-silk dress of white with lilac stripes that set easy over her fine shoulders, and, believe me, bad or good, she was a thoroughbred.

The Chief, turning himself round toward her with a hitch of his chair, began as bland and friendly as if they'd just met at a tea-fest.

" We're very sorry to bother you again, Miss Maitland. But certain facts have come up since you were here that make it necessary for me to ask you a few more questions."

She just inclined her head a little and murmured:

" It's no bother at all, Mr. Whitney. I'm only too anxious to help in any way I can."

Molly's Story

Honest-to-God I think the Chief got a jar; the words came as smooth and as cool as cream just off the ice. For a second he looked at his desk and moved a paper knife very careful, as if it was precious and he was afraid of breaking it.

" I'm glad to hear you say that, Miss Maitland. It's not only what one would expect you to feel, but it makes me sure that you will be willing to explain certain circumstances concerning yourself and your — er — activities — that have — well — er — rather puzzled us."

It was my business to watch her and even if it hadn't been I couldn't have helped doing it. I saw just two things — the light strike white across the breast of her blouse where a quick breath lifted it, and, for a second, her hands close tight till the knuckles shone. Then they relaxed and she said very softly:

" Certainly. I'll explain anything."

"Very good. I was sure you would." He leaned forward, one arm on the desk, his big shoulders hunched, his eyes sharp on her but still very kind. " We have discovered — of course you'll understand that our detectives have been busy in all directions — that nearly a month ago you took a room at 76 Gayle Street. Now that I should ask about this may seem an unwarranted impertinence, but I would like to know just why you took that room."

Miss Maitland Private Secretary

There was a slight pause. Mrs. Price, who was sitting next to me, an empty chair in front of her, rustled and in the moment of silence I could hear her breathing, short and catchy, like it was coming hard. Miss Maitland, who, as the Chief had spoken, had dropped her eyes to her hands, looked up at him:

" I have no objection to telling you. I took it for a school friend of mine — Aggie Brown, a girl I hadn't seen for years. A month ago she wrote me from St. Louis and told me she was coming to New York to study art and asked me to engage a room for her. She said she had very little money and it must be inexpensive. I had heard of that place from other girls — that it was respectable and cheap — so I engaged the room. It so happens that my friend is not yet in New York. She was delayed by illness in her family."

I sent a look around and caught them like pictures going quick in a movie — Mr. Janney glimpsing sideways, worried and frowning, at his wife, Mr. George, his arm on the back of his chair, pulling at his little blonde mustache and twisting his mouth around, and the Chief pawing absent-minded after the paper knife. Miss Maitland, with her chin up and her shoulders square, had her eye on him, attentive and steady, like a soldier waiting for orders.

Then out of the silence came Mrs. Janney's voice, rumbling like distant thunder:

** But you went to that room yourself? "

The Chief's hand made a quick wave at her for silence. Miss Maitland didn't seem to notice it; she turned to Mrs. Janney and answered:

" Yes, several times, Mrs. Janney. I'd had to pay the rent in advance and I had a key, so when I was in town and had time to spare I went there. It was quiet and convenient — I used to write letters and read."

" Would you mind telling me why Mr. Chapman Price went there too ? "

It was the Chief's voice this time, quite low and oh, so deep and mild. Miss Maitland's attitude didn't change, but again her hands clasped and stayed clasped. She gave a little, provocative smile, almost as if she was trying to flirt with him, and said:

" You seem to know a great deal about me and my affairs, Mr. Whitney."

He returned the smile, good-humored, as if he liked the way she'd come back at him.

" A little, Miss Maitland. You see we have had to, unpleasant but still necessary — you have no objection to answering? "

" Oh, not the least, only —" her glance swept over the solemn faces of the others —" I'm afraid Mrs. Janney may not approve of what I've done. I met Mr. Price there to tell him about Bebita; I was sorry for him, for the position he was in. He was fond of her

Miss Maitland Private Secretary

and he heard almost nothing about her. So I arranged to give him news of her, tell him how she was, and little funny things she had said. It wasn't the right thing to do but I — I — pitied him so."

A sound — I can't call it anything but a grunt — came from Mrs. Janney. Mr. George, still pulling at his mustache, shifted uneasily in his chair. Beside me I could hear that stifled breathing of Mrs. Price, and her hand, all covered with rings, stole forward and clasped like a bird's claw on the chair in front. I don't think Miss Maitland noticed any of this. Her eyes were on the Chief, fixed and sort of defiant. Her face had lost its calm look; there were pink spots on her cheek bones.

" A natural thing to do," said the Chief mildly, " though hardly discreet considering the situation. But we won't argue about that — we'll pass on to the business of the moment. Now you told us last time you were here that you left the taxi in front of Justin's. Inquiries there of the doorman have elicited the information that he remembers the cab and the child, and says it was still there when you came out and that you got into it and drove away."

" How can the doorman at a place where hundreds of carriages stop every day remember the people in each one?" All the softness was gone out of her voice and her face began to look different, as if it had

grown thinner. " It's absurd — he couldn't possibly be sure of every woman and child who stopped there. My word is against his, and it seems to me I'm much more likely to know what I did than he is — especially that day."

" Certainly, certainly." The Chief was all kindly understanding. " Under the circumstances every event of that morning should be impressed on your memory. But another fact has come up that seems to us curious. One of our detectives has heard from a clerk in a book bindery at the corner near 76 Gayle Street, that on Friday last, at about half-past eleven, he saw a taxi standing at the curb there. He noticed a child in it talking to the driver and his description of this child, her appearance and clothes, is a very accurate description of Bebita."

He looked at her over his glasses, with a sort of ominous, waiting attention. I'd have wilted under it, but she didn't, only what had been a restrained quietness gave place to a sort of steely tension. You could see that her body all over was as rigid as the hands clenched together, the fingers knotted round each other. It was will and a fighting spirit that kept her up. I began to feel my own muscles drawing tight, wondering if she'd get through and praying that she would — I don't know why.

" It's quite possible that this man — this clerk — 227

may have seen such a taxi with such a child in it. There must be a great many little girls in New York whose description would fit Bebita. I dare say if your detective had gone about the city he would have heard of any number of cabs and children that would have fitted just as well. I can't imagine why you're asking me these questions or why you don't seem to believe what I say. But even if you don't believe it, that won't prevent me from sticking to it."

" A commendable spirit, Miss Maitland, when one is sure of one's facts," said the Chief, and suddenly pushing back his chair he rose. " Now I've just one more matter to call to your attention, a little memorandum here, which, if you'll be good enough to explain, we'll end this rather trying interview."

He went over to her, fumbling in his vest pocket, and then drew out my folded paper and put it into her hand:

" It's the record of a telephone message received by you yesterday at Grasslands, and tapped by our detective, Miss Rogers."

He stepped back and stood leaning against the desk watching her. We all did; there wasn't an eye in that room which wasn't glued on that unfortunate girl as she opened the paper and read the words.

It was a knock-out blow. I knew it would be — I didn't see how it couldn't — and yet she'd put up such a

Molly's Story

fight that some way or other I thought she'd pull out. But that bowled her over like a nine pin.

She turned as white as the paper and her hands holding it shook so you could hear it rustle. Then she looked up and her eyes were awful — hunted, desperate. Yet she made a last frantic effort, with her face like a deatli mask and all the breath so gone out of her she had only a hoarse thread of voice:

"I — I — don't know what this is — oh, yes, yes, I mean I do. But it — it refers to something else — it's — it's — that friend of mine — Aggie Brown from St. Louis — she's come and Mr. Price —"

She couldn't go on ; her lips couldn't get out any words. You could see the brain behind them had had such a shock it wouldn't work.

" Miss Maitland," said the Chief, solemn as an executioner, " we've got you where you can't keep this up. There's no use in these evasions and denials. Where is Bebita?"

" I don't know — I don't know anything about her. I swear to Heaven I don't."

She raised her voice with the last words and looked at them, round at those stony faces, wild like an animal cornered.

"What's the matter with you? Why do you think I'd be a party to such a thing? Why don't you believe me — why can't you believe me? And you don't

— not one of you. You think I'm guilty of this infamous thing. All right, think it. Do what you like with me — arrest me, put me in jail, I don't care."

She put her hands over her face and collapsed down in her chair, like a spring that had held her up had broken. That breathing beside me had grown so loud it sounded as if it came from some one running the last lap of a race. Now it suddenly broke into a sound

— more like a growl than anything else — and Mrs. Price got up, shuffling and shaking, her hands holding on to the chair in front.

" She ought to be put in jail," she gasped out. " She's bad right through — everything she's said is a lie. And she's a thief too."

There was a movement of consternation among them all — getting up, pushing back chairs, several voices speaking together:

" Keep quiet."

" Mrs. Price, I beg of you —"

" Suzanne, sit down."

But she went on, looking like a withered old witch, with her bird-like hands clutched on the chair back:

" I won't sit down, I won't keep quiet. I've sat here listening to all this and I've had enough. I'm crazy; my baby's gone; she's taken it, she's taken everything —" She turned to her mother. " She took your jewels — I know it."

Mr. Janney burst in like a bombshell. I never thought he could break loose that way, with his voice shrill and a shaking finger pointing into his stepdaughter's face.

" Stop this. I can't stand for it — I know something about that — I saw —"

But she wouldn't stop, no one could make her:

" I saw too, and I'm going to tell you. I don't care what you say, I don't care what you think of me — my heart's broken and I don't care for anything but to have my baby back." She addressed her mother again. " / went to take your jewels that night. Yes, I did; I went to steal them — not all of them — just that long diamond chain you never wear. You know why; you knew I hadn't any money and that I had to have it. I was going to sell it and put what I got in stocks and if I was lucky buy it back so you'd never know. It was / who took Bebita's torch — that's why it was lost — and I went down to the safe. I'd found the combination in a drawer in the library and learnt it. And when I opened it everything was gone. Some one had been there before me, the cases were all together in their box but they were empty." She clawed at the embroidered purse hanging on her arm and began to jerk at the cord, pulling it open. " But I found something, something the thief had dropped, lying on the floor just inside the door." She drew out

a twist of tissue paper, and unrolling it held it toward the Chief; "I found that."

He took it, scrutinizing it, puzzled, through his glasses. Every one of us except Miss Maitland, all standing now, craned forward to see. It was a pointed pink thing about as big as the end of my little finger. The Chief touched it and said:

" It looks like a small rose."

" Yes, a chiffon rosebud," Mrs. Price cried, " and she," pointing to Miss Maitland, " wore a dress that night trimmed with them."

We all turned, as if we were a piece of mechanism worked by the same spring, and stared at Miss Maitland. She sat in the chair, not moving, looking straight before her, weary and indifferent. The Chief held out toward her the piece of paper with the rose on the middle of it.

" Have you a dress trimmed with these? "

She moved her eyes so they rested on the rose, ran her tongue along her lips and said:

" Yes."

" Did you wear it on the night of the robbery ? "

" Yes."

" Did you hear what Mrs. Price has just said? "

" Yes."

" What explanation do you make ? "

** None — except that I don't know how it got there." 232

Molly's Story

" You deny that you were there yourself that night?"

" Yes — I was never near the safe that night; I haven't the slightest idea how the rose came to be in it; I never took the jewels; I have had nothing to do with Bebita's disappearance; I haven't done any of the things you think I've done. But what's the good of my saying so — what's the good of answering at all? " She dropped her face into her hands, her elbows propped on her knees. The attitude, the tone of her voice, everything about her, suggested an " Oh-what's-the-use! " feeling. From behind her hands the words came dull and listless. " Do anything you like with me; it doesn't make any difference. You think you've got me cornered; that being the case, I'll do whatever you say."

Mrs. Janney made a step toward her:

" Miss Maitland, I'll agree to let the whole matter drop — hush it up and let you go without a word — if you'll tell us where Bebita is."

Without moving her hands the girl answered:

" I can't tell, for I don't know."

Mrs. Price sank into her chair with a loud, sobbing wail. Some one took her away — Mr. George, I think. Then Mr. Janney had his say:

" If you're doing this to protect Price —"

She cut him off with a laugh, at least it was meant 233

Miss Maitland Private Secretary

to be a laugh, but it was a horrible, harsh sound. As she gave it she lifted her head and cast a look at him, bitter and defiant:

*' Protect him! I've no more desire to protect Mr. Price than I have to protect myself."

The Chief's voice fell deep as the church bell at a funeral:

" If you maintain this attitude, Miss Maitland, there's nothing for us to do but let the law take its course. Theft and kidnaping! Those are pretty serious charges."

She nodded:

" I suppose they are. Let the law do whatever it wants; I'm certainly not standing in its way. But as for bribing and frightening me into admitting what isn't true, you can't do it. All your money," she looked at Mrs. Janney and then at the Chief, " and all your threats won't influence me or make me change one word of what I've said."

No one spoke for a minute. She sat silent, her chin on her hands, her eyes staring past them out of the window. I had a feeling that in spite of the position she was in and what they had on her, in a sort of way she had them beaten. Their faces were glum and baffled, even the Chief had an abstracted expression like he was thinking what he ought to do with her. When he spoke it was to the Janneys:

" Since Miss Maitland persists in her present pose of ignorance and denial, the best thing for us is to get together and decide on our course of action." He glanced across at me. " We'll leave you here, Molly. Stay till we come back."

Away they went, a solemn procession, trailing across the room. When the door into the main office opened I could hear Mrs. Price crying, and I watched them, catching Mrs. Janney's words as she disappeared: " Oh, Suzanne, my poor, poor, girl! Don't give up — don't be discouraged — we'll find her! "

It gripped me, made a sort of prickling come in my nose and a twisty feeling in my under lip. I never could have believed that stern old Roman could have spoken so tender and loving to any one.

When I looked at Miss Maitland I forgot all about suffering mothers. She'd sunk down in the chair, her head resting against its back, her eyes closed. She was as white as a corpse, and I wheeled about looking round the room for some kind of first aid and muttering, " Gee, she's fainted! "

A whisper came out of her lips:

" Nothing — all right — in a minute."

There was a bottle of distilled water in a corner and I went to it, drew off a glass and brought it to her. She couldn't hold it and I took her round the shoulders and pulled her up, saying out of the inner

Miss Maitland Private Secretary

depths of me, that's always mushy about anything hurt and forlorn:

'* You, poor soul, here take this. I'm sorry for you, and I can't help being sorry that I had to give you away."

I held the glass to her lips and she drank a little. Then I let her fall back and stood watching her, and I felt mean. She raised her eyes and sent a look into mine that I'll never forget — it made me feel meaner than a yellow dog — for it was the look of a suffering soul.

" Thanks," was all she said.

CHAPTER XXI

SIGNED " CLANSMEN "

THE consultation in the office resulted in Esther Maitland being taken to O'Malley's flat in Stuyvesant Square, where his wife and sister agreed to be responsible for her. This course had been decided upon after some heated argument. Suzanne had clamored for her arrest, but the others were still determined to keep the affair out of the public eye, which, if Esther was brought before a magistrate, would have been impossible. The Janneys were more than ever convinced that Price was the prime mover, and the girl's attitude had been prompted by the combined motives of love and gain. George, who knew his father's every phase, noticed that the old man was reserved in his comments, and wondered if his conviction had been shaken by Miss Maitland's desperate denials. But if it was he said nothing, agreeing that with the girl hidden and unable to communicate with the outside world, they could concentrate their attention on Chapman and through him locate the child. Miss Maitland was docile to all their suggestions.

237

Miss Maitland Private Secretary

She would go wherever they wanted, place herself under the surveillance of the two women, and do whatever was asked of her. She went off in a taxi with O'Malley, and Molly was sent back to Grasslands. There was no need of her services in town and it was probable that Chapman, believing his confederate to be there, would call up the place.

The Janncy party returned to the hotel, a silent, gloomy trio. The old people were very gentle to Suzanne. On the drive up, Mrs. Janney held her in the hollow of her arm, pressed close, yearning over her in her shame and sorrow and feebleness. To the strong woman she was a child again, a soft, helpless thing. The mother blamed herself for having been hard on her.

After lunch old Sam suggested a drive — the air would do them good. They tried to persuade Suzanne to come, but the young woman, prone on the sofa, a salts bottle at hand, refused to stir. She wanted to be quiet; she wanted to rest. So, knowing the uselessness of argument, they kissed her and went.

Alone, she lay on her back staring at the wall in a trance-like concentration. Her expression did not suggest the state of crushed shame under which her parents thought she languished. In fact her past actions had no place in her mind; she had forgotten her confession in the office. An idea, formidable and

Signed " Clansmen

obsessing, had taken possession of her, settled on her like a shadow. It was possible that their conclusions were wrong.

She had had it from the start, off and on, coming at her in rushes of disintegrating doubt. She had said nothing about it, had tried to force it down, and, talking to them, had been reassured by their unquestioning certainty. Now the scene in the office had strengthened it — something about Esther Maitland, she didn't know what. She had assured herself then — she tried to do it now — that there could be no mistake, they had proofs, the girl hadn't been able to explain anything. But she could not argue it away; it persisted, stronger than thought, power or will, unescapable like the horror of a dream.

It came from an instinct that kept whispering deep down in the recesses of her being, " Chapman couldn't have done it." She knew him better than the others did, the vagaries of his ugly temper, the lines his weaknesses ran upon. She knew him through and through, to what lengths anger might urge him, what he could do when aroused and what he never could do. And trying to convince herself of his guilt, marshaling the facts against him, going over them point by point, she couldn't make herself believe that he had stolen Bebita.

And if he hadn't, then where was she?

This was the hideous thought, pressing in upon her 239

Miss Maitland Private Secretary

recognition, intrusive as Banquo's ghost and as terrible. She writhed under its torment, twisting and turning until her clothes were wound about her in a tangled coil, moaning as her imagination touched at and recoiled from grisly possibilities.

She was lying thus when the door-bell rang. Glad of any interruption she sat up, and, swinging her feet to the floor, called out a sharp " Come in." A bell-boy entered with a letter which he presented with the information that Mr. Janney had ordered all mail to be brought immediately to the rooms. The letter was for her, addressed in typewriting, and as the boy withdrew she rose, heavy-eyed and heavy-headed, and tore open the envelope. The first line brought a thin, choked cry out of her, and then she stood motionless, her glance devouring the words. Dated the day before, typewritten on a single sheet of commercial paper, it ran as follows:

"Mrs. Suzanne Price,
DEAR MADAM:

We have your little girl. She is safe with us and will continue to be if you act in good faith and accede to our demands. We frankly state that our object in taking her was ransom and we are now ready to enter upon negotiations with you. This, however, only upon certain conditions. All transactions between us must be conducted with absolute secrecy. If any member of your family is told, if the police are notified, be assured that we will know it, and that it will react upon your child. Let it be clearly understood — if you inform against us, if you make an attempt to trap or apprehend us, she will pay the

Signed " Clansmen "

price. We hold her as a hostage; her fate is in your hands. If, however, you know of a person in no wise involved or connected with you or your family, having no personal interest in the matter, and of whose discretion and reliability you are convinced, we are willing to deal through them. Copy the form below, fill in blank spaces with name and address and insert in Daily Record personals.

(Xante)

(Address)

S. O. S.

CLAXSMEX."

Suzanne's hand holding the paper dropped to her side and she looked about the room with eyes vacant and unseeing. All her outward forces were shocked into temporary suspension ; for a moment she had no realization of where or who she was. The letter was the only fact she recognized and sentences from it chased through her consciousness: " We hold her as a hostage, her fate is in your hands. She is safe with us if you accede to our demands." She saw them written on the walls, they boomed in her ears like notes of doom. It was confirmation of that instinct she had tried to smother; like the wand of a baleful genii it had transformed her nightmare fancies into sinister reality.

She felt a shriek rising to her lips and pressed her hand against them. Secrecy, silence, her stunned brain had grasped that and directed her restraining hand. Then the one deep feeling of her shallow nature called

Miss Maitland Private Secretary

her shattered faculties into order. Love lent her power, steadied her, gave her the will to act.

She sat down on the sofa and read the letter again, slowly, getting its full significance. For the first time in her life responsibility was cast upon her; she could throw the burden on no one else. By her own efforts, by her own courage and initiative, she must get Bebita back. She whispered it over, " I must do it. I must do it myself," then fell silent, her face stony in its tension of thought. Suddenly its rigidity broke; in an illuminating flash she saw the first step clear, and rising ran to the telephone. The person she called up was Larkin. He answered himself and she told him she wanted to see him on a matter of great importance and would come at once to his office.

Fifteen minutes later, her face hidden by a chiffon veil, her rumpled smartness covered with a silk motor coat, she was knocking at his door.

Mr. Larkin's office was cool and shady, the blinds half lowered to keep out the glare of the afternoon sun. In the midst of its airy neatness, surrounded by an imposing array of desks, card cabinets, typewriters and files, Mr. Larkin was waiting alone for his important client.

She dropped into the chair he set for her, and, pushing up her veil, revealed a countenance so bereft of the petulant prettiness he knew, that he started and stood gazing in open concern. The sight of his astonishment caused the tears to well into Suzanne's eyes, drowned and sunken by past floods, and her story to break without prelude from her lips.

Larkin's surprise at her appearance gave place to a tight-gripped interest when he grasped the main fact of her narrative. He let her run through it without interruption nodding now and then, a frowning sidelong glance on her face.

When she had finished he drew a deep breath and said:

" The moment I saw you, I knew something was wrong. But this —" he raised his hands and let" them drop on the desk —" Good Lord! I hadn't an idea it was anything so serious."

But she hadn't finished — the worst, the thing that had brought her — she had yet to tell. And she began about the letter received an hour ago. At that Larkin forgot his sympathies, was the detective again, hardly concealing his impatience as he watched her fumbling at the cords of her purse. Finally extracted and given to him he read it, once and then again, Suzanne eyeing him like a hungry dog.

" Last evening," he muttered after a scrutiny of the postmark, " Grand Central Station." Then he rose, went to the window and, jerking up the blind, held the paper against the light, sniffed at it, and felt its texture

Miss Maitland Private Secretary

between his thumb and finger. Suzanne saw him shake his head, her avid glance following him as he came back to the desk and studied the sheet through a magnifying glass.

" Nothing to be got that way," he said. " Type-paper — impossible to trace. No amateur business about this."

Suzanne's voice was husky:

" Do you mean it's professional people — a gang? "

" I can't say exactly. But from what you tell me — the way it was accomplished, the plan of action — I should be inclined to think it was the work of more than one person — possibly a group — who had ability and experience."

Suzanne, clutching at the corner of the desk with a trembling hand, cried in her misery:

" Oh, Mr. Larkin, you don't think they'll hurt her. They wouldn't dare to hurt her? "

The detective's glance was kindly but grave:

" Mrs. Price, I'll speak frankly. I think your child is in the hands of a pretty desperate person or persons. But I have no apprehension that they'll do her any harm. They don't want to do that — it's too dangerous. What they might do if their plans fail is a thing we'll not consider — it'll only weaken your nerve. And that's what you've got to keep hold of. You'll get her back all right, but you must be cool and brave."

Signed fr Clansmen "

" I'll be anything; I'll be like another person. I'll do anything. No one need be afraid I'll be weak or silly now"

" Good — that's the way to talk. Now let me know a little about the way the situation stands. It's odd I've seen nothing about this in the papers — heard nothing. Your family must be active in some direction. What are they doing? "

A sudden color burnt in her wasted cheeks.

" They suspect my husband. They think he did it — to — to — get square. We'd quarreled — separated — and he'd made threats."

" Ah, yes, yes, I see — kidnaped his own child, and they're keeping it quiet. I understand perfectly. But you didn't believe this ? "

She shook her head and bit on her underlip to control its trembling.

" No — I couldn't, though I tried to. I knew he wouldn't have done it — it's not — it's not — like him. And then while I was thinking the letter came, and I knew, no matter what they thought, no matter what the facts were, that that was true."

" Urn," Larkin, his mouth compressed, nodded in understanding. " You would know better than any one else. In these matters instinct is one of the most important factors." He was silent for a moment, then looked at her, a glance of piercing question. " Do I

understand that you are willing to enter into these negotiations? "

*' Willing! " she cried. " Why should I be here if I wasn't willing? "

" Yes, yes, exactly, but let us understand one another. What I mean is are you willing — realizing what they are — to deal with them on their own terms? In short, pay them what they ask and let them

go?"

" Of course." She almost cried it out in her effort to make him comprehend her position. " That's what I want to do ; that's why I haven't told any of my own people and won't. I'd have gone straight to my mother with this but I knew she wouldn't agree to it, she'd get the police, want to fight them and bring them to justice."

" Could you be relied on to maintain the secrecy necessary ? "

" I can be relied on for anything. Oh, Mr. Larkin, if you knew what I feel you wouldn't waste time asking these questions."

He answered very gently:

" Mrs. Price, I appreciate your feelings to the full, but this is a hazardous undertaking. You don't want to rush into it without realizing what it means. There is the question of money for example — the ransom. Your family is known for its wealth. You can be

Signed fe Clansmen

pretty certain that the parties you're dealing with will hold the child for a large sum."

Suzanne clasped her hands on her breast and the tears, brimming in her eyes, spilled over, falling in a trickle down her cheeks.

" Oh, what's money ! " she wailed. " I'd give all the money I have, I've ever had, I ever thought of having, to get my baby back."

Larkin was moved. He looked away from that pitiful, quivering face and his voice showed a slight huski-ness as he answered:

" Well, that's all right, Mrs. Price — and don't take it so hard, don't let your fears get the upper hand. There's no harm can come to her; it's to their interest to take care of her. If we do our part cleverly, follow their instructions and keep our heads, you'll have her back in no time." He stopped, arrested by a sudden thought. " I say * we,' but maybe I'm presupposing too much. Was it your intention to ask for my assistance ? "

She dashed her tears away and leaned forward in eager urgence:

" Of course — that's why I came. And you will give it — you will ? The letter says it has to be some one having no ties or interests with the family — some one I could trust. I couldn't think of any one at first, and then when I remembered you it was like an inspiration.

Oh, you must do it — I'll pay you anything if you will."

Larkin's face satisfied her; she dropped back with a moan of relief.

" I'll undertake it willingly — not only to give you any help I can, but because it will be a good thing for me. Don't be shocked at my plain speaking, but I want to be frank and straight with you. I'm not referring to pay — we can arrange about that later — it's work done for the Janney family, successful work. And with your cooperation, Mrs. Price, this is going to be successful. Now let's get to business." He picked up the letter and glanced over it. " Headed * Clansmen ' and signed ' S. O. S.' I'll copy it, insert my name and address, and have it in to-morrow's Daily Record. Then we'll see what happens."

He smiled at her, reassuring and kindly. There was no response in her tragic face.

" It may be days before they answer," she murmured.

But he was determined to uphold her fainting spirit.

" I think not. They want to end this thing as quickly as they can — get their loot and go. You've got to remember that their position is terribly dangerous and at the first sign from us they'll get busy."

She rose, took the letter and put it in her purse:

" I hope to Heaven you're right. It's so awful to wait."

£48

Signed " Clansmen

" I don't think you'll have to. They'll see our answer to-morrow morning and I'll expect a move from them by that evening or the next day. If they communicate with me, I'll let you know at once, and if you hear, do the same by me. It's going to be all right. Keep up your courage and remember — not a word or a sign to any one."

" Oh, I know," she said, drawing down her veil with limp hands, " you needn't be afraid I'll spoil it. You thought me a fool, perhaps, when I first consulted you, and I was, bothering about things that didn't matter— jewels! There isn't one of us that hasn't forgotten all about them now. Good-by. No, don't come out with me. I have a taxi waiting."

SUZANNE FINDS A FRIEND

ON Monday evening Ferguson heard from Molly of the scene in the Whitney office. He was incredulous and enraged, refusing to accept what she insisted were irrefutable proofs of Esther's guilt.

" What do I care about your 'phone messages and your suppositions! " he had almost shouted at her. " What do I care about what you think. You say she didn't answer the charges — she did, she denied them. That's enough for me."

There was no use arguing with him, he was beyond reason. She lapsed into silence, letting him rage on, seething in his wrath at the Janneys, the Whitneys, herself. When he tried to find out where Esther was, she was obdurate — that she couldn't tell him. All the satisfaction he got was that Miss Maitland was not under arrest, that she was " put away somewhere " and had agreed to the arrangement. He left, too angry for good-nights, with a last scattering of male-

250

Suzanne Finds a Friend

dictions, leaping down the steps and swinging off across the garden.

The next morning he telephoned in to the St. Boniface Hotel and heard that the Janney party were out. Then he tried the Whitney office, got George on the wire, and was told brusquely that Miss Maitland's whereabouts could not be divulged to any one. He spent the rest of the day in a state of morose disquiet, denying himself to visitors, short and surly with his servants. Willitts was solicitous, inquired after his health and was told to go to the devil. In the kitchen quarters they talked about his queer behavior; the butler was afraid he'd had " a touch of sun."

Wednesday wore through to the early afternoon and his inaction became unendurable. He decided to go into town, look up the Janneys and force them to tell him where Esther was. He laid upon his spirit a cautioning charge of self-control; he must keep his head and his temper, use strategy before coercion. He had no idea of what he intended doing when he did find her, but the idea of getting to her, seeing her, championing her, transformed his moody restlessness into a savage energy. His servants flew before his commands; in the garage the chauffeur muttered angrily as orders to hurry were shouted at him from the drive.

Tuesday had been a day of strain for the Janneys. According to the telephone message, that night Chap-

man was to move the child from the city. He had been under a close surveillance for the two preceding days, and every depot and ferry housed watching detectives. Hope ran high until after midnight when reports and 'phone messages came dropping in upon the group congregated in the library of the Whitney house. No child resembling Bebita had left the city at any of the guarded points. Chapman had been in his office all day, had dined at a hotel and afterward had gone to his rooms and remained there. The plan of moving her had either been abandoned or had been intrusted to unknown parties who had taken her by motor through the city's northern end.

On Wednesday morning a consultation had been held at the Whitney office. This had been stormy, developing the first disagreements in what had been a unity of opinion. Mr. Janney was for going to Chapman and demanding the child and was seconded by the elder Whitney. Mrs. Janney was in opposition. She had no fear for Bebita's welfare — Chapman could be trusted to care for her — and maintained that a direct appeal to him would be an admission of weakness and place them at his mercy. In her opinion he would threaten exposure — he was shameless — or make an offer of a financial settlement. George agreed with her; from the start he had thought Chapman was actuated less by a desire for vengeance than a hope of gain. Mrs. Jan-

ney, thus backed up, became adamant. She would have no dealings with him, would run him to earth, and when he was caught, crush and ruin him.

Suzanne had listened to it all very silent and taking neither side. Her hunted air was set down to mental strain and she was allowed to remain an unconsulted spectator, treated by everybody with subdued gentleness. Back in the hotel, Mrs. Janney had suggested a doctor, but her querulous pleadings to be let alone had conquered, and the old people had gone for their afternoon drive, leaving her in the curtained quietness of the sitting room.

The door was hardly shut on them when she drew out of her belt a letter. She had found it in her room on her return from the office and had read it there before lunch. It was a prompter answer than she had dared to hope for.

"Mrs. Suzanne Price, DEAK MADAM:

In answer to your ad. we would say that we are willing to deal through the agent you name. We take your word for it that he is to be trusted, that both you and he understand any attempt to betray us will be visited on your child.

Remember Charley Ross!

The sum necessary for her release will be thirty thousand dollars. On payment of this we will deliver her over at a time and place to be specified later. If you agree to our terms insert following ad. in the Daily Record. 'John — O. K. See you later. Mary.'

(Signed) CLAXSMEK."

Miss Maitland Private Secretary

On the second perusal of this ominous document Suzanne felt the strangling rush of dread, the breathless contraction of the heart, that had seized her when she first read it. Horrors had piled on horrors — as she had risen to each new step of her progress up this Via Dolorosa, another more fearful and unsurmountable had faced her. When she had spoken to Larkin of the money she had never thought of it, how much it might be, how she was to get it. Now, with a stunning impact, she was brought against the appalling fact that she had none of her own and did not dare ask her mother for any.

There was no use in lies; she had lied too much and too diversely to be believed. She would have to tell what it was for, and she knew the mood in which her mother would meet the demand. Money would be forthcoming — any amount — but Mrs. Janney, with her iron nerve and her implacable spirit, would never consent to a tame submission. Suzanne knew that her fortune and her energies would be spent in an effort to apprehend the criminals, and Suzanne had not the courage to take a chance. All she wanted was Bebita, back in her arms again, the fiends who had taken her could go free.

She sat down, pushing the damp hair from her forehead and trying to think. One fact stood out in the midst of her blind, confused suffering. She could not

Suzanne Finds a Friend

go to Larkin till she had the thirty thousand dollars. Every moment she sat there was a moment lost, a moment added to Bebita's term of imprisonment. She stared about the room, the gleam of her shifting eyes, the rise and fall of her breast, the only movements in her stone-still figure.

Suddenly, piercing her tense preoccupation with a buzzing note, came the sound of the telephone. It made her jump, then mechanically, hardly conscious of her action, she rose to answer it. A woman's voice, languidly nasal, came along the wire:

" Mr. Richard Ferguson is calling."

" Send him up," she gasped and fumbled back the receiver with a shaking hand. With the other she steadied herself against the wall; the room had swung for a moment, blurred before her vision. She closed her eyes and breathed out her relief in a moaning exhalation. It was like an answer to prayer, like the finger of God.

Of course Dick was the person — Dick who could always be trusted, who could always understand. He would give it and say nothing; she could make him. He was not like the others — he would sympathize, would agree with her, in trouble he was a rock to cling to. A broken series of answers to unput questions coursed through her head; she could go to Larkin now !— she needn't tell him how she'd got it, he thought

Miss Maitland Private Secretary

she was rich — after it was all over her mother would pay Dick back — in a few days she'd have Bebita, the kidnapers would have made their escape — and it would be all right, all right, all right!

Ferguson had come up, grim-visaged, steeled for battle, but when he saw her his fighting spirit died. There was nothing left of her but a blighted shadow, the cloud of golden hair crowning in gay mockery her drawn and haggard face. Before he could speak she made a clutch at his arm, drawing him into the room, babbling a broken greeting about wanting him, wanting his help. He put his hand on hers and felt it trembling; he would not have been surprised if she had dropped unconscious at his feet.

" Lord, Suzanne, you don't want to take it this way," he soothed, guiding her to the sofa. "

You must get hold of yourself; you've been brooding too much. Of course I'll help you — anything I can do — and we'll get her back, it'll be only a few days." He didn't know what to say, he was so sorry for her.

She was past parleys and preliminaries, past coquetry and artifice. The whole of her had resolved itself into one raw longing, and before they were seated on the sofa, she had broken into her story. He didn't at first believe her, thought grief had unsettled her brain, but when she thrust the two letters into his hand all doubts left him.

Suzanne Finds a Friend

He read them slowly, word by word, then turned upon her a face so charged and vitalized with a fierce interest that, had she been able to see beyond the circle of her own pain, she would have wondered. If he forgot to ask for Esther's hiding place it was because the larger matter of her vindication had swept all else from his mind. The proofs of her innocence were in his hands; he did not for a moment doubt their genuineness. It was what he had thought from the first.

His manner changed from that of the sympathizing friend to one of stern authority. He shot questions at her, tabulating her answers, discarding cumbering detail, seizing on the important fact and separating it from the jumble of confused impressions and fancies that she poured out. A few inquiries set Larkin's position clear before him. The money he dismissed with a curt sentence; of course he would give it, she wasn't to think of that any more.

" Thank heaven you decided on me," he said. " I'll straighten this out for you and I'll do it quick."

She was ready to take fright at anything and his eagerness scared her.

" But you'll not do anything they don't want ? You'll not tell the police or try to catch them? "

He had seen from the start that she was dominated .by terror, as the kidnapers had intended she should be:

Miss Maitland Private Secretary

and seeing this had recognized her as a negligible factor. To keep her quiet, soothe her fears, and employ her services just so far as they were helpful was what he had to do with her. What he had to do without her was shaping itself in his mind.

" You can rely on me. I won't make any breaks. And you have to be careful, not a word about me to this man Larkin. He must think the money is yours."

She assured him of her discretion and he felt he could trust her that far.

" Now listen," he said slowly and impressively as if he was speaking to a child, " we've both got to go very charily. A good deal of the threat-stuff in these letters is bluff, but also men who would undertake an enterprise of this kind are pretty tough customers and we don't want to take any risks. When I'm gone you drive over to Larkin's, tell him you have the money for the ransom, and to put in the ad. As soon as either you or he get an answer let me know. I'll be at Council Oaks; I'll go back there now. It's probable you're watched and if they saw me hanging about here they might think I was in the game and take fright. Do you understand? "

She nodded:

" Yes, you've put some courage into me. I was ready to die when you came in."

" Well, that's over now. What you've got to do is 258

Suzanne Finds a Friend

to follow my instructions, keep your nerve and have a little patience."

He smiled down at her as she sat, a huddled heap of finery, on the edge of the sofa. She tried to return the smile, a grimace of the lips that did not touch her somber eyes. No man, least of all Dick Ferguson, could have been angry with her.

" She was crazy," he said to himself as he walked down the hall. " They were all crazy and I guess they had enough to make them so. I'll get the child back, and when I do, I'll make them bite the dust before my girl."

Several people who knew him saw Dick Ferguson driving his black car down Fifth Avenue late that afternoon. He saw none of them, steering his way through the traffic, his eyes fixed on the vista in front. He stopped at Delmonico's for an early dinner, telling the waiter to bring him anything that was ready, then sat with frowning brows staring at his plate. Here again were people who knew him and wondered at his gloomy abstraction — not a bit like Ferguson, must have something on his mind.

Night was falling as he crossed the Queensborough bridge, a smoldering glow along the west glazing the surface of the river. When he left the straggling outskirts of Brooklyn and reached the open country the dark had come, deep and velvety, a few bright star

Miss Maitland Private Secretary

points pricking through the cope of the sky. He lowered his speed, his glance roving ahead to the road and its edging grasses, startlingly clear under the radiance of his lamps.

Round him the country brooded in its rest, silence lying on the pale surface of fields, on the black indistinctness of trees. Here and there the lights of farms shone, caught and lost through shielding boughs, and the clustered sparklings of villages. The air was heavy with scents, the breath of clover knee-high in the grass, grain still giving off the warmth of the afternoon sun, and the delicate sweetness of the wild grape draped over the roadside trees. All this night loveliness in its fragrant quietness, its rich and penetrating beauty,, reminded him of her. He looked up at the sky, and its calm and steadfast splendor came to him with a new meaning. She was related to it all, in tune with the eternal harmonies, part of everything that was stainless and noble and pure. And he would show the world that she was, clear her of every spot, place her where she would be as far from suspicion, as serenely above the meanness of her accusers, as the stars in the crystal depths of the sky.

When he reached Council Oaks he had a vision of her, belonging there, a piece of its life. He saw a future, when, coming back like this to its friendly doors, she would be waiting on the balcony to greet him..

Suzanne Finds a Friend

There was no one there now; the house was still, its lights shining across the pebbled drive. Obsessed by his thoughts, he jumped out, and leaving the car at the steps, entered. From the kitchen wing he could hear the servants' voices raised in cheerful clamor. Crossing the hall, he had a glimpse through the dining room door of the table, set and waiting for him, two lamps flanking his place. He had no mind for food and went upstairs, dreams still holding him. In his room he switched on the lights and his vacant glance, sweeping the bureau, brought up on the box with the crystal lid.

In his mind the robbery had faded into a background of inconsequential things. It had become a side issue, a thread in the tangled skein he had pledged himself to unravel. When Molly had told him of the evidence against Esther his interest had centered on the charge of kidnaping — the monstrous and unbelievable charge of which she almost stood convicted. Even now, as he looked at the box and remembered what he had hidden there, it came to his memory not as another weapon to be used in her defense, but as a souvenir of the moment when his present passion had flamed into life. A picture rose of that night, the silver moon spatter-ings, her hand, white in the white light, with the band on its third finger. He opened the box to take it out

— it was not there.

He had seen it a few days before, was certain he had, shook up the contents, then overturned the box, strewing the studs and pins on the bureau. But it was fruitless — the band, crushed and flattened as he remembered it, was gone. He muttered an angry phrase, its loss came as a jar on the exaltation of his mood. Then a soft step on the staircase caught his ear, and looking up he saw Willitts' head rise into view. The man came down the passage and spoke with his customary quiet deference:

" I saw the car outside, sir, and knew you'd come back. Would you like dinner — the cook says she can have it ready in a minute? "

" No," Ferguson's voice was short, " I dined in town. Look here, I've lost something—" he pointed to the scattered jewelry —" I had a cigar band in that box and it's gone. Did you see it ? "

Willitts looked at the box and shook his head:

"No, sir. A cigar band, a thing made of paper? " There was the faintest suggestion of surprise in his voice.

" Yes, you must have seen it. It was there a few days ago, underneath all that truck — I saw it myself."

The man again shook his head and, moving to the bureau, began to shift the toilet articles and look among them.

" I'm afraid I didn't see it, sir, or if I did I didn't 262

notice. Maybe it's got strayed away somewhere."

He continued his search, Ferguson watching him with moody irritation:

" What the devil could have happened to it? I put it in there myself, put it in that particular place for safekeeping."

Willitts, feeling about the bureau with careful fingers, said:

" Was it of any value, sir? "

" Yes," Ferguson having little hope of finding it turned away and threw himself into a chair, " it was of great value. I wouldn't have lost it for anything. It was evidence —" he stopped, growling a smothered " Damn." He had said enough; he didn't want the servants chattering.

" I'm very sorry, sir, but it doesn't seem to be here. Perhaps the chambermaid threw it away, thinking it had got in the box my mistake."

" I daresay — it sounds likely. I wish the people in this house would let my room alone, control their mad desire for neatness and leave things where I put them. Have the car taken to the garage, I'm not coming down again. If any one calls up I'm out. Good-night."

"Good-night, sir," said Willitts, and softly withdrew.

CHAPTER XXIII

MOLLY'S STORY

AFTER that Monday night when he went off in a rage, Ferguson didn't show up at Grasslands for several days and I had the place to myself and all the time I wanted. Believe me, I wanted a lot and made use of it. While the others were concentrating on the kidnaping — the big thing that had absorbed all their interest — I went back to the job I was engaged for, the robbery. And I went back with a fresh eye, the old idea cleared out of my head by Mrs. Price's confession.

She'd explained the light, the light by the safe at one-thirty. With that out of the way, I could get busy on the cigar band. I was just aching to do it, for, as I'd told Ferguson, it was an A

1 starting point. Given that, there's nothing more exciting in the world than tracking up from it, following different leads, seeing if they'll dovetail, putting bits together like a picture puzzle.

So I started in and for two days collected data, ferreted into the movements of every person on the

Molly's Story

place, gossiped round in the village, picked up a bit here and a scrap there, and made notes at night in my room. I broke down Dixon's dignity and had a long talk with him; I got Ellen to show me how to knit a sweater and before I'd learnt had her inside out. I spent two hours and broke my best scissors spoiling the lock of the bookcase in my room and had Isaac up to try keys on it. When I was done I knew the movements of everybody in the house on the night of July seventh as if I'd personally conducted each one through that important and exciting evening.

It wasn't love of the work alone, or the feeling that I ought to earn my salary, that pushed me on. There was something else — I wanted to clear Esther Mait-land. I wanted it bad. I kept thinking of her eyes looking at me when I gave her the drink of water and it made me sort of sick. In my thoughts I kept telling my husband about it, and I always tried to make out I'd acted very smart and some way or other I knew he wouldn't think so. It wasn't that I felt guilty — I'd done nothing but what I was hired for — but there's a meanness about beating a person down, there's a meanness about staring into their white, twisted face and saying, " Ha — Ha — you're cornered and I did it! " You have to be awfully good yourself to do that sort of thing.

Thursday morning I'd got all I could and with my 265

Miss Maitland Private Secretary

notes and my fountain pen I went out on the side piazza by Miss Maitland's study; there was a table there and it was quiet and secluded. So I fixed everything convenient and set to work. Taking the cigar band as the central point I built up from it something like this:

It had been dropped by a man — so few women smoke cigars you could put that down as certain. It had been dropped between half-past eight when the storm stopped and half-past ten when Miss Maitland found it. The man could not be Mr. Janney who had driven both ways, nor Dixon or Isaac who had walked to the village by the road and come back the same route. It couldn't have been Otto the chauffeur as he had stayed at Ferguson's garage visiting there with Ferguson's men. The head gardener had gone to the movies with the other Grasslands servants, and the under gardeners had been in their own homes in the village as I had taken pains to find out. Therefore it was no man living on the place at that time.

But that it was some one who was familiar with the house and its interior workings was proved by two facts: — that the dogs, heard to start barking, had suddenly quieted down, and that a rose from Miss Mait-land's dress had been found inside the safe.

An expert burglar could have got round all the rest, had a key to the front door, worked out the combination — the house was virtually empty for over two

Molly's Story

hours — it was known that the family and servants were out. But the most expert burglar in the world couldn't have controlled those dogs — Mrs. Price's Air-dale was as savage to strangers as a wolf and had a bark on it like a steam calliope.

The rose figured as a proof this way: It had been put inside the safe to throw suspicion on Miss Maitland, the thief was aware that she knew the combination. This would argue that he was acquainted with the habits of the household. All social secretaries are not given the leeway Miss Maitland was; all social secretaries aren't given the combination of a safe where two hundred thousand dollars' worth of jewels are kept. The man knew she had it, and tried to fix the guilt on her. Where his plan slipped up was Mrs. Price coming later, finding the rose, salting it down in a piece of tissue paper, and, for some reason of her own, not saying a word about it.

How did he get the rose ? As far as I could see there was just one way. Esther Maitland had spent part of the afternoon of July the seventh altering her evening dress. Ellen had pinned it up on her and she'd taken the waist down to her study to sew on as her room was too hot. When she'd gone upstairs again — it was Ellen who gave me all this — she'd left part of the trimming on the desk. The next morning the parlor maid had given it to Ellen — all cut and picked apart,

some of the roses loose in a cardboard box — to put in Miss Maitland's room. It had lain on the desk all night and, in my opinion, the thief had either known it was there or found it, taken the rose, and made his " plant " with it.

Now one man who would be familiar to the dogs and might know Miss Maitland's privileges and habits, was Chapman Price. But it wasn't he, for at nine-thirty, the hour when the thief was busy, Mr. Price was crossing the Queensborough bridge, headed for New York. And anyway, if he hadn't been, you couldn't suspect him of trying to lay the blame on the girl who was his partner. No — Chapman Price was wiped off the map with all the rest of the Grasslands crowd.

When I'd got this far I sat biting my pen handle and sizing it up. A thief, professional, had taken the jewels. He was some one unknown, having no connection with Mr. Price or Miss Maitland. The two crimes that had nearly shaken the Janney family off its throne had been committed by different parties. I was as sure of that as that the sun would rise tomorrow.

After dinner that evening I went out on the balcony and sat there, turning it all over in my head, and looking at the woods, black-edged and solid against the night sky. It was very still, not a breath, and presently, off across the garden, I heard the gravel crunch

under a foot, a soft padding on the grass, and then a long, lean figure came into the brightness that shot out across the drive from the hall behind me — Ferguson.

He dropped down on the top step, settled his back against one of the roof posts, and took out a cigarette case. He was right where the light shone on him, and I could see he had a serious, glum look which made me think he still " had a mad on me " as they say on the east side. That didn't trouble me; people getting mad when they've a reason to never does, and he'd reason enough, poor dear.

Puffing out a long shoot of smoke, he said:

" I've come over to speak to you about that idea of mine — that cigar band I told you about."

" Oh," I answered, " you've got round to that, have you? "

" I have, or perhaps you might say half way around."

" Well, I'm the whole way. I've spent three days getting there."

" I thought you'd beat me to it. What have you arrived at? "

" The certainty that the man who dropped the band was the thief."

" We're agreed at last. Have you gone far enough round to come to a suspect? "

"No, I'm stuck there."

He blew out a ring, watched it float away into the darkness and said:

" So am I. But I've a small, single compartment brain that can't accommodate more than one idea at a time. And it's busy just now in another direction. If you'll put that forty horse-power one of yours on this we ought to get round the whole way." He glanced sideways at me, his eyes full of meaning. " You'll find I can be a very grateful person."

" Gratitude's a kind of pay I like."

" Yes — it's stimulating and it can take more than one form." He flung away the cigarette, leaned back against the post and said: " The worst of it is that our main exhibit, the cigar band, is gone. I looked for it last night and found it was lost."

" Lost! " I sat up quick. He'd told me where he kept it and right off I thought it was funny. " Gone out of that box you had it in? "

" Yes. I wanted to see it when I came in — I'd been in town — and it wasn't in the box."

" Had it been there recently ? "

" Um — I can't tell just how recently — perhaps a week ago."

" Did you ask about it ? "

" Yes, I asked Willitts. He said he hadn't seen it."

" Didn't you tell me you kept studs and jewelry in that box?"

" I did; that's what it's for. I don't see how he could have helped seeing it. I daresay he did and, thinking it was of no use, threw it away and then, when he saw I wanted it, got scared and lied."

A thing like a zigzag of lightning went through me. It stabbed down from my head to my feet, giving my heart a whack as it passed. My voice sounded queer as I spoke:

" He could have known, couldn't he, of that walk you and Miss Maitland took, that walk when you found the band?"

He had been looking, dreamy and indifferent, out into the darkness. Now he turned to me, a little surprised, as if he was wondering at my questions:

" I suppose so. He knew all my crowd up there; they're forever running back and forth from one place to the other. They know everything, and they're the greatest gossips and snobs in the country. I've no doubt he heard it talked threadbare — the boss walking home with Mrs. Janney's secretary. Probably gave their social sensibilities a jolt."

Something lifted me out of my chair, carried me across the balcony, plunked me down beside him on a lower step. I craned up my head near to his and I'll never forget the expression of his face, sort of blank, as if he wasn't sure whether I'd gone crazy or was going to kiss him.

Miss Maitland Private Secretary

" Some one who knew the family, some one who knew it was out that night, some one who knew Miss Maitland had the combination, some one who could have got a key to the front door, some one the dogs were friendly with!"

He was staring at me as if he was hypnotized — getting a gleam of it but not the full light. I put my hands on his shoulders and gave them a shake.

" You simp, wake up. It's Willitts! "

CHAPTER XXIV

GAUDS ON THE TABLE

IN spite of Molly's excited certainty that Willitts was the thief, Ferguson was not convinced. He met her impetuous demand for the valet's arrest with a recommendation for a fuller knowledge of his activities on the night of the robbery. Willitts had gone to the movies with the Grasslands servants and if he had been with them the whole evening he was as innocent as Dixon or Isaac. She had to agree and promised to do nothing until she had satisfied herself that his movements tallied with their findings.

Ferguson had a restless night. There was matter on his mind to keep him awake; he was fearful that Suzanne might make some false step. She was at best a shifty, unstable creature, how much more so now strained to the breaking point. He felt he ought to be in town where he could keep her under his eye, and decided to motor in in the morning. Also he began to think that Molly was probably right; she was shrewd and experienced, knew more of such matters than he. He would go to the Whitney office and put the Willitts'

affair in their hands, then run up to the St. Boniface, take a room, and have a look in at Suzanne.

He left the house at nine-thirty, telling the butler he was called to the city on business, and might be gone a day or two. At the Whitney office he was informed that Mr. and Mrs. Janney were in consultation with the heads of the firm, and, saying he would not disturb them, waited in an outer room from whence he telephoned to Suzanne, telling her he would be at the hotel later. When the Janneys had gone he was ushered into the old man's office where he found the air still vibrating with the clash of battle. A combined attack had been made on Mrs. Janney who, under its pressure and the slow undermining of her confidence by a week of failure, had given in and consented to a move on Price. It had been planned for that afternoon, when he was to be summoned to the office, charged with the kidnaping and commanded to render up the child.

Whitney and his son listened to Ferguson's story of the cigar band with unconcealed interest. George, however, was skeptical — it was ingenious and plausible, showed Molly's fine Italian hand; but his mind had accepted the theory of Esther's participation and was of the unelastic, unmalleable kind. His father was obviously impressed by it, admitting that his original conviction of the girl's guilt had been shaken. To George's indignant rehearsal of the evidence, he ac-

corded a series of acquiescing nods, agreed that the facts were against him and maintained his stand. He would see Willitts as soon as possible and put him through a grilling examination. O'Malley could be sent to Council Oaks at once to bring him in, and his business could be disposed of before they got round to Price. As Ferguson rose to go George had the receiver of the desk telephone down and was giving low-voiced instructions to O'Malley to report immediately at the office.

It was nearly one when the young man found himself on the street level. There was no use going to the St. Boniface now as the family would be at lunch and speech alone with Suzanne impossible. On the way uptown he stopped at a restaurant, ordered food which he hardly touched, filling out the time with cigarettes. By half-past two he was on the move again, threading a slow way through the traffic, his eye lingering on the clock faces that loomed at intervals along the Avenue. Suzanne had told him that the old people always went for a drive after lunch and he scanned the motors that passed him, hoping to see them. He was in no mood for polite conversation — felt with the passing of the hours an increasing tension, a gathering of his forces for a leap and a struggle.

At the desk in the St. Boniface he heard that Mr. and Mrs. Janney had just gone out, and waited while

Mrs. Price's room was called up. There was no response; Mrs. Price must be out too. The information made him uneasy; she had told him she went nowhere except to Larkin's. More than ever anxious to see her, he engaged a room and left the message that he would be there and to be called up when she came in. The door shut on him, his uneasiness increased; wondering what had taken her out, wondering if she had done anything foolish, cursing the fate that had placed so much in her feeble hands, perturbed and restless as a lion in a cage.

Suzanne had gone to Larkin's, called there by a telephone message. It had come almost on the heels of her parents' departure and was brief — a request to come to him as soon as she could. She had scrambled into her street clothes, and, shaking in every limb, slipped out of the hotel's side door and sped across town in a taxi to hear how Bebita was to be found.

She was hardly inside the door, her veil lifted from a face as pale as Cassar's ghost, when Larkin answered her look of agonized question:

" Yes, the letter's come — what we expect, very clear and explicit. It was sent to me this time — came on the two o'clock delivery."

He turned to the desk and took up a folded paper. Before he could offer it to her, she had leaned forward

Cards on the Table

and snatched it out of his hand. Instantly her eyes were riveted on the lines:

" Mr. Horace Larkin, DEAH SIR:

In answer to the ad. in the Daily Record, we are dealing through you as the agent named by Mrs. Price. We do this as we realize that a lady of Mrs. Price's type and experience would be unable to handle alone so important a matter. Before we enter into details we must again repeat our warnings — not only the return of the child but her life is dependent on the actions of her mother and yourself. If you are wise to this and follow our instructions Bebita will be restored to her family on Saturday night.

The plan of procedure must be as follows: At eight-thirty a roadster, containing only the driver and marked by a handkerchief fastened to the windshield, must leave the village of North Cresson by the Cresson turnpike, at a rate of speed not exceeding fifteen miles an hour. It must proceed eastward along the pike for a distance of ten miles. Somewhere during this run a car will pass it and from its tonneau flash an electric lantern twice. Follow this car. Make no attempt to hail or to overtake it. It will turn from the main road and proceed for some distance. When it stops the driver of the roadster must alight, place the money at a spot indicated, and submit, without parley, to being bound and gagged. When this is done the child will be left beside him. If agreed to insert following personal in The Daily Record of Saturday morning: ' James, meet you at the time and place specified. Tom.'

(Signed) CLANSMEX."

The letter fluttered to the desk and Suzanne sank into a chair. Larkin looked at her; his glance showed some anxiety but his voice was hearty and encouraging:

" Well, you agree, of course ? " 277

Miss Maitland Private Secretary

She nodded, swallowing on a throat too dry for speech.

He picked up the letter and ran a frowning eye over it:

" It simply confirms what I thought — old hands. It's about as secure as such a thing could be. I don't see a loose end."

She made no answer and he went on still studying the paper:

" I'm not familiar with this country, but they wouldn't have picked it out unless it offered every chance of escape."

" Escape! " she breathed. " They've got to escape."

It made him smile, the eye he turned on her showed a quizzical amusement:

" You're almost talking like an accomplice, Mrs. Price." But he quickly grew grave as he met her tragic glance. " Pardon me, I shouldn't have said that, but the fact is, with the climax in sight, I'm a bit on edge myself." Then with a brusque change of tone, " Do you know this section of Long Island? "

" Yes, well — I've driven over it often."

" Am I right in thinking there are numbers of roads leading from the Cresson Turnpike? "

" Lots of them, to the Sound and inland."

" Umph!" he threw the letter on the desk and sat 278

down. " I don't think you need worry about their getting away. Now we must settle this up and then I'll go out and have the ad inserted. We've got to hustle — they've only given us a little over twenty-four hours."

She looked dazedly at him and murmured:

" What have we got to do ? "

" Why —" he was very gentle as to a stupid and bewildered child —" we have to arrange about this car — our car, the one that gets the signal."

" We can hire it, can't we? "

" Well, we could hire the car, but the driver — we can't very well hire him. He must be some one upon whom we can rely."

She stared at him, her eyes dilating:

" Yes, yes, of course. I'd forgotten that."

" Is there any one you can suggest — any one that you know you could trust and who would be willing to undertake it? "

" Yes," the word came with a sudden decision. " I know some one." Larkin eyed her sharply. She looked more alive than she had done since her entrance, seemed to be vitalized into a roused, responsive intelligence. " I know exactly the person."

" Entirely trustworthy? "

"Absolutely. Mr. Ferguson — Dick Ferguson."

" Oh, yes, Ferguson of Council Oaks." He mused a 279

moment under her hungry scrutiny. " Do you think he'd be willing to — er — agree to their demands as you have? "

" Yes, he'd do it to help me. He's an old friend; I know him through and through. He'd do it if I asked him."

The detective was silent for a moment, then said:

" Well, we have to have some one and if you're willing to vouch for him I'll abide by what you say. Before you came in I was thinking of offering to do it myself. But there are reasons against that. I don't mind helping you this way — quietly, on the side — but to be an actual participant in the final deal, handle the money, be more or less responsible for the person of the child — I'd rather not — I'd better not. And anyway I think I can be more useful as an observer, an unsuspected spectator who may see something worth while."

She gave a stifled scream and caught at his hand, resting on the edge of the desk:

" No, no, Mr. Larkin, please, I beg of you. You're not going to try and catch them."

Her fingers gripped like talons; he laid his free hand over them, soothingly patting them:

" Now, now, Mrs. Price, please have confidence in me. Am I likely, at this stage of the game, to do anything to queer it ? "

She did not reply, her eyes shifting from his, her teeth set tight on her quivering underlip. He waited a moment and then spoke with a new note, dominating, authoritative, as one in command:

" My dear lady, you've got to get hold of yourself. I can't go on with this if you don't trust me. We're launched on an enterprise by no means easy and if we don't pull together we'll fail, that's all."

That steadied her. She dropped his hand and broke into tremulous protestations:

" I do, I do, Mr. Larkin. It's only that I'm so terribly afraid, so upset and desperate. Of course I trust you. Would I be here, day after day, if I didn't?"

He was mollified, dropped back with the crisp, alert manner of the detective.

" All right, we'll let it go at that. Now as to Ferguson — you'll have to get word to him at once. Is he in the country? "

" No — he's here. I had a telephone from him this morning to say he was in town and would be at the hotel later in the day. He's probably there now, waiting for me."

" Um! " Larkin considered for a moment. " That's lucky. There's no time to waste. Get his consent and then 'phone me here. Just a word. And you understand he'll have to know the circumstances; he'll have to be wise to everything if he's to play his part."

Suzanne had lied so long and so variously that she did it with a natural ease. No one, having seen her as Larkin had, would have guessed the knowledge she hid. Her air of innocently comprehending his charge was a triumph of duplicity.

" Of course, I know, I understand. It'll be a dreadful surprise to him but he'll see it as I do. And he'll do what I ask —I 'm as certain of that as I am of his secrecy."

She would have to have the letter to show him, and Larkin, after a last, careful perusal of it, handed it to her. Then she went, cutting off his heartening words of farewell, making her way out in a quick, noiseless rush. At the desk in the hotel she learned that Ferguson was there, asked to have him apprised of her return and sent at once to her sitting room.

MOLLY'S STORY

THE morning after that talk with Ferguson I rose up " loaded for bar." At breakfast I led Dixon round to the old subject — we were good friends now and he'd drop his professional manner when we were alone and talk like a human being. Of course he remembered everything, and opened up as fluent as a gramophone. Willitts hadn't found them at the movies till nearly ten — been delayed on his way in from Cedar Brook, his landlady's little girl had been took bad with croup and he'd gone for the doctor — Dr. Bernard, who was off on a side road half way between Cedar Brook and Berkeley.

That ought to have been enough for me, but having started I thought I'd clear it all up, so I borrowed a bike off Ellen and set out on the double quick for Dr. Bernard's. I saw Mrs. Bernard and heard all I wanted. Willitts had been there on the night of July seventh, came on a bicycle, saw the doctor and gave his message about the sick child. She thought it was somewhere between eight and half-past — the storm

283

was just stopping. I lit out for home; I'd got it all now. He'd gone straight from the doctor's to Grasslands, taken the jewels, and made a short cut back to the main road through the woods to where he'd hidden his wheel.

When you get this far on a case there comes over you a sort of terror that you may slip up. You have it all in your hand, your fingers are stretched to lay hold on the criminal, and an awful fear takes possession of you that right on the threshold of success you may lose. The cup and the lip — that's the idea.

This seized me on the ride back to Grasslands. Why was the cigar band gone if he wasn't wise to what it meant? It was a powerful hot day, smothering on the wood roads, but the way I made that machine shoot you'd suppose it was a hard frost and I was peddling to get up my circulation. He might be gone already, taken fright and skipped! I had a vision of telling the Chief and what he'd say, and the perspiration came out on me like the beads on a mint julep glass. I'd go to town right now — there was an express at eleven — but before I left I'd call up Council Oaks and find out if he was there.

As I ran up the piazza steps the hall clock chimed out a single note, half-past ten — I had plenty of time. I called to Dixon to order the motor — I was going to town — whisked into the telephone closet, and

Molly's Story

made the connection. The voice that answered lifted me up out of the depths — for I guessed it was Willitts by the dialect, English, with the " H's " hanging on sort of loose and wobbly. To make sure I asked, and it answered, smooth as a summer sea — yes, I was talking to Mr. Ferguson's valet, Willitts. Mr. Ferguson was not at 'ome, 'ed gone to the city to be away a day or two. Was there any message? There wasn't — you could bet on that — and I eased off in a high-class society drawl.

With a deep breath I dropped back to normal, smoothed my feathers, powdered my nose, and when the motor came round looked like a shy little nursery governess, snitching a day off in town.

It was at the station that something happened which ended my peaceful state and gave me an experience I'll remember as long as I live.

Just as I was stepping on the train I took a glance back along the platform and there, close behind me, dressed as neat as a tailor's dummy, was Willitts with a bag in his hand. He didn't notice me, and if he had he wouldn't have known me, for I'd only passed him onc'e in the village and then he wasn't looking my way. I mounted up the steps and went into the car. From the tail of my eye I saw him in the doorway and when he'd taken the seat in front of me, I dropped against

flfiss Maitland Private Secretary

the back of mine, saying to myself: " Hully Gee, he's going! "

All the way into town, I sat with my eyes on his hat, thinking what I'd better do. There was one thing certain — that stood out like the writing on the wall — I mustn't let him out of my sight. Where he went I'd have to go, tight as a barnacle I'd have to stick to that desperado. I tried to think how I could get a message to the Whitneys' office, but I didn't see how I was going to find the time or the opportunity. If the worst came to the worst I could call a cop, but if I knew anything of men like Willitts, he'd keep a watch out like a warship for periscopes, for anything that wore brass buttons and connected with the law.

The " Penn " station was as hot as a Turkish bath and through it you can imagine me, trying to trip light and airy, and keeping both eyes as tight as steel rivets on that man's back. I've never shadowed anybody — it's not been included in my college course — all I knew was I mustn't lose him and I mustn't get him suspicious, and if you're making away with a fortune in a handbag, suspicion ought to be your natural state. So I trailed after him as far in the rear as I dared, sometimes, a gang rushing for a train coming in between us, sometimes the space clear with him hurrying to the exit and me sort of loitering and gawking up at the maps on the ceiling.

Molly's Story

Out in the street he turned and shot a glance like a searchlight round behind him. It swept over me and took no notice, which was qonsiderable of an encouragement. If it was warm in the station, it was sizzling outside. Men were carrying their coats on their arms, some of them using palm leaf fans, careful ones keeping to the edge of shade along the house fronts. But Wil-litts didn't mind the sun; I guess when you're making off with a fortune you're indifferent to temperature — it's another proof of mind over matter.

After walking down Seventh Avenue for a few minutes he turned to the left and struck across a side street to Sixth. Half way down the block he went into a men's furnishing store, and sauntering slow past the window, I saw him looking at collars. There was a stationer's just beyond and I cast anchor there, by a counter near the door set out with magazines. A sales girl lounged up, chewing her gum like the heat had made her languid, and looking interested over my clothes.

" Awful warm, ain't it?" she said, and I answered, picking up a magazine:

" It's something fierce. I'll take this one."

" You got that one already," says she, pointing to the magazine I'd bought at Berkeley and was still clinging to. " Don't you wanna try something new ? "

"Oh — it's the heat; the sun gets my head woozy." 287

Miss Maitland Private Secretary

I picked out another and gave her a dollar, the smallest change I had. As she was walking to the cash register, Willitts passed the door and I was out on the sill, moving cautious to the sidewalk.

" Say," comes the girl's voice from behind me, " what are you doin'? You ain't got your change yet. You'd oughtn't to be let out in this sun."

" Keep it," I called back. " I was a working girl once myself."

At the corner of Fifth Avenue he stopped and, a bus coming along, he haled it. " Lord," thought I, '* if he gets into that without me I'll have to run after it and they'll arrest me for a lunatic." Being quite a ways behind, I had to make a dash for it, waving my magazine and hollering like the rubes from the country. He was up on the roof, and the bus was moving when I lit on the step, and was hauled in friendly by the conductor.

We jolted downtown, me sitting sideways in a rear seat watching the stairs for Willitts' legs. It wasn't until we were below Twenty-third Street that they came into view, stepping lightly down. The bus heaved up against the curb and he swung off, me behind him. I was terribly scared that he'd begin to suspect me, and all I could think of that would look natural was to roll my eyes flirtatious at the conductor, who seemed to like it so much I was afraid he wouldn't let me off.

Molly's Story

When I got down on the pavement Willitts was walking along the cross street back toward Sixth Avenue. Midway down the block, he stopped and disappeared through a doorway. I was quite a piece behind him and when I saw him fade out of sight I forgot everything and ran. At the door I came up short, panting and purple in the face — the place was a restaurant. It had a large plate glass window with white letters on it and a man making pancakes where he'd show plainest. Inside I could see Willitts seating himself at a littered up table.

" Lunch!" I said to myself. " He's going to eat, the cool devil. Now's my chance! "

Almost directly opposite was a drug store with telephone booths close to the window. I could get a message to the office, and if I caught the chief or Mr. George, I could have a man up in twenty minutes. If they weren't there I'd try headquarters, but I was afraid of that — they'd ask questions, waste time, want to know who I was and what it was all about. If only Willitts was hungry, if he'd only eat enough to last till I got some one, if he'd only order pancakes. As I waited for the connection I found myself sort of praying " Pancakes — make him order pancakes. They're made in the window and they take quite a while. Please make him eat pancakes ! "

Right in the midst of my prayer came the voice of 289

Miss Maitland Private Secretary

Miss Quinn, the switchboard girl in the office, and for me it was:

" Quick, Miss Quinn — it's Mrs. Babbitts. Is Mr. Whitney or Mr. George there ? Give 'em to me — on the jump — if they are."

She didn't waste a word, and in a minute Mr. George's voice came sharp:

"Hello, who is it?"

" Molly, Mr. George. And I've got Willitts — and I've got enough on him to know he's the thief — I can't tell you now but —"

He cut in with:

"I know, I know, Ferguson's told us. O'Malley's here now going to Council Oaks for him."

I almost screamed:

" Send him here. Willitts is off; he's left and I've trailed him. I'm waiting at the door and he's inside."

" Inside what, where the devil are you? "

I gave him the directions and then:

" It's a restaurant; he's eating. But it may only be a doughnut and a glass of milk. If it's pancakes we're safe, but a man lighting out with a fortune in a handbag don't generally want anything so filling. I'll follow him until I drop, but I don't want to travel round with a jewel thief unless I have to."

" I'll send O'Malley now. You stay right there and 290

if Willitts finishes before he comes, hold him any way you can. Get a cop. I'll 'phone to headquarters for a warrant. So long."

Of course I thought of the cop, but spying out from the doorway, there wasn't one in sight. And by this time I was considerably worked up, afraid to move in any direction, afraid to take my eyes from the restaurant entrance. I pulled up one of the chairs they have for people getting prescriptions filled, and sat down by the doorway, watching the place opposite, like a cat camped in front of a mouse hole.

Ten minutes had passed. If the traffic wasn't too thick on Broadway O'Malley could make it in less than twenty. But the traffic was thick — it was the middle of the day; if he was stalled or had to make a detour it might run toward half an hour. He might be — The door of the restaurant opened and out crept the mouse.

The cat rose up, soft and stealthy, with her claws ready. As I crossed the street I sent a look both ways — not a taxi in sight, not a cop, only the whole thoroughfare tangled up with drays and delivery wagons. There was nothing for it but to stop him, first put out the velvet paw and then shoot the claws. Jumping quick on the curb I came up alongside of him, a smile on my face that felt like the grin you get when you make a j oke that no one sees.

Miss Maitland Private Secretary

" Why, hullo," I said, going at him with ray hand out, " I couldn't at first believe it — but it is you."

He drew up quick, all on the alert, looking at me with hard, ferret eyes.

"Who are you?" he said, fierce and forbidding. "What do you want?"

I put my head sideways, and tried to take the curse off the smile, changing it to a sort of trembly sweetness.

" Why, don't you know me? I can't be changed that bad. It's Rosie."

I didn't know what his Christian name was and anyway, if I had it wouldn't have helped — a man like Willitts changes his name as often as he does his address. But I had to call him something, so when I saw the anger rising in his eyes, I said, all broken and tender like the deserted wife in the last act:

" Dearie, don't pretend you don't remember me — it's Rosie from the old country."

He began to look savage, also alarmed:

" I don't know what you're talking about. I never saw you before in my life."

He made a movement to pass on, but I drew up close, wiped off the smile, and put on the look of true love that won't let go.

"Oh, dearie, don't say that. Haven't I worn the soles off my shoes hunting for you ever since, ever

Molly's Story

since —" Gee, I didn't know how to finish it, then it came in a flash. I moaned out, " ever since we parted."

" Look 'ere, young woman," he said, low, with a face on him like a meat ax, " this doesn't go with me. Now get out; get off or I'll 'ave you run in."

I knew he wouldn't do that; he'd hand over the jewels first. I raised up my voice in a wail and said:

" Oh, dearie, you're faking; I won't believe it. You can't have forgot — back in the old country, me and you."

A messenger boy, slouching by, heard me and drew up, hopeful of some fun. Willitts saw him and began to look like murder would be added to his other offenses. I gave a glance up the street — still only drays and wagons, not a taxi in sight. Fatima with Sister Anne reporting from the tower, had nothing over me for watchful waiting.

" It's Rosie," I whined, " it's your own little Rosie. If I don't look the same it's the suffering you've caused me and Gawd knows it."

I laid my hand on his arm. With a movement of fury he shook it off and began to back away from me. Another boy had come up against the messenger and lodged there like a leaf in a stream, caught in an eddy. I heard him say, "What's on?" and the other answered :

" Don't know but I guess it's the movies." 293

Miss Maitland Private Secretary

And they both looked round for the camera man.

I don't think Willitts heard them. His back was that way and his face to me, hard as iron and savage as a hungry wolf's. He tried to speak low and soothing:

" Now 'old your tongue, don't make such a fuss. I'll give you something and you go off quiet and respectable." His hand felt in his pocket and I raised a loud, tearful howl:

" Money! Is it money you're offering? What's money to me whose heart you've broken? "

" I don't see no camera man," came the messenger boy's voice.

" Aw, he's in one of them wagons," said the other. " I've seen 'em in wagons."

The perspiration was on Willitts' forehead in beads, he was whitening round the mouth. Putting his face close down to mine he breathed out through his teeth:

" What in 'ell do you want? "

" You! " I cried and out of the tail of my eye I saw a taxi shoot round the corner from Fifth Avenue. Willitts drew away from me, shrunk together for a race. I saw it and I knew even now, with O'Malley plunging through the traffic, it might be too late. Embracing is not my strong suit, no man but my lawful husband ever felt my arms about him. But duty's a strong word with me and then my sporting blood was up. So with

my teeth set, I just made a lunge at that crook and clasped him like an octopus.

I didn't know a man was so much stronger than a woman. Willitts wasn't much taller than I and he was a thin little shrimp, but believe me, he was as tough as leather and as slippery as an eel. I could see the two boys, delighted, drinking it in, and a dray man in a jumper, drop a crate and come up on the run, bawling: " Say, you feller, let the lady alone," The boys chorused out: " Aw, keep out — it's the movies! " Willitts must have heard too, and I guess he saw his chance, for he suddenly squirmed one arm loose, and whang! came a blow on the side of my head. It might have seemed part of the play but he did it too hard — calculated wrong in his excitement. I let go, seeing everything — the houses, the sky, the crowd that seemed to start up out of the pavements — whirling round and shot over with zigzags. There was a roaring noise in my ears and all about, and I dropped over into somebody's arms, things getting swimmy and dark.

When I came out of it I was sitting on a packing box with a man fanning me and O'Malley, red as a tomato and Willitts the color of ashes in the middle of a mob. There was a terrible hubbub, people jamming together, the wagons stopped and the drivers yelling to know what was up, heads out of every window, and then two policemen, fighting their way through. I felt

queer, sickish, and as if the muscles of my face were all slack so my mouth wouldn't stay shut. But the gentleman fanning me acted awful kind and a clerk came out of a store with ice water and a wet handkerchief that he patted soft on the side of my head.

I could see O'Malley and the policeman (they'd come from headquarters I heard afterward) go off into a vestibule with Willitts and the crowd that couldn't get a look-in came squeezing round me, heads peering up over heads. They'd got the idea that Willitts was my husband, seeming to think only a lawful spouse would dare to hit a woman before witnesses in the public street. The guys in the front were explaining it to the guys in the back and calling Willitts names I couldn't put down in these refined pages.

It got me laughing, especially when an old Jew who had been sizing me up like a piece of goods nodded slow and solemn and said: " And she ain'd zo bad lookin' neither." I burst right out at that and the man with the fan waved his arms at them, shouting:

" Give way there — back — back! She wants air — she's hysterical. She's gone through more than she can bear."

Gee, how I laughed!

Presently in the center of a surging mass we crowded our way to the taxi, the policemen going in front and hitting round light with their clubs. O'Malley with

Willitts handcuffed to him got in the back seat, me opposite, with my hat off, holding the handkerchief against my head. As we pulled out I looked back over the sea of faces and caught the eye of one of the policemen. He straightened up, very serious and dignified, and saluted.

CHAPTER XXVI

THE COUNTER PLOT

FERGUSON'S knock on Suzanne's door was promptly answered by the lady herself, still in her hat and wrap. She clutched at him as she had done when he came to 'her in her dark hour, drawing him into the room and gasping her news. He was in no mood to follow her ramblings and, as soon as she spoke of a letter, interrupted her with a brusque demand for it. After he had mastered its contents he told her to 'phone at once to Larkin that it was all right, and while she delivered the message, stood by studying the paper. When she turned back to him he laid his hands on her shoulders and looked into her eyes. The touch that once would have sent the blood burning to her cheeks called up no responsive thrill now: " This lets you out — it's the end of your responsibility. Your part now is to be quiet and wait. Tomorrow night you'll have Bebita back. Just nail that up in your mind and keep your eyes on it." " Back where ? Will you bring her here ? " It was so like her — so indicative of a mental atti-298

The Counter Plot

tilde invariably small and personal, that he could have smiled:

" I can't say, but probably Grasslands. The end of the route laid down isn't so far from there."

" Shall I go back to Grasslands? "

He pondered a moment, then decided it was wiser to trust nothing to her, even so simple a matter as her withdrawal to the country.

" No, stay where you are. There'd be a lot of questioning if you went, bothersome, hard to answer. When we have her I'll let you know. For the rest of this afternoon I'll be in town, in my room here on the floor below. If anything of moment should happen send for me, but don't unless it's vital. I'll be busy getting things ready. Be silent, be grave, be hopeful — that's all you have to do now."

He left her, going directly to his room on a lower floor of the hotel. She felt numb and dazed, wondering how she was to live through the next twenty-four hours. Her parents returned from their drive and

close on their entrance came a communication from the i

Whitney office, saying the jewels had been found and Mr. and Mrs. Janney were wanted downtown. In the midst of their bustling excitement she sat mute, following their movements with vacant eyes. She saw them leave in agitated haste, Mr. Janney forgetful of her, her mother throwing out phrases of comfort as she hurried

Miss Maitland Private Secretary

to the door. She was glad when they were gone and she could be still, draw all her energies inward in the fight for endurance and courage.

His coat off, the windows wide for such breaths of air as floated across the heated roofs, Ferguson paced back and forth with a long, even stride. His uncertainty was ended, the tension relaxed; he stood face to face with the event and measured it.

His assurances to Suzanne that he would make no attempt to apprehend the kidnapers had been sops thrown to pacify her terror. He had no more intention of a supine acquiescence than Mrs. Janney would have had. Beyond the clearing of Esther, stood out the man's desire to bring to justice the perpetrators of a foul and dastardly deed. Now, with their cards laid on the table, it rose higher, burned into a steady, hot blaze of rage and resolution.

But between his desire and its fulfilment stretched a maze of difficulties. He saw at once what Larkin had seen — that their plan was as nearly impregnable as such a plan could be. Though he knew every mile of the country they had selected, he knew that the chances of waylaying or flanking them were ten to one against him. Numerous roads, north and south, led from the Cresson Pike, some to the shore drive along the Sound, some inland crossing the various highways that threaded the center of the Island. Any one of these might be

The Counter Plot

chosen as the road down which their car would turn, and any one of them, winding through woods and lonely tracts of country, would offer avenues of escape.

He thought of stationing men along the designated route but it would take an army, impossible to gather at such short notice and impossible to place without his opponent's cognizance. Hundreds of men could not be picketed along a ten-mile stretch of highway without those who were the authors of so daring a scheme being aware. They would be on the watch; no move of such magnitude could be hidden from them. It would be the same if he called in the police. They would know it, and what could the police do that he could not do more secretly, more efficiently?

A following car was also out of the question. There was no reason to suppose that they would not have several cars of their own, passing and repassing him, making sure that he was unescorted. The threats of injury to the child he had set down as efforts to reduce Suzanne to a paralyzed silence. But if they saw an attempt was on foot to trap them they might not show up at all — go as they had come, unknown and unsighted, their car lost among the procession of motors that passed along the Cresson Pike. Then taken fright, they might not dare another effort, might drop out of sight with their hostage unredeemed. A chill crept over the young man, he had a dread vision

Miss Maitland Private Secretary

of the old people's despair, of Suzanne distraught, crazed perhaps. It behooved him to run no risks; to make sure of the child was his first duty, to strike at her abductors his second.

The course he finally decided on was the only one that made Bebita's restoration certain and offered a possibility of routing his opponents. At the hour named he would place on the road six motors, driven by his own chauffeurs and garage men, and entering the turnpike at intervals of ten minutes. Three would start from its eastern end, meeting him en route, three from its western, strung out behind him, now and then speeding up, overhauling him and passing on. Of a summer's Saturday night the Cresson Pike was full of vehicles, and the six, merged in the shifting stream, would suggest no connection with him or his mission.

Where his hope of success lay was that one of these satellites, to whom the character and marking of his roadster would be visible at some distance, might be within sight when he was signaled and see him turn into the branch road. Its business would be to wait until another of the fleet came up, pass the word, and the two follow on his tracks. This halt would give the kidnapers time to complete the transaction, get the money, give up the child, and bind him. If they were interrupted the situation would be too perilous to permit of delay — he had thought of an attack on the

The Counter Plot

child — and if they had finished and gone the rescuing cars could fly in pursuit.

He was far from satisfied with it; it was very different from the schemes he had had in his head before he measured his resourcefulness against theirs. He dropped into a chair, sunk in moody contemplation of its deficiencies. The men he had to rely on were not the right kind, loyal and willing enough, but without the boldness and initiative necessary to such an enterprise. He wanted a lieutenant, some one he could look to for quick, independent action if the affair took an unexpected turn. You couldn't tell how it might develop, and he, pledged to his ungrateful role, would be powerless to meet new demands, might not know they had arisen.

He was roused by a knock on the door. It surprised him for his presence in the city was unknown except to his own household and the Janney family. Then he thought of Suzanne coming down to him to pour out her fears, and his " Come in " was harsh and unwelcoming. In answer to it the door opened and Chapman Price entered.

Ferguson rose, looking at his visitor, startled and silent. His surprise was caused by the man's appearance, by a fierce disturbance in the handsome face, pale under its swarthy tan, by the eyes, agate-black and gleaming in a bovine glare. He had seen Chapman

angry but never just like this, and from a state, keyed to anticipate any new shock from any direction, said:

" What's happened now? "

Price had closed the door and backing up, leaned against it. His answer came, hoarse and broken:

" I've been to those hounds, the Whitneys."

It illuminated the ignorance of his listener, who was readjusting his mind for a reply when the other burst into a storm of invective against the lawyers and the Janneys. It broke like a released torrent, sentences stumbling on one another, curses mingled with wild accusations, its cause revealed in a final cry of: " Stolen — my child — kidnaped — gone! "

Through Ferguson's head, full of weightier matters, flashed a vision of Chapman raging at the Whitneys and a wonder as to what effect his rage had had. Kicking a chair forward he spoke with a dry quietness :

" That's all right — you needn't bother to go over it. Pull yourself together and sit down."

But he might as well have counseled self-control to an angry lion. The man, still standing against the door, jerked out:

" I can get nothing from any of them. They know nothing. They've Jet all this time pass — following me, suspecting me. I don't know why I didn't kill them!"

"Probably because you've sense enough left not to 304

The Counter Plot

complicate what's complicated enough already. What brought you here? "

He seemed unable to answer any direct question, staring with dilated eyes, his thoughts fastened on the subject of his pain:

" Spent a week — lost a week! Good God, Dick, they ought to be held responsible. Where is she? Not one of them knows — not an effort made. She's gone, lost, been stolen, spirited away, while they've been sitting in their office, turning their d d detectives loose on me."

" Look here, Chapman, I'm not saying you're not right, but the milk's spilled and it's no good trying to pick it up. If you'll sit down and listen to me —"

Price cut him off, leaving his post by the door to begin a distracted striding about the room:

" I couldn't stand it — when I'd got it through me I left. Then I tried to get hold of Suzanne — telephoned her, here somewhere in this place. She's half crazy, I think — I don't wonder, she's fonder of Bebita than anything in the world. She wouldn't see me, crying and moaning out that she couldn't, that she couldn't bear any more. And when I begged — I thought that she and I might arrange some combined effort, that whatever we had been we were partners now in this — she told me to come to you, that you could tell me more, that you could help." He swerved round on

Ferguson, the hard passion of his glance softened to a despairing urgency, " For God's sake, do. I'm penniless, I know almost nothing except that I've got to act now, at once, before any more time is lost. Give me a hand, help me to find her."

Ferguson's voice had an element of endurance in its level tones:

" That's just what I want to do. And if you'll stop talking and let me explain, you'll see I'm on the way to do it. But it's not my help that you want, it's the other way round — *I* want yours."

It was almost dark and Ferguson turned on the lights. Under their thin, white radiance, the two men sat, drawn close to the open window, and Ferguson told his story. The other listened, the storm of his anger gone, his dark face growing keen and hard as he heard the plan unfolded. An hour later they parted, Price to go to Council Oaks and lie low there until the following night when he would command the fleet of motors in the chase along the Cresson Turnpike.

CHAPTER XXVII

NIGHT ON THE CRESSON PIKE

THE night fell stifling and airless, unfortunately favorable for the kidnapers, as the sky was covered with clouds and the country wrapped in a thick darkness.

At half-past eight the roadster, with Ferguson driving, glided into the little village of North Cresson and swung out into the Cresson Turnpike. Ten minutes behind him was his touring car with Saunders, his chauffeur, at the wheel. Twenty minutes later a limousine was to strike into the pike from a road just beyond the village, and a runabout, emerging from an opposite direction, complete the chain. At the other end of the ten-mile limit Chapman Price in the black racer, was running up from the shore drive, with two satellites, one his own motor, one a hired Ford, strung out behind him.

Of a hot summer night at this hour the pike was alive with autos; returning holiday-makers, city dwellers taking a spin in the country to cool off, joy riders rioting by, belated business men speeding to the sea-

side for the Sunday rest. They bore down on Ferguson like a procession of fleeing monsters with round, goblin eyes staring in affright. They came from behind, swinging across his path in a blur of dust, laughter and shrill cries rising from their crowded tonneaus. Keeping to their narrow track between the borders of the fields they were like a turbulent, flashing torrent, dividing the darkness with a stream of streaked radiance, cutting the silence with a current of continuous sound.

Ferguson's glance ranged ahead, dazzled by the glare of advancing lamps that enlarged on his vision, grew to a blinding haze and swept by. He could see little, blackness and brightness alternating, the motors emerging as dim solidities, realized for a passing moment, then gone. Once a small car, cutting across his bows from a side road, made him slacken, but it slowed round showing the gnarled face of a farmer with a fat woman on the seat beside him and a bunch of children behind.

As he went on the press of vehicles thinned, the line of the road showed bare for longer stretches. The runabout overhauled him, kept by his side for a few yards, then drew ahead, its red tail lantern receding with an even, skimming smoothness ; a spot, a spark, nothing. He calculated he had covered nearly half the distance when the black racer passed in a soft, purring rush, his eye, through the yellow fog that preceded it, catching

a glimpse of Price's face. Then came a long, straight level between fields where only two cars went by, both going cityward. He looked back and tried to see the road behind him, straining his vision for a following shape, but the darkness lay close and unbroken, no goblin eyes peering through it in anxious pursuit.

The road took a dive into woods, black as a cavern, the air breathless. It wound in sharp curves, his lamps sending their swinging rays into thickets, then out again on a hilltop, and down, swooping with a long, smooth glide into a valley. Here the touring car passed him and he met a limousine, traveling at a pace as sober as his own, in its lit interior two men talking; after that a farmer's wagon drawn up against the roadside grasses, the horse prancing in fractious fear. Then nobody — a wide strip of open country with the sky setting down like an arched lid over the low circular surface of the land.

It was very still and his listening ear caught the buzzing hum of a vehicle behind him. This time he did not turn but drew off further to the right, and a closed coupe swung by, with the jarring rattle of an old and loose-geared body. He was on the alert at once, its hooded shape suggesting secrecy, the surrounding loneliness apt for its design. Its tail light cast a bobbing, crimson blot on the bed and he saw its back, dust-grimmed and rusty, and the numbered ob-

Miss Maitland Private Secretary

long of its license tag. That caused his expectancy to drop — the tag stood for respectability and honest wayfaring, then, with a quickened leap of his heart, he realized that its speed was slackening. It slowed down to his own gait, and at the limit of his lamp's illumination, moved before him, a square bulk, its back cut by a small window. He felt sure now, and with his hand on the wheel took a look over his shoulder. In the distance, cresting a rise, he saw two golden dots, too far for a speedy overtaking, and even if that were possible he had no reason to suppose they belonged to any of his followers.

A belt of woods spread across the way and the road entered it as if tunneling a vault. It wound, looped and twisted, tree trunks and leafy hollows starting out as the long bright tubes swept over them. As one of these, slewing wide in a sharper turn, crossed the bank of the forward car, Ferguson saw an arm extended and from the hand a white spark flash twice. Almost immediately the coupe turned to the left, and plunged into a by-way, black as a pocket, the woods' thick growth crowding on its edges.

The roadbed was good and the leading car accelerated its speed racing onward under the arching boughs. Ferguson, close on its heels, knew that the sounds of their going would be muffled by the enshrouding woodland, absorbed in its woven density. No chance either

Night on the Cresson Pike

of meeting any one; the way was one of those forest trails, sought by the rich on their afternoon drives, but at night deserted by all but the birds and the squirrels. Cursing at the failure of his schemes, powerless now to protest or to retaliate, he followed until he knew by a freshening of the air that they were near the Sound. The coupe's speed began to lessen and it came to a halt.

Ferguson drew up a few rods behind it. He could see the trees about him picked out in detail and behind them the engulfing darkness. The machine in front still seemed to shake and vibrate; he caught the sound of a step and then a voice, a man's, deep and low-keyed:

" This is the place. Get out."

He jumped to the ground, discerning a shape by the coupe's door. He advanced, peering through his lantern's intervening glare, and made out it was alone. Stung with a quick fear, he halted and said.

"Where's the child?"

" Here. Put the money on the rock to your right."

The man came forward, a raised hand pointing to where the top of a rock showed among the wayside grasses. From the lifted hand, the light struck a silvery gleam, touching the barrel of a revolver. Ferguson, without moving said:

" I must see her first."

Miss Maitland Private Secretary

He thought he detected a moment's hesitation, then the man stepped back to the car and called a gruff:

" All right — quick — look."

He swung the coupe door open and from an electric torch in his left hand sent a ray into the interior. The white shaft pierced the murk like a pointing finger. Its circular end, a spot of livid brightness, played on Bebita curled on the floor asleep. Ferguson saw her as if cut from an encompassing blackness, transparently clear like a picture suspended in a void. Then the ray was extinguished, and as he stood, blinking against the obscurity, heard the man's voice, " The money — on the rock there," and caught the gleam of the revolver barrel level with his eyes.

He walked to the rock and laid the money, in an envelope clasped with rubber bands, on its flat surface. The whole thing seemed to him like a cheap melodrama and he could have laughed as he righted himself and saw the round, shining end of the revolver covering him, and the silent figure behind it.

" Come on," he said, " get to the rest. You tie me — where ? "

" The oak — behind you."

It was a large-sized tree back from the edge of the road, and he walked to it hearing the man trampling the underbrush in his wake. He had a sense of a dreamlike quality in the whole fantastic performance, as if

Ferguson saw him in silhouette, a large, humped body with bent head
Night on the Cresson Pike

he might wake up suddenly and find he'd been having a nightmare.

But there was nothing dreamlike in the force with which the rope was thrown about him and tightened round the tree. As he felt it strained across his chest, lashed round his legs, girding him to the trunk close at its bark, he recognized expertness and strength in the hands that bound him. The thing was done with extraordinary speed and deftness, and ended by a lump of waste, that smelled of gasoline, being thrust into his mouth.

The heavy tread moved again through the underbrush, the man passed to the rock, and, his back to Ferguson, crouched on the light's edges counting the money. Ferguson saw him in silhouette, a large, humped bod\'7d 1 with bent head. This done, he went to the door of the coupe and lifted out the child. He had some difficulty in getting hold of her, muttered an oath, then drew her out, carried her to the roadside and set her down on the grass. There was a moment when he crossed the full gush of illumination and Ferguson had a clear glimpse of him, a chauffeur's cap on his head, the lower part of his face covered by a thick beard. Returning to his car, he jumped in. Its lurching start broke into a sudden flight, it rushed; Ferguson could hear the bounding of stones, the creaking and wrenching of its body as it hurtled down the road.

Miss Maitland Private Secretary

Silence settled, the deep, dreaming quiet of the woods. The young man tried to struggle, to writhe and work himself loose, but his bonds held fast, and he found himself choked for air, stifling and snorting over his gag. He gave it up and looked at the child. By straining his eyes he could just see her, a small, relaxed bod\'7d r , one hand outflung, her profile, held in a trance-like sleep, marble white against the grass. A hideous fear assailed him: — she might be dead. Some drug had evidently been administered to keep her quiet — an overdose! He wrenched and pressed at the cords, almost strangled and had to stop, the sweat pouring into his eyes, his heart pounding on the rope that cut into his chest. He called on his will, felt himself steadied, his smothered breath came easier, the only sound on the silence.

Then another broke upon it, far away, from the direction of the Sound — a thin, clear report. He stiffened, all his faculties strained to listen, heard it again, several in a spattering run, dropping distinct, like little globules piercing the stillness. " Shooting! " he thought with a wild surge of excitement, " out toward the water — Oh, Lord, have they got him ? "

He listened again, but heard nothing. And then from the ground rose a moaning breath, a sleepy cry — Bebita was awake. He wrenched his head till he could see her plainly, her face turned upward, the eyes

Night on the Cresson Pike

still closed, the forehead puckered with a look of pain. He tried to emit some word, heard it only as a guttural mutter, and watching, saw her stir, the outstretched arm sway upward, her eyes open, dazed and aeavy, and heard her drowsy whimper of, " Mummy," and then, " Oh, Annie, where are you? " Slowly, her head moving as her glance swept the unfamiliar prospect, she sat up.

He remembered the next few minutes as something incredibly horrible, the child's consciousness clearing to an overwhelming fear. She looked about, saw him, scrambled to her feet and began to scream, shrill, terrified cries, crouching away from him like a scared animal. She made a rush for the motor, climbing in, cowering down, calling on the names that meant safety: " Mummy ! Oh, Mummy ! Gramp, Daddy — Come! Come to me! "

An answer came, the hollow bray of a motor horn, the shout of a man's voice, then the twin spears of light, the whirring buzz of a machine shooting out of the road's dark tunnel — Chapman Price in the black car. He leapt out and ran to her, caught her up, strained her to him, held her head back to look into her face, kissed her, babbled words of love that broke on his lips and he hid his face on her neck. She twined round him, arms and legs clutching and clinging, sobbing out, "Popsy, Popsy! " over and over.

CHAPTER XXVIII

THE MAN IN THE BOAT

PRICE took Bebita to Grasslands, handed her over to Annie and telephoned in to the Janncys. Then he left to rejoin Ferguson who was to go to the shore and find out the meaning of the shots. Price, missing the leading car, had decided that it had turned from the pike and scouring the side roads in a blind chase had heard the shots, agreeing with Ferguson that they came from the direction of the Sound.

Ferguson went that way, driving at breakneck speed. He had almost reached the shore, felt the water's coolness, saw the wood's vista widen when, to avoid a deep rut, he slewed his machine to the left. The lights penetrated a thicket, revealing behind the woven foliage, a dark, large body, black among the tangled green. He drew up, peering at it — it was not a rock; its side showed smooth through the boughs. He jumped out and pushed his way through the bushes. It was a taxi, its lamps extinguished, broken branches and crushed foliage marking its track.

It gave evidence of a violent flight and a hasty deser-316

tion, careened to one side, its door open, a rug hanging over the step. He went to the back, struck a match and looked at the license tag — the number was that of the motor he had followed. Covered by the darkness, driven deep among the trees, it could easily have passed unnoticed until the daylight betrayed it.

The plan of escape revealed a new artfulness — the man had made off either on foot or in another vehicle. It accounted for the license — he knew his pursuers would mark it and look for a car carrying that number. In the face of such a crafty completeness of detail the young man felt himself reduced to a baffled indecision. Cogitating on the various routes his quarry might have taken, he ran out on to the shore road and here again halted.

Before him the Sound lay, a smooth dark floor, along which glided the small golden glimmerings of river craft. He looked up and down the road, discernible as a gray path between the upstanding solidity of the woods and the flat solidity of the water. Some distance in front a black blot took shape under his exploring glance as a small house. He started the car and ran toward it, seeing as he approached a dancing yellow spot come from behind it in swaying passage. He stopped, the yellow spot steadied, rose, swung aloft — a lantern in the hands of a man, half dressed, who came toward him spying out from under the upraised glow.

317

\

Ferguson spoke abruptly :

" Did you hear shots a while ago ? "

The man setting his lantern on the ground, spoke with the slow phlegm of the native:

" I did — close here. I bin down to the waterside seein' if I could make out what they was."

The house was skirted by a balcony along which a second light now came into view; this time from a lamp carried in the hand of a woman. She was wrapped in a bed gown, a straggle of loose hair hanging round a frightened face.

" We was asleep and they woke us up. They was right off there," she jerked her head to the Sound behind her.

" From the water? " Ferguson asked.

" Sounded that way," the man took it up. " We wasn't sure at first what it was; then they come crack, crack, one after the other, from somewheres beyont. My wife, she said it was motor boats, said she heard 'em off across the water. But by the time we got something on and was outside it was over. There wasn't no more and we couldn't see nothing. I bin down on the beach lookin' round, thinkin' they might have come from there, but I ain't found no tracks or signs of anybody."

" I was wonderin'," said the woman, " if may be it was that patrol boat — the one they got this sum-

mer runnin' along the shore for thieves — That they caught a sight of one and went after him."

Ferguson was silent for a moment then said:

" Is there any place round here where a boat could be hidden, deep enough water for a launch? "

The man answered:

" Yes, right down the road a step there's a cove and an old dock; used to belong to the folks that lived on the bluff but the house burned down a while b£.ck and ain't been rebuilt and no one's used the dock since. A feller could hide a boat there fine; it's all overgrown so you can't see it unless you know where it is."

" I'd like to take a look at it," said Ferguson. " Come along with the lantern."

The place was only a few yards from the mouth of the wood road. Trees and shrubs sheltered it, concealing with their rank growth a small wharf, rotted and sagging to the water line. The lantern rays revealed a recent presence, scattered leaves and twigs on the wooden planking, the long marshy grasses showing a track from the road to the wharf's edge.

" Yes, sir," said the native, much impressed; " some one's been here to-night and not s'long ago either. You can see where the dew's been swep' off the grasses right to the water."

Ferguson said nothing; he now saw the whole plan of escape — the coupe left in the woods, a short run

to the cove where a boat had been concealed, the getaway down on across the Sound. What had the shots meant? Was the woman right in thinking the police patrol had come upon the fleeing criminal? And if they had what had been the result?

Lantern in hand, the man at his heels, he crushed through the swampy copse to the shore. There his glance swept the long stretch of the water, sewn in the distance with a pattern of moving sparks. Two of them, red and green, stole over the ebony surface toward him, advancing with an even, gliding smoothness, piercing and steady, like the eyes of a stealthily approaching animal, fixing him with a meaning scrutiny. He snatched up the lantern and ran for a point that jutted out in a pebbly cape. Standing on its tip he raised and waved the light, letting his voice ring out across the stillness :

" Boat ahoy! "

The lights drew closer, their reflections stabbing down into the oily depths, gleam below gleam. The pulsing of a muffled engine came with them, a prow took shape, a shine of wood and brass above the lusterless tide. Ferguson called again:

"Who are you?"

An answer rose in a man's surly voice:

"What's that to you?"

"A good deal. I'm Ferguson of Council Oaks and 320

I'm looking for the boat that fired on some one round here about an hour ago."

The voice replied, its tone changed to sudden conciliation:

" Oh, Mr. Ferguson; couldn't see who it was. We're what you're looking for — the police patiol. We have the launch here in tow."

" Have you got the man? "

" Yes, sir. He didn't answer our challenge and fired on us. We chased and gave it back to him — a running fight. One of us got him — he's dead."

" Go on to my wharf; I'll be there when you come."

On his way along the shore road he met Price, paused for a quick explanation, and the two cars ran at a racing clip to Ferguson's wharf. The men were standing on its end when the police boat glided into the gush of light that fell from the high electric lamps at either side of the ship. Behind it, lifted and dropped by the languid wavelets, was a launch, a covered shape lying on the floor.

The story of the police was quickly told. The night, dark and windless, was the kind chosen by the water thieves for their operations. The men had been on the watch faring noiselessly with engine muffled and hooded lamps. It was nearly the end of their run, a length of shore with few estates, when they saw a boat glide from a part of the beach peculiarly dark and

deserted. The craft carried no lights, a fact that instantly roused their suspicions, and they waited. As it drew out for the open water they challenged. There was no answer, but a sudden acceleration of its speed, shooting by them like a streak for the mid reaches of the Sound.

They started in pursuit, repeating their challenge and then an order to lie to. Again there was no response and they clapped on top speed and raced in its wake. They were gaining on it when, in answer to a louder hail, the man fired on them, the bullet passing between two of them and burying itself in the gunwale. They replied with a return fire, there was a fusillade of shots, and the two boats sped in a darkling rush across the Sound. They knew something was wrong with their opponent ; his launch headed in a straight line swept through the wash of steamers, cut across the bows of tugs and river craft, rocking like a cockleshell, menaced by destruction, shouts and objurgations following its mad course. They were up with it, almost alongside on the last lap. He made no answer to their hails, sat upright and motionless, sat so when his bow crashed against the rocks of the Connecticut shore. They found him dead, a bullet in his brain, the wheel still gripped in his hands.

Ferguson dropped into the launch and drew down the coat that had been thrown over the body. The face, the

The Man in the Boat

false beard gone, was handsome, the body large and powerful, the hands fine and well kept — it was not the type he had expected to see. He felt in the pockets and found the money still in its envelope, clasped by the rubber bands. There were no other papers, no means of identification. After a short colloquy with the men, he and Price drove back to Council Oaks.

Price left the next morning. His presence was necessary in the city, he said, and he seemed preoccupied and anxious to go. He hinted at forthcoming revelations which would clear up what was still unexplained, but declared himself unable at present to say more.

When he had gone, Ferguson walked to Grasslands where he found the family recuperating in a relief too deep for words. Bebita was in bed still asleep. The doctor, sent for the night before, said she was suffering from the effects of a drug, but that rest and quiet would soon restore her.

They collected on the balcony to hear his story. When it was over, questions answered, amazement and horror vented in various forms, Mr. Janney said he would like to walk over to the wharf and have a talk with the police himself. Ferguson decided to go with him; there would be a lot of business to be gone through, an inquest with all its unpleasant detail.

As they rose to leave, Suzanne announced that she wanted to come too. She looked a wreck, in her hysteri-

cal jubilation forgetful of her rouge and powder; a worn little wraith of a woman whose journey to the heart of life had stripped her of all coquetry and beauty. They tried to dissuade her, but, as usual, she was insistent; she wanted to see the men herself, she wanted to hear everything.

On this day of thanksgiving no one had the will to thwart her, so they accepted with the best grace they could and she walked through the woods with them.

There was a group of men on the wharf, the local police, the coroner, some of Ferguson's emploj'ees. The body had been put in the boathouse, laid on a table under a sheltering tarpaulin. Ferguson and Mr. Jan-ney drew off to the end of the dock in low-toned conference with the officials. They were relieved to see that Suzanne had no mind to listen, but stayed by herself in the shade of the boathouse wall.

She leaned against it, looking out over the sparkling reaches of the Sound. Her thoughts were of the dead man, close behind her there, on the other side of the wooden partition. She wondered with an awed amaze at his wild act and its dark ending. She wondered what manner of man he was, what he was like — a human creature, unknown to her, who could want only to cause her such anguish.

She shot a glance over her shoulder and saw that the door of the boathouse was half open — the coroner

The Man in the Boat

had been in and had neglected to close it. She looked at the men at the end of the wharf; they stood in a little cluster, backs toward her, heads together in animated discussion. She moved from the wall, advanced on tiptoe through the slant of shade, and slipped through the open doorway.

The place was very still, its clear, varnished brown-ness impregnated with the sea's salty tang, through its windows the golden gleam of the waves reflected in rippling lights that chased across its peaked ceiling. She stole to the table where the grim shape lay and lifted the tarpaulin with a trembling hand. The other shot suddenly to her mouth, strangling a scream, and she dropped the heavy cloth as if it burned her. Both hands went up over her face, flattened there until the nails wcre empurpled, and she stood, bent as if cramped with pain, for the moment all movement paralyzed.

Ferguson, informed of all he wanted to know, turned from the others to join her. She was not where he had left her, and moving down the wharf he looked about and, seeing no sign of her, decided that she had gone home. He was passing the boathouse doorway when she came through it almost upon him.

" Good heavens! " he said angrily, " have you been in there? " Then, seeing her face, he caught her arm and held her. Would there ever be an end to her willfulness !

Miss Maitland Private Secretary

" Come home," he said, sharply, and led her away. She tottered beside him, drooping and ghastly. As they crossed the road to the path up the bluff he could not forbear an exasperated:

" What in the name of common sense did you do that for? Didn't you know it was not a thing for you to see?"

Her hands locked on his arm; she leaned against him lifting a haggard glance to his face. Her voice was a husky whisper:

" It's not that, Dick. It wasn't just the dead man. It was — it was — he was my detective — Larkin! "

MISS MAITLAND EXPLAINS

ON Saturday afternoon several telephone messages were sent to Esther Maitland at O'Malley's flat. They came from Ferguson, from Grasslands, and the Whitney office. In the two latter cases they were conciliatory and apologetic and asked that Miss Maitland would see the senders and explain the circumstances that had so strangely involved her in the case.

To both her employers and the Whitneys Miss Maitland returned an evasive answer. She would be happy to do as they asked, but would have to let a few more days pass before she would be free to speak. Meantime she would remain with Mrs. O'Malley, who had offered to keep her, and who had treated her with the utmost kindness and consideration. One request she made — this to the Whitneys — she would like Chapman Price to be advised of her whereabouts. It would be necessary for her to communicate with him before she would be able to explain her share in the mystery. Ferguson's message had been an importunate demand 327

to let him come to her. She refused, said she would see no one until she was at liberty to clear herself, which would not be for some days yet. Her voice showed a tremulous urgency, a note of pleading, new to his ears and infinitely sweet. But he could not break down her resolution; she begged him to do as she asked, not to seek her out, not to demand any explanations until she was ready to give them. The one favor she granted him was that when the time was up and she could break her silence, he could come for her.

This did not happen until Wednesday. That morning she 'phoned to them all that she could now see them and tell them what they wanted to hear. A meeting was arranged at the Whitney office for three that afternoon and Ferguson went to fetch her.

They met in Mrs. O'Malley's front parlor, considerately vacated and with the folding doors closed against intrusion. Without greeting Ferguson took her hands and held them, looking down into her face. She was beaming, her cheeks flushed, her eyes shy. She began to say something about being at last able to vindicate herself, but he cut her off :

" Before you go into that, I want to say something to you."

" No, that's not fair; I must speak first and you must let me. It's my privilege."

" With the others maybe, but not with me. What I 328

Miss Maitland Explains

have to say has to be said before I hear. Esther, do you know what it is ? "

She was silent, her head drooping, her hands growing cold in his grasp. He went on, very quietly and simply:

" It's that I ask you to be my wife. And I must ask it before the clearing or vindicating or any rubbish of that sort. I don't know what you'll say to it and I don't want any answer now. That's at your own good time and your own good pleasure. It's just that I wanted you to see how I stand and have stood since that night when we walked through the woods together. Come along now — it's nearly three, and we mustn't keep them waiting."

It was a very different Esther who sat in Wilbur Whitney's private office, facing those who had once been her accusers. She gave no evidence of rancor, greeted them with a frank friendliness, smiled with a radiance they set down to the rebound from long tension and strain. Suzanne, her jealous fires burned out, could acknowledge now that she was handsome; Mr. Janncy wondered at her look of breeding. " A fine girl," old Whitney thought, as he studied her through his glasses, " spirited and high-mettled as a racer."

" It's a long story," she said, " and for you to understand it I'll have to go back to a time when none of you had ever heard of me. And before I begin, I want to say to Mrs. Janney," she turned to the older woman

eagerly earnest, " if I had understood people better, if I hadn't been hardened and made suspicious by the struggle I'd had, I would have trusted you and told you more, and all this misery would have been averted. So, in a way it was my fault, and being such I've suffered for it.

" I have a half-sister, Florence Jackson, nine years younger than I am; that would make her eighteen. When my stepfather died, ten years ago, he left us penniless and I had to start in at once to make our bread. I boarded Florry out with friends and found a position as a school teacher. That was only for a year or two; soon I advanced into the secretarial work which was less fatiguing and better paying. In the first place I got, Florry was living near me and on Sundays she used to come and see me. My employer didn't like it — did not want a strange child about the house and told me so without mincing words. I was angry — J was hot-tempered and sensitive in those days and I made a vow to keep my life to myself, be nothing to my employers but a machine who rendered certain services for a certain wage. When I came to you, Mrs. Janney, I should have seen that I was with some one who was big-hearted and generous, but I had been molded and the mold had set in a hard and bitter shape.

" Earning more money I was able to put Florry in good schools. It was my intention to give her a fine

Miss Maitland Explains

education, and equip her for the task of earning her living. She was quick and clever, but willful and hard to control. I suppose it was because she had had no home influences, no place that belonged to her. She had to spend her vacations anywhere — sometimes at the school, sometimes with classmates. It was a miserable life for a child.

" She was always pretty — when she was little people used to stop on the streets to look at her — and as she grew older she grew prettier. She was charming, too, there was something about her very willfulness that was captivating. The combination worried me; if she had had more balance, been more reasonable, it wouldn't have mattered. But she was the kind who is always full of wild enthusiasms, going off at a tangent about this, that and the other. Not a promising temperament for a girl who has to support herself.

" A year ago I got her into a first class school near Chicago — I had met the principal, who had been very kind and taken her at a greatly reduced rate. It was to be her last year; in June she would graduate and with her education finished, I felt sure I could get her a position in New York where I could help her and watch over her. During the winter — last winter — her letters made me uneasy. She was discontented, tired of study, wanted to be out in the world doing something.

I was prepared for a struggle with her, but not for what happened.

" One day — it was in March — I had a letter from her saying she had run away from school, was in New York and was looking for a job. I was angry and bitterly disappointed, also I was frightened — Florry in New York without a cent, with no one to be with her, with no home or companion. I went to the address she gave me and found her in the hall bedroom of a third rate boarding house — a woman on the train had told her of it — full of high spirits and a sort of childish joy at being free. She did not understand my disappointment, laughed at my fears. I lost my temper, said more than I ought — and — well, we had a quarrel, the first real one we ever had.

" That night I couldn't sleep, blaming myself, knowing that whatever she did it was my duty to stand by her. The next day I went to the place and found she'd gone, leaving no address. For three days I heard nothing from her and was on the verge of going to you, Mrs. Janney, and imploring your aid and advice, when a letter came. She was all right, she had found paying employment, she was independent at last. In my first spare hour I went to her and found her in another boarding house, a cheap, shabby place, but decent. A good many working women lived there, the better paid shop girls and heads of departments. It was through

one of these, a fitter, at Camille's, that she had got work. With her beauty it had been easy — she had been employed as a model at Camille's."

" Camille's! " the word came on a startled note from Suzanne. Esther turned to her:

" Yes, Mrs. Price, and you saw her there — you ordered a dress from a model that Florry wore."

" The girl with the reddish hair — the tall girl? "

" Yes, that was Florry. She told me afterward how she walked up and down in front of you."

" But —" Suzanne's voice showed an incredulous wonder, " she was beautiful; they were all talking about her."

" I said she was — I was not exaggerating. She was satisfied with her work, liked it, I think she would have liked anything that was novel and took her away from the grind of study. / didn't like it, but at least it wasn't the stage, and I set about trying to find something better. That was the situation till April and then —" She paused, her eyes dropped to the floor. The color suddenly rose in her face and raising them she shot a look at Ferguson. He answered it with a slight, almost imperceptible nod and smiled in open encouragement. She took a deep breath and addressed Mrs. Janney:

" What I have to tell now isn't pleasant for me to say or for you to hear, but I have to tell it for all the

subsequent events grew from it. Mr. Price had been to Camille's that first time with his wife."

There was a slight stir in the listening company, a sudden focusing of intent eyes on the girl, a waiting expectancy in the grave faces. She saw it and answered it:

" Yes, he saw Florry. He went again — Mrs. Price was buying several dresses. After that second visit he waited one night at the side door used for employees and spoke to her. I can't condone what she did, but I can say in extenuation that she was very young, very inexperienced, that she knew who Mr. Price was, and that she had never in her life met a man of his attractions.

" She didn't hide it from me, was frank and outspoken about the meeting and his subsequent attentions. For he saw her often after that, took her for walks on Sunday, sent her theater tickets and books. I was filled with anxiety, besought of her to give it up, but she wouldn't, she couldn't. Before I went to Grasslands I realized a situation was developing that made me sick with apprehension. She was in love, madly in love. I couldn't reason with her, I couldn't make her listen to me; she was blind and deaf to anything but him and what he said.

" I went to Mr. Price and implored him to leave her alone. I had to catch him as I could — in the halls, at

odd moments in the library, for he hated the scenes I made and tried to avoid me. He assured me that he meant no harm, that her position was hard and he was sorry for her. I threatened to tell Mrs. Janney, and he said I could if I wanted, that he would soon be done with them all and didn't care. I saw then that he too, like Florry, was growing indifferent to everything but the hours when they were together — that lie was in love.

" That was the situation when I went to Grasslands. It was much worse there — I couldn't see her often, I was in ignorance of how things were going with her, for her letters told me little. It was unbearable, and I went into town whenever I could; all the extra holidays were asked for so that I could go into the city and see how Florry was getting on. On one of these visits she told me something that, at the time, I paid little attention to, setting it down as one of her passing fancies; she was interested in the working girls' unions. At Camille's and in the boarding house she had fallen in with a group of girls of Socialistic beliefs and, through them, had met their organizers and backers. She was much more deeply involved than I guessed. Her fearlessness, her ardor for anything new and exciting, making her a valuable addition to their ranks. It carried her far, to the edge of tragedy."

She turned to Mr. Janney: 335

" Do you remember, Mr. Janney, one morning early in July, how I read you an account of a strike riot among the shirtwaist makers when one of the girls stabbed a policeman with a hatpin? "

The old man nodded:

" Yes, vaguely. I have a dim memory of arguing about it with you."

" That was the time. Well, that girl was Florry. She lost her head completely, stabbed the man, and in the tumult that followed, managed to get away through the hall of a tenement house. She was hidden by friends of hers, Russian socialists called Rychlovsky. I have met them; they seem decent, kindly people, and they certainly were very good to her. When I read you the article I had no more idea that the girl was Florry than you had. It was not until the next morning that I received a letter from her, telling me what she had done and where she was.

" She wrote two letters, one to me and one to Mr. Price. He had told her that he would spend his weekends with the Hartleys at Cedar Brook and she sent his there. Mine was delivered on the morning of July the seventh but he did not get his until the same evening when he came to Cedar Brook from the city. Each of us acted as promptly as we could, but he went to her before I did, going in that night in his car.

" It seems incredible that he should have done what 336

he did, dared to take such a risk. But when he found her cooped up in the rear room of a tenement, lonely and frightened, he prevailed on her to go out with him in his motor. He took her for a drive far up the Hudson, not returning until after midnight. The Rych-lovskys, who had missed her and were in a state of alarm, were furious. When I went there the next day they were vociferous in their desire to be rid of her, saying she would land them all in jail. I was her sister; it was up to me, I must find another lair for her.

" I had heard of the house in Gayle Street from two girls, art students, who had once lived there. It was the only place I could think of; and when I found that the top floor was vacant, I realized that she could be hidden in one of the rooms and no one suspect it was occupied. I engaged it and paid the rent, telling the janitor the story of a friend coming from the West. Then I took the key back to Florry. The Rychlovskys, pacified by the thought that she would be out of their house, undertook to furnish her with food. They made her promise that she would keep to the room, light no gas at night, make no noise, and stay away from the window. Florry was by this time thoroughly cowed and agreed to everything. It was through their adroitness that the room passed as vacant. They visited her in the evening, a time when many people came and went in the house, bringing in her food and carrying away

Miss Maitland Private Secretary

what was left in newspapers. They had two extra keys made, one for me, one for Mr. Price. I brought her money, Mr. Price books and magazines. He saw her oftener than I did, and gave me news of her. This I asked him to do by letter. I had once met him by Little Fresh Pond, and another time he had telephoned. I was afraid of repeating the meeting at the pond — we had both come upon Miss Rogers and Bebita on the way out — and I dreaded being overheard at the 'phone.

" All went well for two weeks, though we were terribly frightened, for the policeman developed blood-poisoning, and for some time hung between life and death. Then the Rychlovskys suggested a plan that seemed to me the only way out of our dangers and difficulties. A friend of theirs, a woman doctor, was one of a hospital unit sailing from Montreal to France. This woman, allied with them in their Socialistic activities, agreed to get Florry into her group as a hospital attendant, take her to France and look after her. It struck us all as feasible and as lacking in danger as any plan for her removal could be. The doctor was a woman of high character who told the Rychlovskys she would keep Florry near her as the unit was shorthanded and needed all the workers it could get. The one person who showed no enthusiasm was Florry herself. I knew perfectly what was the matter — she did not want to leave Chapman Price. He tried to persuade her, was as

Miss Maitland Explains

worried and anxious as I was. The situation between them had cleared to a definite understanding — when his wife had obtained her divorce he would go to France and marry Florry there.

" And now I come to the day of the kidnaping, that dreadful, unforgettable day!

" The morning before — Thursday — I had seen her and found her in a state of nervous indecision, weeping and miserable. I knew I was to be in town with Mrs. Price the next day and told her if I could get time I would come to her. Mrs. Price had told me how we were to divide the errands and I realized, if I could finish mine earlier than she expected, I would have a chance of seeing Florry. I had just been paid my salary and that, with some money I had saved, I brought with me. My intention was to give all this to Florry and implore her to go with the hospital unit, which was scheduled to leave Montreal early the following week.

" Things worked out as I had hoped. The commissions took less time than Mrs. Price had calculated and I found that I would be able to spend a few minutes with Florry. In case Bebita should mention the excursion downtown, I ordered the driver to drop me at a bookbindery on the corner of Gale Street. I could easily explain our stop there by saying that I had left a book to be bound.

" When I reached the room I found her in a state of 339

hysterical terror — she said the house was watched. Peeping out through the coarse lace curtains that veiled the window, she had several times noticed a man lounging about the corner. At first she had thought nothing of him, but the day before he had reappeared, and stayed about the block most of the afternoon covertly watching the entrance and the upper floor. I was nearly as frightened as she was — the thing was only too probable. There was no difficulty in getting her to go with the hospital ship. She had only stayed on in the hope of seeing me and having me tell her what to do.

" I gave her the money and told her to wait until nightfall and then slip out and go to the Rychlovskys. They had promised to help her in any way they could, and with Bebita waiting in the cab, I couldn't go with her. It was a simply hideous position to have to leave her that way. But it was all I could think of — it came so unexpectedly I was stunned by it.

" When I reached the bookbindery the taxi was gone! Can you imagine what I felt? I told the truth when I said my first thought was that Bebita might have played a joke on me. I did think that, for my mind, confused and crowded with deadly fears, could not take in a new catastrophe. Then, when I saw Mrs. Price and realized that the child had mysteriously disappeared, while with me, while in my charge — I — well, I hope I'll never have to live over moments like those again. I had to

Miss Maitland Explains

keep one fact before my mind — to be quiet, to be cool, not to do or say anything that might betray Florry. If I'd known what you suspected, I couldn't have done it. But, of course, I hadn't any idea then you thought I was implicated.

" Florry had told me she would communicate with Mr. Price and he would give me word of her. The telephone message that Miss Rogers tapped was that word; all I received. It relieved me immensely, I began to feel the dreadful strain relaxing, I began to think we were on the high road to safety. And then came that day here in the office. Shall I ever forget it! "

She turned to Mrs. Janney:

" If I had had the least idea of what was going to be done here, I would have tried to get to you and have thrown myself on your mercy. But I was completely unsuspecting and unprepared, and with Mr. Whitney as the judge, representing the law, I did not dare to tell the truth, I had to lie.

" As you saw, I lied as well as I could, puzzled at first, not knowing what you were getting at, to what point it was all leading. Then, when you caught me with the tapped message, I saw — I guessed how circumstances had woven a net about me. I realized there was nothing to be done but let you believe it, let you do what you wanted with me. You couldn't make me speak, and if I could stay silent till Florry was in Europe, hidden, lost

in the chaos of a country at war, it would be all right."

She swept their faces with a glance, half pleading, half triumphant.

" She is there now — this morning Mr. Price had a cable from her. I have told this to Mr. Whitney as well as the rest because I have thought — shut up in O'Malley's flat I had much time for thinking things out straight and clear — that after my explanation, no one would want, no one would dare, to bring that unfortunate girl back here to face a criminal charge. She has had her lesson, she will never forget it, the man she wounded is back on the force as good as ever. No human being with a conscience and a heart —" she-looked at Whitney — " and you have both — could want to make her pay more bitterly than she has. She is safe, under intelligent supervision. She can work, be useful, where her youth and strength and enthusiasm are needed. I did not trust you before, Mr. Whitney, but I do now and I know that my trust is not misplaced."

A murmur, a concerted sound of agreement, came from her listeners. Whitney, pushing his chair back from the desk, said gravely:

" You can rest assured, Miss Maitland, that the matter will die here with us to-day. As you say, your sister has had her punishment. She will stay in France of course? "

** Yes, make her home there, I think. When Mr. 342

Price is free he is to go over and marry her. He intends to sell his business out and offer his services to the French government."

There was a moment of silence, then Mrs. Janney spoke, clearing her throat, her face flushed with feeling:

" As you've said, Miss Maitland, none of this would have happened if you'd seen fit to come to me. But it's no use going over that now — we've all made mistakes and we're all sorry. What we — the Janneys — want to do is to be fair, to be just, and now — if it is not too late — to make amends. The only way you can show your willingness to forget and forgive, is to come back at once to Grasslands and take things up where you left them."

The girl for a moment did not answer, her face reddening with a sudden embarrassment. Mrs. Janney saw the blush, read it as reluctance and exclaimed:

" Oh, Miss Maitland, don't say you refuse. It's as if you wouldn't take my hand held out in apology, in friendship."

" No, no "— Esther was obviously distressed — " don't think that, Mrs. Janney, it's not that. It's that I can't — I've — I've made another engagement — I'm going to marry Mr. Ferguson."

CHAPTER XXX

MOLLY'S STORY

IT'S my place to finish, tell the end of the story and straighten it all out. Some of it's been cleared up clean, with the people on the spot to give the evidence, some of it we had to work out from what we knew and what we guessed. Willitts, who was a gamy guy, told his tale from start to finish, and loved doing it, they said, like an actor who'd rather be dead in the spotlight than alive in the wings. Larkin's part we had to put together from what we could get from Bebita and what Mrs. Price gave up.

Bebita, the way children do, saw plain and could tell what she saw as accurate as a phonograph. It made tears come to hear the dear little thing, so sweet and innocent, making us see that even the crooks she was with couldn't help but love her.

When Miss Maitland got out of the taxi at the book-bindery the driver told the child that he knew her Daddy and could take her round to see him while Miss Maitland was in the store. He said it wouldn't take long, that Mr. Price was close by, and they would come back

in a few minutes and pick up Miss Maitland. Bebita was crazy to go, and he started, giving her a box of chocolates to eat on the way. Of course she never could tell where he went but it could not have been a long distance, or Larkin — we all were agreed that he drove the cab

— couldn't have reached the Fifth Avenue house as soon as he did. The place was evidently a flat over a garage. He told her her father was waiting there, went upstairs with her, and gave her in charge of a woman called Marion who opened the door for them.

During the whole time she was gone she stayed here with Marion, who every morning assured her her Daddy would come that day. She said Marion was very good to her, gave her toys and candies, cooked her meals and played games with her. She cried often and was homesick, and Marion never scolded her but used to take her in her arms and kiss her and tell her stories. She never saw the man again until he came to take her away, but sometimes the bell rang and Marion went out on the stairs and talked to some one.

One evening Marion said she was going home; it would be a long drive and she must be a good girl. . Marion dressed her and then gave her a glass of milk, and kissed her a great many times and cried. Bebita cried too, for she was sorry to leave Marion, but she wanted to go home. After that the man came and took her downstairs to the taxi and told her to be very quiet

Miss Maitland Private Secretary

and she'd soon be back at Grasslands. It was dark and they went through the city and then she got very sleepy and laid down on the seat.

No trace of Marion, Larkin's confederate, could be found, and in fact no especial effort was made to do so. The man was dead, the woman, who had evidently treated the child with affectionate care, had fled into the darkness where she belonged. The family, even Mrs. Janney, was contented to let things drop and make an end.

When it came to Larkin we had to piece out a good deal. We agreed that he had started in fair and honest, had tried to make good and had failed. At just what point he changed we couldn't be sure, but Ferguson thought it was after Mrs. Price threatened to end the investigation. Then he realized that his big chance was slipping by, determined to get something out of it, and hit on the kidnaping. It was easy to see how he could worm all the data he wanted out of Mrs. Price. From what she said he'd evidently pumped her at their last meeting in town, finding out just what her plans were, even to the fact that she intended taking the extra cab from the rank round the corner. / thought that one thing might have given him the whole idea.

When they stopped at the book bindery he heard Miss Maitland tell Bebita she would be gone a few minutes and knew that was his opportunity. He took the child

Molly's Story

to the place he had ready for her, made a quick change — not more than the shedding of his coat, cap and goggles — and ran his car into the garage below, which of course he must have rented. Then he lit out for the Fifth Avenue house, a bit late but ready to report in case Miss Maitland didn't show up before him. Miss Maitland did — he must have seen her go in — but he rang just the same, which showed what a cunning devil he was.

He must have been surprised when he didn't see anything in the papers, but after he'd written the first " Clansmen " letter to Mrs. Price she explained that and it made it smoother sailing for him. Knowing her as well as he did, he planned the letters to scare her into silence, and saw before he was through he had her exactly in the state he wanted. The one place where his plot was weak was that an outsider had to drive the rescue car. But he had to take a chance somewhere, and this was the best place. He'd fixed it so neat that even if the outsider had informed on him, he'd have been wary, and, as Ferguson thought, not shown up at all.

He'd done it well; as well, we all agreed, as it could be done. What had beaten him had been no man's cleverness, just something that neither he, nor you, nor any of us could have foreseen. Ain't there a proverb about the best laid plans of mice and men slipping up when you least expect it? It was like the hand of some-

thing, that reached out sudden and came down hard, laid him dead in the moment when the goal was in sight.

As to Willitts, he was some boy! They found out that he was wanted in England, well-known there as an expert safe-cracker and notorious jewel thief. That's where he's gone, to live in a quiet little cell which will be his home from this time forth. He said he hadn't been in New York long before he heard of the Janney jewels and went into Mr. Price's service. But he couldn't do anything while the family were in town. The safe was right off the pantry — too many people about — and anyway it was a new one, the finest kind, that would have baffled even his skill. He would have left discouraged but one day Dixon let drop that the safe at Grasslands was old-fashioned, put in years before by the former owners, so he stayed on devoted and faithful.

At Grasslands he had lots of time to try his hand on the ancient contraption in the passage. He worked on it until he found the combination and then he lay low for his opportunity. When the row came and Mr. Price left, he stayed on .with him. It was the best thing to do as he could run in and out from Cedar Brook seeing the servants, with whom he was careful to be friendly.

Before this he'd got wise to the fact that something was up between Miss Maitland and Mr. Price. He said it was his business to snoop and his profession had

Molly's Story

got him into the way of doing it instinctive, but I'd set it down as coming natural. Anyway he'd found out that there was a secret between them; he'd surprise them murmuring in the hallways and the library, quieting down quick if any one came along. He made the same mistake as the rest of us, thought it was an affair of the heart and grew mighty curious about it. He didn't explain why he was interested, but if you asked me I'd say he had blackmail in the back of his head.

On the afternoon of July the seventh he biked down from Cedar Brook to take a look round and see how things were progressing. Familiar with the ways of the house, he knew the family would be out and stole round past Miss Maitland's study. No one was there, and, curious as he was, he slipped in to do a little spying — Miss Maitland and Mr. Price separated would be writing to each other and a letter might throw some light on the darkness.

He rummaged about among the papers but found nothing. Scattered over the desk were bits of the trimming Miss Maitland had been sewing on; a pile of the little rosebuds was lying on the top of her work basket. Reaching over toward a bunch of letters he upset the basket, and, scared, he swept up the contents with his handkerchief, putting them back as quick as he could. This was the way he explained

the presence of the rose in the safe. He was shocked at any one thinking that he had tried to throw suspicion on such a fine young lady. That night, taking the jewels, hot and nervous, his glasses had blurred the way they do when your face perspires. He had whisked out his handkerchief to wipe them, and no doubt a rosebud lodged in the folds had fallen to the ground. Mr. Ferguson didn't believe this — he thought the rose was a plant — but I did. It was one of those queer, unexpected things that will happen and that, for me, always puts a crimp in circumstantial evidence.

After that he went round to the kitchen and heard of the general sortie for that evening. Then he knew the time had come. He hiked back to Cedar Brook, saw Mr. Price, and went to his lodgings. Here he found his landlady's child sick with croup and offered to go for the doctor, whose house was not far from Berkeley. It fitted in just right, for if there was any inquiry into his movements he could furnish a good reason why he was late at the movies. Before he got to Grasslands he hid his wheel by the roadside and took a short cut through the woods, lying low on the edge of them until he saw the kitchen lights go out. Crossing the lawn, the dogs ran at him barking, then got his scent and quieted down. At the balcony he slipped off his rain coat, put on sneakers, unlocked the front door with Mr. Price's key, and crept in. The

Molly's Story

job didn't take him ten minutes; just as he finished he saw the box of Mr. Janney's cigars and helped himself to one. He rubbed off his finger prints with an acid used for that purpose, left the broken chair just where it was and departed.

In the woods he lit the cigar, carelessly throwing the band on the ground. Fifteen minutes later he was at the movies with the Grasslands help. When he saw in the papers that a light had been seen by the safe at one-thirty every fear he had died, for at that time he was back at Cedar Brook helping his landlady look after the sick child.

He was too smart a crook to disappear right on top of the robbery, and hung around saying he was looking for another place. He met up with Larkin but at first didn't know he was a detective. When the offer came from Ferguson he took it, intending to stay a while, then say his folks in the old country needed him and slip away to Spain. It was the day after he'd accepted Ferguson's offer that he learned what Larkin was, and saw that both he and the Jan-neys had their suspicions of Chapman Price. This disturbed him, but he couldn't throw up the job he'd just taken without exciting remark. To be ready, however, he dug up the jewels—he'd buried them in the woods — and put them handy under the flooring of his room.

Miss Maitland Private Secretary

One day, looking over Ferguson's things, he came on the cigar band in the box on the bureau. It gave him a jar, for he couldn't see why it was put there. He'd heard from the servants about Ferguson and Miss Maitland walking home that night through the woods and began to wonder if maybe they'd found the band. The thought ruffled him up considerably, and then he put it out of his mind, telling himself it was one from a cigar Ferguson had brought from Grasslands and smoked in his room. Nevertheless, to be on the safe side, he threw it away, very much on the alert, as you may guess.

It wasn't a week later that he had the interview with Ferguson about the band. Then he saw by the young man's manner and words why the little crushed circle of paper had a meaning of its own, and knew that the time had come to vanish. He still felt safe enough to do this without haste, not rousing any suspicion by a too sudden departure. His opportunity came quickly — on Friday morning he heard Ferguson tell the butler that he was going to town and would be away for a day or two; by the time he came back his valet would be far aSeld.

Right after Ferguson's departure he put the jewels in a bag, and, telling the butler the boss had given him the day and night off, prepared to leave. He was crossing the hall when the telephone rang — my mes-

Molly's Story

sage — and being wary of danger, answered it. It was only a lady asking for Mr. Ferguson, and, calm and steady as his voice had made me, started out for the station. Mice and men again! — I was the mouse this time. Gracious, what a battered mouse I was!

Well — that's all. The tangled threads are straightened out and the word " End " goes at the bottom of this page. I'm glad to write it, glad to be once again where you can say what you think, and talk to people like they were harmless human beings without any dark secrets in their pasts or presents, and, Oh, Gee, how glad I am to be home! Back in my own little hole, back where there's only one servant and she a coon, back where I'm familiar with the food and know how to eat it, and blessedest of all, back to my own true husband, who thinks there's no sun or moon or stars when I'm out of the house. I'm going to get a new rug for the parlor, a fur-trimmed winter suit, a standing lamp with a Chinese shade, a pair of skates — oh, dear, I'm at the bottom of the page and there's no room for " End," but I must squeeze in that I got that reward — Mrs. Janney said I'd earned every penny of it — and a wrist watch with a circle of diamonds round it from Dick Ferguson, and — oh, pshaw! if I keep on I'll never stop, so here goes, on a separate line

    THE END

Made in the USA
Coppell, TX
20 April 2024

31508351R00079